**"I COULDN'T READ IT
FAST ENOUGH . . ."**

"It's the reality of boxing, the reality of people and most of all, the reality of Peter Hamill's brilliance."
—Dave Anderson, *The New York Times*

"A MOVING NOVEL WHICH SHOWS US WHAT WE ARE—an ambivalent mix of love and hate, of strength and weakness, of success and failure. But always human."
—*Los Angeles Times Book Review*

"AN OEDIPAL THRILLER, powerful, savvy, authentic."
—Christopher Lehmann-Haupt, *The New York Times*

"PETE HAMILL HAS CREATED A PUBLISHING SENSATION."
—Liz Smith, *New York Daily News*

FLESH AND BLOOD
A sensational novel of passion and rage

FLESH and BLOOD

Pete Hamill

BANTAM BOOKS · TORONTO · NEW YORK · LONDON

FLESH AND BLOOD
*A Bantam Book / published by arrangement with
Random House, Inc.*

PRINTING HISTORY
*Random House edition published November 1977
Bantam edition / August 1978*

*Bantam Books are published by Bantam Books, Inc. Its trade-
mark, consisting of the words "Bantam Books" and the por-
trayal of a bantam, is registered in the United States Patent
Office and in other countries. Marca Registrada. Bantam
Books, Inc., 666 Fifth Avenue, New York, New York 10019.*

This book is for

ANNE DEVLIN HAMILL
of Madrid Street, Belfast, Northern Ireland

Lay your sleeping head, my love,
Human on my faithless arm;
Time and fevers burn away
Individual beauty from
Thoughtful children, and the grave
Proves the child ephemeral:
But in my arms till break of day
Let the living creature lie,
Mortal, guilty, but to me
The entirely beautiful . . .

—"Lullaby," W. H. Auden

BOOK
ONE

IT WAS YOU, BABE.

Remember that.

It was you, lying there that night: before the arena had even filled; before the newsmen had left the casinos to take their seats at the press tables; before the celebrities had stepped off the charter flights from New York and L.A. and Miami Beach; before your own people had climbed out of the subways, a continent away, heading for the closed-circuit theaters from their homes in Brooklyn and Queens and the high Bronx; before the Puerto Ricans had carried their cases of beer to the Academy of Music and the Mexicans had piled out of Boyle Heights; before the pimps had assembled their women; before Harlem and Hough, Watts and Newark and Roxbury had emptied of high rollers to scream for the other guy. Before any of it, it was you, babe, and you already knew how it would end.

3

You lay there, alone in the desert, the taste of pennies in your mouth, your back sticking to the plastic covering of the exercise mat, a towel over your groin; your feet already sweating, your palms wet, your scalp itching from sweat. You lay there with your eyes closed so you wouldn't see a clock or a wrist watch, controlling your breath to feign sleep, so you wouldn't have to discuss it with anybody. But you listened: for a word of doubt or fear; for the small nuances of betrayal. And you heard only a whisper, a mumble; the door opening and closing, the growing murmur outside, and the water tap-tapping in the shower.

You knew that you made all of it come to this final place. You. Bobby Fallon. You had insisted. You had forced the appointment. You had used the weapons of refusal against them, the weapon of departure. That final night.

A gull skims low over the waves, his body still, frozen in the glide. A slight move, his head vanishes, the wings beat, and he rises. I sit here, beside the Pacific, and watch him until he circles away over the Colony. It's been a long time since I've seen anything clearly.

Down the beach, two old people walk together along the edge of the sea. The tide is out. Sticks of legs jut from the man's Bermudas; he bends over to pick up a rock. There are rocks on the beach around me, too. Smooth and old, glistening in the tame surf. They've tumbled across sea bottoms to get here. All the way from Honolulu, someone said. All the way from China. Under the toy sailboats. Under the gulls and the fish.

The old couple is larger now. She wears a straw hat, flapping in the morning breeze. A broad, formless cloud seeps into the sky over San Pedro to the south. Dark, and loaded with rain. The sea is gray. I fiddle with my sunglasses. The stitches itch. My feet dig into the cool sand.

I hope the old people don't stop to talk.

I hope nobody stops to talk.

1

It STARTED IN THE RAIN. Back then, in Brooklyn. In the rain beating across the New York harbor in sheets. On a payday Friday, in the parking lot at Bush Terminal.

Kirk and I are running for the shelter of the Belt Parkway, the rain drumming on the rooftops of cars around us. He's older than I am, by ten years at least, and when we reach the elevated structure of the parkway, he holds his side in pain. His black face glistens.

"Dammit, Bobby, *no!*" he says. "I'm too *old* for the Shamrock."

"Twenty-eight ain't old," I tell him.

"Too old for them hardhat muthafuckas."

I laugh, tap him on the arm, and move out into the rain again, heading for the Shamrock.

"Crazy honky."

"Chickenshit nigger."

6

Kirk is about six foot, looks shorter because of his paunch. Skin the color of bittersweet chocolate. Good teeth. Thin lips. But the first thing you always notice is his eyes: gray with yellow glints, and always moving. He is smart as hell and talks a lot, but when he wears shades there's no way of knowing him. At this time, he's my closest friend. Maybe my only friend, because we've moved around so much, Ma and I. Kirk doesn't give a shit, and that's why I like him. Doesn't give a shit for bosses, the job, money, skin or tomorrow. He wears work clothes on the job and pimp threads on weekends. He has girls in a lot of places. Or so he says. I don't know because I've never seen them. Every payday we go drinking, a kind of reward for a week of drill presses banging through the brain. Usually we drink in the Tip Top, where there's a Puerto Rican bartender and a mixed crowd. Spanish music on the jukebox, right alongside deep black dirty blues. But the Tip Top is four blocks further than the Shamrock.

"We can have a drink at the Shamrock and wait for the rain to die," I tell Kirk.

"*We* could be dead before the *rain*," he says.

But we go to the Shamrock.

Which is kind of funny, I guess, considering what happened later, when I had shamrocks coming out of my ass.

We went in the front door. The bar was crowded and smoky, smelling of wet wool, and country music was playing on the jukebox. Heads turned as we walked in. To stare at Kirk, then at me. One customer stopped a beer halfway to his mouth. A Schlitz sign bubbled over the cash register, and rows of whiskey bottles filled the back of the bar, stacked up against a big mirror. In the mirror, I saw the way these people were looking at me: at my goddam choirboy face, at my goddam yellow hair and blue eyes. I wished I had a mashed-in mug, all rough and ugly, and I wished I was six foot three instead of six foot even and had big broad shoulders like a goddam lumberjack. I could almost hear them thinking: Who's the fuckin' choirboy with the jigaboo?

Kirk must have picked it up, too, the way they were staring at us through the mirror as we walked the length of the bar to an empty spot close to the rear door. Right then, he started to swagger. I mean, he was diddy-bopping, like some dude on Lenox Avenue. Just to piss them off. And I was swaggering behind him. We moved into the empty space, and I peeled a crisp ten off the payday roll and reached into the bar.

"Give us a—"

The bartender got busy at the register, breaking rolls of coins into the drawer.

I looked at Kirk and his eyes moved in the direction of the rear door, but I stayed put. I leaned close to him and whispered:

"No, man. Fuck it. I want a drink."

We were standing a few feet from the end of the bar. The rear door was to the right and there was another room on the other side of an arch, filled with a shuffleboard machine and dusty tables. Four shuffleboard players had stopped their game and were eying Kirk. One of them leaned against a phone booth, pulling drags on a cigarette.

The bartender started filling glasses for a couple of fat guys beside us. I tapped the creased bill on the bar.

"A Schaefer for me and a bourbon rocks."

He didn't even raise his head. He was dunking glasses in the wetsink and slipping them on a wire rack to dry. And then he turned to the front door. A very large customer was walking in, wearing a white T-shirt under a zipper jacket. He had about a size 22 neck and was built like a weightlifter.

"Oh, wow," one of the fat guys said. "Oh, wow, it's Kingsize."

Kingsize took a stool near the front, and the bartender almost ran to put a bottle of Four Roses and a glass in front of him.

"Wait till Kingsize clocks this dinge," the fat guy said.

The shuffleboard players were sitting on the machine now, and one of them was slowly hefting the puck, over and over in his hand. On the juke, Bing Crosby was singing about Galway Bay.

Kingsize took off his jacket. It looked like a couple of bowling balls had been sewn into his arms. He popped peanuts into his mouth from a Planters bag and listened to the bartender. But he had already spotted Kirk and me, and his eyes never left us.

"Let's go," Kirk said. "This cat's got muscles in his shit."

"Fuck him," I said.

Then I decided to stare back at Kingsize. More regulars were coming in, but I just kept staring. Finally the bartender said something to him that he had to answer. The bowling balls shifted in his arms, and he blinked, and talked and blinked again, all the while looking past the bartender at me and Kirk. He might have muscles in his shit, all right, but goddam him, he blinked first. Not me.

Then two cops came in through the rear door. They were wearing visored caps and heavy rubber raincoats with white stripes down the front, and they were dripping with rain. One of them was tall, with a pouchy face and pink skin. The other one was smaller, with a neat sandy mustache that made him look like he'd been sad all his life. The regulars made room for them a few feet away from us and started dropping hellos and first names. The sad cop leaned on the bar and his raincoat made a sound like the crumpling of heavy paper.

The bartender hurried past us to serve them.

"Hey!" I yelled. "Hey, *you!* I asked for a *Schaefer* and a *bourbon rocks!* Before these guys got here!"

The bartender's eyes went from me, to Kirk, to Kingsize, all in one move, and then he turned around to serve the cops. I bulled my way in front of them and pointed a finger at him.

"I said a beer and a bourbon rocks, Mac."

The sad cop said, "Easy, boy."

"It's got nothing to do with you," I said. "I've been waiting a while. Me and my friend here."

The cop gazed past me and I shifted around to see what he was seeing. Everything in the bar seemed frozen: customers, bartender, even the Schlitz sign. Down at his end of the bar, Kingsize sipped a straight shot. He had the face of a man about to get laid.

"You got any I.D. on you, pal?" the sad cop said.

I tapped the ten on the bar. "Yeah. This."

"A wit," the tall cop said. "We got a fuckin' *wit* here, Henry." He lifted his glass, holding it between his thumb and forefinger like a woman drinking tea. "I mean such fuckin' wit makes you not see certain things. I mean it fuckin' *dazzles* you. It dazzles *me* so fuckin' much I don't even see Kingsize gettin' off his fuckin' stool."

I turned in time to catch Kingsize standing up like a wall that had learned how to walk. He was heading for me.

"You oughtta leave, boy," Henry said.

"Come on," Kirk said. "There's a thousand bars."

"I like this one," I said. "I like the service. The friendly atmosphere."

The tall cop picked up a fresh shot and said, "You better split, pretty boy, while you can still fuckin' breathe."

I knocked the glass out of his hand. It bounced and rolled. He looked at me as if he had just met a crazy man.

And then Kingsize was there. Up close, he was the biggest man I'd ever seen.

"Pick that glass up, boy."

He had a small voice that didn't go with his body and I smiled, working hard to hold back a laugh.

"And after that, take the jig and get your ass outta here."

The cops eased back, giving him room. The bartender laid a sap on the bar. The only sound was Tony Bennett singing "Boulevard of Broken Dreams" on the juke.

I shrugged and bent down to pick up the shot glass.

And suddenly twisted and hurled myself at him from the squat, driving a left hook into his face. The face exploded in a jumble of teeth and blood, and I moved in, whipped a right hand to his balls, and in the same motion bashed his head again with the left hook.

He went down in sections, like a house collapsing.

When his shoulders hit the floor, I stomped his face, to keep him there.

But even then I wasn't finished. Kingsize was, but not me. I grabbed the sap and heaved it through the back mirror. Then I reached for the bartender with both hands, yanking him forward, and smashed his face into the glasses on the bar.

Hands were all over me now, but it was as if twenty men were inside me trying to get out and I was no longer just fighting a guy in a saloon. Now I was trying to kill.

I don't remember hitting the tall cop. He was just there suddenly, sitting on the floor against the shuffleboard machine, his eyes surprised. I remember that, and Kirk near the back door, winging punches, and

the man with the shuffleboard puck lying on his face,
and then the sad cop with his gun out. And a high
piercing hurting siren going off in my head.

I can't move my arms. They're hitting me and I can't
move my arms. I'm slammed, lifted, dropped.

Nigger-loving bastard.

Give it to him.

I'm on the ground, my back against a wall. I hear
rain making a drumming sound and see the tall cop
standing over me, blood leaking from his nose. The
rain is hitting his rubber coat. There's a streetlight a
hundred yards away, at the far end of the alley.

Now the bartender staggers out, holding a bloody
towel to his face. The sad cop moves into the yellow
light and stands beside his partner while the rain turns
the alley to mud. I touch my face and my fingers come
away red. I see a lot of legs and shoes, and then something moves and pain rips through me. Jarring, heavy,
shocking pain. Again. And again. The mud is sticky.
I'm lying beside some garbage cans face down in the
mud. I try to get up, but I'm kicked backwards.

I see Ma's face. Angry. Pissed off.

There's another hard bone-jerking pain, one final
thump, and then I don't feel anything at all.

2

You WAITED FOR HER in the holding room of the Kings County Jail. Your hands were skinned, your jaw was swollen, your face bruised and raw. When you breathed, pain stabbed through your chest from your rib cage. Your legs ached. Your hair was matted with blood and mud, your clothes covered with dried muck from the alley. You waited for her, and you were afraid.

Then you saw her on the other side of the door, talking to a guard. In that place of steel walls and ceaseless drilling noise, she looked more beautiful than you'd ever seen her before. She was thirty-six years old that year, as far as you could figure it out, with dark skin, high cheekbones and good teeth. Her eyes were shiny brown, her mouth thick-lipped but small. Her hips were a little too narrow and her shoulders a little too wide to look movie star perfect, but when she walked there was a softness and a grace to her that made people look twice. Men and women.

She told you once that she was Shoshone on her father's side, that father who had run off before the Second World War and ended up killed in Italy with an artillery battalion. When she was ten, her mother died in a car crash in Alabama and she came to New York to live with aunts. You didn't know much more, but the Indian thing was a piece of the mystery, hidden by a smile you could never quite understand. The smile said: Come on. And then it said: Stay back. It told you to know her and it told you to forget her. It told you that everything was possible, that you would always be loved and cherished and cared for, and then it said that you did not matter, that you were unworthy, that you would be easily forgotten. You had studied that smile across kitchen tables, in the booths of restaurants out there in America. And it had teased and turned you away.

You watched her arrive in the outer room, in her lime-green dress, a green hat, a frilly yellow scarf tossed over one shoulder, holding a dripping black raincoat. She talked quickly to the outside guard and then was brought into the room. A second guard leaned against the back wall. You were separated by a table. She smiled and shook her head and you wanted to cry.

You look wonderful, she said.

I feel terrific.

She lit a Marlboro and her eyes took in the room: mesh and bars on the windows, black and Puerto Rican wives and girl friends at the other tables talking to their men.

You blew the job at the plant, she said.

That's like blowing a ticket on the Hindenburg.

Funny. A real wit.

That's what the cop said last night.

Your father was a wit, too. A real wit.

Your heart lurched. The smile froze. She shut you

off for a moment. She was remembering him. Jack Fallon.

You said: No ghost stories, Ma. I'm in the can.

Well, she said, I saw him hit people every Saturday night for four years. A lot of good it did him. Or us.

What about the lawyer, Ma?

She leaned in close, smelling of soap and rain. You looked at her lips and wanted to bite them.

I talked to the lawyer, she said. He's on a murder in Jersey and is trying to get loose. He thinks he can fit you in.

She fiddled with the green hat and took a drag on the Marlboro. How soft she looked. How young and fresh.

He thinks you'll probably do time . . .

Time?

You couldn't believe it. You couldn't believe that she was saying you would go to jail and you couldn't believe that she was saying it so calmly, with such a cool low voice. She rubbed a knuckle on her teeth. You could not do *time*. Not for hitting a guy who was trying to hit you.

She said: Hitting a cop is a felony, Bobby.

You told her that you didn't remember hitting any cop. You hit Kingsize. You hit him coming up from the floor and you remembered his face exploding, but you didn't remember hitting a cop. The cops saw what happened, they saw the guy coming at you, they could have stopped it. If anything, you should sue the goddam city. That's what.

She listened to you, smiling as you poured out your anger. Some of the other visitors were getting up and saying goodbyes. There were hugs. Muttered words. A heavy black woman was crying. You looked at your mother's face. The make-up was streaked by the rain.

She said: The lawyer says he'll try to get a friendly judge. Some judge who can knock it down from a felony to a simple misdemeanor and try to get you a suspended sentence. But he says things are tough now. He says there's an election coming up and nobody wants to look soft on punks.

I'm not a punk.

I know you're not a punk. I'm just telling you what the lawyer said.

If he thinks I'm a punk, then we should get another lawyer.

He doesn't think you're a punk, either. He's saying what the newspapers might say. That's all. I—

Her eyes welled with tears. The smile vanished completely. You took her soft hand in yours, the table between you.

I'm sorry, Ma. You're doing your best. I'm sorry about—

And then the guard was there, leaning over slightly:

Let's go, folks. Visiting's over.

She stood up slowly, still holding the raincoat. From where you were sitting she seemed very tall.

Hey, Ma?

Yes?

Thanks. Thanks for coming. Thanks for getting the lawyer.

She leaned forward across the table, balanced on one hand, and kissed you on the cheek. You smelled bedrooms. And the Botanical Garden.

She whispered: See you tomorrow, dummy.

Don't worry, Ma. I'll just flash the baby blues at that judge, and Kirk and I will both walk.

She winked at you and turned quickly, following the blacks and Puerto Ricans into the hall. The guard looked at her legs. They were long and tan, and she was not wearing stockings.

Jesus Christ. What a kid. What a dummy. I flash the baby blues, all right. I give them the blondie boy look. I tell them yes, my name is Robert Fallon. My father ran off. A long time ago. When? When I was six. Where'd he go? Away, somewhere, I don't know where. What do you want to do? I don't know. You don't know? No. Why not? It's none of your fucking business, asshole.

The judge is a little fat Italian. He sweats a lot and pats at his face with a monogrammed handkerchief. He pulls the handkerchief from somewhere under the bench. I wonder if he has it wrapped around his prick. He listens carefully to the cops when they testify but they never mention Kingsize or what caused the fight. He listens to the bartender talk about these two punks who were looking for trouble, namely, Kirk and me. When we tell our stories, he looks bored and writes notes on a yellow pad. Ma is in the second row, sitting with the black mothers and Puerto Rican wives, all of them waiting for their men's cases to come up. Uniformed black guards lounge against the walls.

In the end, we're guilty, all right, and the judge tries to give me a year and a day, and three years for Kirk.

"Hey, that's bullshit, man!" I yell, kicking the table.

The lawyer's brief case hits the floor. Papers scatter. Guards rush over and wrestle me to the floor.

"I'm *white* and he's *black*, so he does three times more time? What *is* this shit?"

"Yeah, what *is* this shit?" a black guy shouts from the back of the courtroom.

And now everybody in the room is standing, various black people screaming about *honky justice*, and bull*shit*, and what the *fuck*, muffuck. The judge sweats and raps for order. The door in the back opens and more people rush in, blacks, and guards, and reporters.

"Clear this courtroom!" the judge bellows.

And all the while, a huge black guard has his forearm dug into my Adam's apple, and he's whispering: "Don't move, cocksucka, or I break your fuckin' neck."

I look at Ma. They're shoving her along to the door. Her face is worried and angry, like a young girl caught in someone else's argument.

Then my lawyer finishes picking up his papers and stuffs them into the brief case. He looks at me.

"You Irish asshole," he says, very quietly.

And he turns around and walks straight down the middle aisle and out of the courtroom.

The judge compromises. He gives us each two years.

I want to puke. Then Ma bursts back into the room. She calls the judge a lot of bad names and tells him he doesn't know what he's doing, and she has friends and he'll be sorry.

"Put the crooked *cops* in the can! Lock up the crooked *judges!*"

Guards are grabbing at her, but when I try to move, the big black guard slams the hammerlock on me.

"Leave her alone!" I yell. "Get your hands off her or I'll break your ass!"

The guard presses and suddenly I can't feel my legs. They're dragging Ma out of the courtroom. She kicks at them with spiked heels. I never loved her more.

We went upstate in a closed van, with benches along the sides. Seven of us: Kirk and three other black guys, two Puerto Ricans, and me. We couldn't see out through the frosted glass, so most of the trip was a series of sounds. I could hear hard city noises as the van moved us through the tunnel to Manhattan and then the sound of engines idling as we waited at a tollbooth, and then cars whizzing by as we drove out onto a highway. The stink of the city drifted away, and I could smell trees and dirt and country. Kirk sat there staring at his hands. He never brought up what happened in the Shamrock that rainy payday. He had been right and I had been wrong, and now we were going to the can. Once in a while, he would look up, shake his head, smile, and chuckle in a dry kind of way. But he didn't say anything and I liked him for that.

Gradually, the others began to talk. What I learned later was con talk. About bum raps and bad lawyers, crooked judges and evil women. They were all sad and pissed off and smoking too much, and they talked in short bursts as if they knew the words didn't really mean very much. A million words couldn't cut our way out of that van. They ignored me. I was white and I had nothing to do with them. I wasn't too sure what the Spanish guys were saying, but I could understand the blacks well enough and it all sounded empty.

After a while, a Puerto Rican named Fuentes cleared his throat, looked at me and said: "What's a white cat going to the can for, man?"

Kirk leaned forward, before I could answer. "He's an ay-dult molester, man."

Fuentes backed up slightly, as if I might have some terrible disease. "Yeah?"

"The worse kind," Kirk said. I could see the yellow glints dancing around in his eyes.

"Hey, you better *watch* it in the can," Fuentes said to me. "No little girls up dere, mister."

"No, wait, man, he don't molest little *girls*," Kirk said. "He does it to big people."

"Yeah?" That was even worse.

"*Cops,* man. That's why he's here. He banged out some bacon."

Suddenly Fuentes understood. He laughed with a mouthful of gold teeth and offered me a cigarette. "No shit? You beat up a cop?"

"In a bar 'n' grill," Kirk said.

Fuentes looked at the blacks. "Fuckin' guy is hot shit," he said.

I took a long drag on the cigarette. Thinking: I'm hot shit, all right. I'm also going to the can.

3

YOU SPENT THAT FIRST DAY being fingerprinted, photographed, stripped, inoculated, lectured. A man with a rubber glove roaming around in your rectum. You were given a gray uniform, a blanket and a cell in D Block. You said goodbye to Kirk as he left for A Block across the great open yard. You did all of this mechanically, without feeling, shoving down the fear, surrendering to the routine. You found it was easy. That first day, you let yourself become someone who was moved around by others.

Your cell was on the third tier of D Block and it was empty. You dropped your gear and followed a guard to the main commissary, where you ate a stew full of gristle-streaked meat. And that night you listened to the sounds of prison: footsteps clacking on metal, iron bars sliding into place, the coughing, snoring, spitting and humming that came from the other cells.

You stood up suddenly and climbed into the top bunk, kneeling close against the wall, leaning over to look through the barred window. There was a town out there, and farms. But you couldn't see the streets, or the fields, or the hills of the countryside. You saw only more jail: red brick; dirty iron; rivets and wires and walls; men standing near corner turrets, holding machine guns; slowly turning lights. Your breath made a blotch of steam on the cold glass. You climbed down. The lights were out now, and somewhere a voice hummed a song whose words you didn't know.

You tried to sleep, remembering the Easter smell of wax candles in Holy Name Church, when the statues were all draped in purple and the old Italian women shuffled in the darkness like black dwarfs. That was the time of death and judgment. But at Christmas the smell of wax was erased by the smell of pine needles, sticky at the root where the sap had clogged like gluey blood. Four winters after Jack Fallon left, you went to Midnight Mass to see what it was about, to feel the eerie contact with mystery. And death was all around you, except for the pines. The bearded young man hung from his cross, a crucified son, the wound of the lance dripping from his side; the statue of the Virgin was like ice, no character or detail betrayed her face, no color stained her skin, no mysterious smile beckoned and sent you away. Only death, cold as granite. The church was crowded but you sat by yourself, because your mother would never go to Mass. An old Italian man was suddenly beside you, toothless, deep holes where his eyes should be; his hand touched your leg; you looked, afraid to scream, and felt fear enter you like a spider. Before that Christmas minute, you have no memory of fear. Suddenly the spider came from the old man's gnarled hand, scurried up your leg, and entered you. You tried to move away, but the ancient hand clamped your leg. Like a claw. Like iron. As the sightless eyes stared up at the Virgin.

You made a smothered sound, and a few faces at the end of the aisle turned, and an altar boy hesitated, but then the priest was holding up the host: a circle: white: pure: making God enter this round disk so that all there could eat small broken parts of it. The cardboard disk of God. And the old man held your leg.

And when they got up to go for Communion, you slashed at him with an elbow, hitting him in the worn face, and his hand came free, and you ran out, down the side aisle to the street.

You ran that night, full of the spider, moving past crowded saloons, heading down darkened avenues, finished with Midnight Mass and cardboard Gods. Ran until you got home, and she was there, smiling her cool smile, holding you close to her. Soft and warm in the Christmas night.

That was in the place on 10th Street, on the second floor. The place with the backyard, where you dug holes in the dirt and pulled great earthworms from the clay. That was the place you lived in that year, together.

And you remembered other places where you had lived with her. With Kate Fallon. With Ma. A place in California, low and bright with dust in the yard and a car in the driveway; the seat covers were split and the two of you patched them with adhesive tape. A place near Buffalo; she took you to see the steel mills, their walls the color of jail. Those were the years when you went away a lot, you and Ma, you and Kate, heading off in buses and cars, on railroad trains and airplanes; the two of you together; moving on, from house to house and town to town. But you knew you would always come home. One morning the suitcase would be packed again, and you would be heading home: back to the neighborhood.

The neighborhood where Jack Fallon was famous. They would tell his tale in the bars, in Farrell's and Rattigan's, in McCauley's and the Caton Inn. From the time you were seventeen, after you'd dropped out of high school, you were in those places, too, drinking beer, fighting on the sidewalks. Or listening as they told you how good he was with his hands, and how all the ladies loved him, and what a handsome bastard he was, and Jesus, how he had *heart*. They never said he had a good heart. That's not what they meant. They meant Jack Fallon could be hit with a ball bat and would still be there, coming at you.

Jack Fallon, the gambler. He had a lot of heart.

You beat the shit out of enough people so that some of the older men started to say: Jack Fallon had a lot of heart, like you. But you knew they didn't mean it. They were his friends, not yours, and they were in love with his ghost. The ghost of the gambler with the murderous hands. Jack Fallon, who could play poker for three days without sleep and still have enough left to take on the house. Jack Fallon, who left them all so empty when finally he went away and never came back.

Wherever he went, alive or dead, you wished someone would tell him about you. Tell him how, through you, he was still beating people in the bars of Brooklyn. Tell him how when you bent someone over a jukebox and hammered him with your hands you were doing it to get Jack Fallon out of the room forever.

Him.

Jack Fallon.

With the big shoulders. Smelling of tobacco.

The man who made Ma laugh.

Once he lathered your face with his shaving brush as you stood beside him in the small bathroom, and then laughed with his heavy laugh, and when Ma yelled, he lathered her, too. She punched him in the chest. He called her a dirty redskin and pulled her hair back and kissed her all over her lathered mouth. Laughing all the time. Before sending you out to play.

Jack Fallon had a lot of heart.

When you were five, he took you on the ferry to the Statue of Liberty. The water rolled and fell away below the ship and then rolled high, smashing against the bow of the ferry. He picked you up and put you on his shoulders, holding your arm tight. You were afraid you would fall together into the sea. But he carried you into the statue that way, climbing up through the iron belly of the giant woman, right into her head. Nobody was ever that strong.

And then one night he and Ma were in the kitchen, with you in the bed in the next room. He was slapping cards against the table. They talked but you couldn't hear the words. First low, then louder, then very loud. He slammed the table. Glasses fell. Ma shouted at him to stop and he kicked the glasses. Then he grabbed the tall white metal cabinet that stood against the wall and jerked it over, mashing glasses and food together, and kicked over the table. And then he yanked the refrigerator away from the wall. He pulled it over on its side, and she ran through your room, screaming. You covered your head with a pillow and lay there shaking.

When you came home from school the next day, he was gone.

Except for you. He was still there in your head for years after that. He took you to ball games, in your head, sat with you in the bleachers, bought you hot dogs, talked about the weather and the starting pitchers. In your head. He took you to Coney Island. To South America when the snow was deep. He showed you how to make kites, start fires with pieces of wood, hunt animals with knives, fish the great streams, climb the tall mountains. You made him do all those things. The things fathers did with sons.

And then one day, not in your head, you were eleven. He had been gone for five years. You and Kate had circled back to Brooklyn again, to the neighborhood. And that afternoon she dressed up in her best clothes, smoking too hard while she got ready, dropping her lipstick in the sink, cursing, dropping it again. She said goodbye, told you there was soup in the pot, and a TV dinner in the freezer, and then went out, smiling her mysterious smile. But you went out, too. You followed her. She was on one side of the street, walking fast, her head down. You hugged the wall on the other side, moving from doorway to doorway. She went down into the subway. You rushed to the entrance on the other side of the street, running on sneakered feet, faster than she was. You bought a token, went down the end stairway to the platform, and hid behind a pillar. She came down, looked vaguely in the direction of the train. She bought a one-cent pack of gum from a machine. She chewed the gum, staring down at the rails.

It was early afternoon and the train was half empty. You went into the car behind hers, so you could keep her in sight. She got off at 49th-50th Street, near Radio City Music Hall. You followed. She came up into a lobby of Rockefeller Center, where lines of people were waiting to see some TV show, and went past them to the street. You followed her up Sixth Avenue. She turned at 52nd Street, moving more urgently now, looking at her watch. She went into Toots Shor's. You waited across the street.

You waited for hours. It got dark, and you were very hungry, and wondering if you would remember which train to take home. You wondered if the restaurant had a back door, and if she had left from that other secret door, was already home, waiting for you, angry with you, or afraid, calling the police, searching the neighborhood.

Then she came out. With Jack Fallon.

The long-gone man. Wearing a dark gray coat with a velvet collar and shiny black shoes. She was holding his arm. The smile played on her face.

You wanted to run across the street. To jump on him. To wrap your arms around him. To sit on his shoulders again.

But you didn't move. Afraid that you would ruin things if you went to him. Thinking maybe he wanted to come home. Back to Ma, back to you. Maybe they were going to talk about it, but if they saw you, she might get mad. And worse, he might leave again. So you stayed back, in the shadows of doorways, and followed them to Broadway. To the Hotel Taft. Ma leaning close against him, her hand in his overcoat pocket. They went in together. You waited two hours, but they didn't come out, and you were starving and heartbroken and confused and afraid. You took the subway back to Brooklyn.

She came home at four in the morning. Her hair mussed, her make-up gone. You asked her where she'd been. She told you she'd been to the movies, that's all. Then she cracked a tray of ice and poured herself a drink. She picked up the drink and headed for the bedroom. You heard her cry for a while, and then silence.

4

I'M A NEW PRISONER and that means I'm a fish. All
new guys are called fish, and every fish must learn the
laws of the pond. Right away, I learn that I'm supposed to join a clique or get left to the fags. There's a
Spanish clique, a lifer clique, a white clique, a black
clique. The blacks break down into regular blacks and
Muslims. I see them every day in the yard, nobody
mixing. The Puerto Ricans play ball with the Puerto
Ricans. The blacks sit with the blacks at the movies.
The whites do their number against the west wall.
Everybody conning, scheming, bullshitting, complain-
ing or just checking out their shoeshines.

   The leader of the white clique is a short little
Italian with thin blond hair and fading tattoos. He
tells everybody that on the outside he was a soldier in
the mob. What mob? Some fucking mob. A Brooklyn
mob one week. A Bronx mob the next. It doesn't

matter. Every week he gets packages: hard salamis, provolone, Nestle's Crunch bars. He uses the stuff to buy loyalty, but after a few hours around him, I decide to stay away. I don't like pricks like him on the outside. No point starting to like them on the inside. Not for a bite of a Nestle's Crunch.

The third day, I catch up with Kirk. He's already acting different, though I don't know exactly what it is. He stands different, his eyes shift around, his voice is slower, like he's trying to remember some line he made up the night before in bed. We're standing in a corner of the Big Cube, which is what the cons call the yard because of the shape. Kirk asks how I am. I tell him lousy. He jingles a few coins in his pocket.

Then he nods over to a very large spade leaning against the west wall. This spade has on an immaculate, starched uniform. His shoes gleam. He is very clean. Around him is a group of smaller, thinner, not so sharp blacks and whites.

"See that cat?"

"Yeah?"

"That's Elizabeth Taylor."

"No shit. I'm Burt Lancaster."

"That's what they call him," Kirk says. "And you better watch your white ass, babe. 'Cause he done passed the word he wants to own your swipe."

Just then, one of the smaller cons leans down with a yellow handkerchief and flicks some dust off the gleaming shoes.

"You mean he's the boss fag?"

"You got it. Elizabeth Taylor. Queen of Sheba. Head dick-chewer. Pimp of all pimps, princess of the fuck boys. And I'm tellin' you, Bobby, don't pull any wise-ass jitterbug bullshit on *him*. He is *bad*."

"He don't look so fuckin' bad to me."

Kirk is exasperated. "I'm *tellin'* you, man, don't do nuthin' dumb. This joint's like an armory. Wire hangers sharpened to a point. Plain old shivs from the kitchen. Rolled metal blackjacks from the machine shop. Be cool, boy."

We drift across the yard. The whites stare at us one way, wondering what I'm doing with a yom. The blacks stare at Kirk. I feel this Elizabeth Taylor's eyes on me. I look back at him, see shiny hair, long lashes, and I'm afraid. And ashamed that I'm afraid.

Kirk whispers: "The first week is the worse. I ast them lifers, babe. They know." He lights a cigarette. "They gonna come on strong, the Fagola Army, and try and make you a jailhouse punk. Buy your ass with a pack of smokes."

"Shit, I come higher than that," I tell him.

"Maybe," he says. "Remember, you're *valuable*, babe. A piece of fresh white ass."

The piece of fresh white ass nods, and Kirk walks over to a group of blacks, lolling against the east wall. He's smiling.

That Friday, I was in the shower on the first floor of D Block. The water was very hot, the floor scummy with old soap, and I stood in the thick steam soaping my arms, legs, balls, letting the water boil me. Then I felt it: a hand reaching around from behind, rubbing my stomach, followed by a hard penis sliding along the crack of my buttocks. Not forcing. Just taking a look.

I whirled, sliced my elbow into the steam and smashed something bony. A body fell heavily and I wished I had boots on to stomp with.

"Who the fuck *is* that?"

I saw nothing, then started for the door and stepped on a slippery body. I heard laughter from another part of the shower room as I groped along the wet tile wall for the door. The laughter was eerie. Dark black mustached laughter. Water poured against the floor. I found the door but the handle was stuck. I jiggled it, rattled it, suddenly panicky, afraid there were more of them back there in the steam. I began to pound on the door.

It opened from the other side.

A guard was holding the doorknob and I pushed past him into the cool air of the dressing room, where my clothes were hanging on a peg.

"Wud is it, boy?" the guard said.

"Some son of a bitch in there just tried to corn-hole me."

"Yeah?"

"I gave him a good rap in the head."

"Tough guy, huh?"

"He's on the floor in there. He might drown."

"So?"

"So go in and get the son of a bitch and *do* something!"

"Wuddya gettin' *excited* for, pretty boy? You gonna piss your *pants*, you get any more excited. I think you oughtta get back to your cell, pretty boy. Right now, hear? Just get your ass dressed and get on back to that cell of yours."

I dried myself quickly, while the guard sat down at a wooden desk and watched me. Inside, the water kept pouring on the slimy floor.

Back in the cell I was no longer alone. Someone was lying face down in the top bunk. He turned his head as the door locked behind me. I saw a frog-eyed black face and hair braided in very tight curls. He said his name was Roy. I shook hands and grunted, got undressed and slid into the bottom bunk. The 10:30 bells were tolling away for lights out, but some light seeped into the cell from outside. My elbow hurt.

Then Roy dropped down from the top rack. I heard him taking off his clothes, shoes falling, buttons popping, the sound of a zipper. I turned to look at him.

He was barefoot. Wearing a brassiere. Stuffed with something. And a pair of flowered women's panties.

"You can have me," he whispered.

"Aw, come on, man. That's the second time *to-night*. It's just not my *scene,* man."

His voice was very soft now. "Nobody will know."

"I will," I said.

I faced the wall. We were all in this cage now, whites and blacks and Puerto Ricans, two thousand three hundred and forty cocks. And not a cunt in sight. I lay on my belly, trying not to think of women, of the smell of hair and pussy and tongue, of softness, and breasts, and white teeth. Roy moved his back against the cell wall and slid down. I knew he was looking at me, probably playing with himself, but I just didn't want to see it. I hooked my elbow around the side of my head and stared out of the cell, across the tier. Something was moving in one of the other cells. A large bulky coal-black body. On his knees, with his head working hard on a pale young Puerto Rican.

Roy groaned.

Oh, man.

After a month, Kirk shaves his head. And one day in the yard, with a lot of blacks hanging around, he starts coming on to me with a brand-new rap:

"You know somethin'? It was the *black* man set the universe in motion. Bet you didn't know that, did you? White history never tells you that. Black scientists in a million-man spaceship, flyin' from the mouth of Allah, driftin' through the galaxies, man, until it came to the earth and they saw the white apes: a million years ago, when blacks lived on sixty-six billion planets all over the universe: arrived on the earth and taught the white apes how to *stand,* and then how to *hunt:* placed the *moon* in its orbit, commanded the *sun* to stand still: all for Allah! And Allah then sent us his *Messenger!* Sent him to cleanse and *purge* the earth! And the Messenger conquered all of the white man's world, warnin' the blue-eyed devil that corruption and fornication shall *not* be passed to the black man! The spaceship hovers ovuh this planet even now, awaitin' the final battle, awaitin' Armageddon."

His voice gets louder and more Southern, and the blacks begin to listen carefully.

"And in the final battle the so-called Negro will stand up and take what is *his,* restore the earth to its greenness and delight, all to please Allah! The so-called Negro will throw off his chains and purge the Lost-Found-Nation-in-the-West! What has the white man given the so-called Negro? Whiskey! Tobacco! Dope! Clothes he can't afford and cars he can't gas! He made whores of the black man's women, connived at his downfall, gave him easy credit and welfare and all the other pollutions of Babylon! We do not live in a country, we live in a *jail with a flag,* and we can break that jail only under the Sword and the Crescent!"

"What kind of act *is* this, Kirk?" I whisper.

"I speak of my love for Allah. Of my new-found knowledge, my love of Self and Kind. We here are in prison 'cause we robbed or we killed! But if we *robbed* the white man, we can never get all that is owed to us. If we *killed* the white man, well, he has always been our tormentor!"

"Right on!" yells one of the blacks.

Others drift over. I ease back and away. From the towers, the guards look down at the little crowd. More than six blacks talking loud together and the screws get nervous.

Kirk points a finger at one of the blacks. "The cop who arrested you, what color was he?"

"White!"

"The D.A. who possicuted you, what color was he?"

"White!"

"The jury that sat in judgment, and the judge that passed sentence, what color wuh they?"

"White!"

Kirk rolls, his accent blacker and thicker. The crowd cheers him on. The Muslims move in closer. They look at him suspiciously, glowering at him, watching me. I'm the only white man in this corner of the yard. And the only young white con in the entire prison.

"And here in the white man's prison, what color are the guards?"

"White!"

"And even the chaplain. Even the speaker faw the Christian god, that wolf in sheep's clothes, that agent who tells you to console yawsef to these four walls. What color?"

"White!"

"So I say to you, throw off the white man's trick-nology! Learn your history, black men! Remember that Aesop was black, and that the man who showed Columbus the way to the New World was black! Remember that when the white man was eatin' raw meat, the University of Sankore in Timbuktu—that's in Africa! —was sendin' its wise men to all the cities of the known world, to Cairo and Granada, to Morocco and Italy! You are all of the Tribe of Shabazz, on this earth for sixty-six trillion years, and you were chartin' the stars when the white man slept with dogs in caves!"

The Muslims are paying close attention now; they move in even tighter.

"So we close as brothers. *As-salaam-alaikum!*"

The Muslims answer together: *"Wa-alaikum-salaam!"*

"As-salaam-alaikum!"
"Wa-alaikum-salaam!"
"As-salaam-alaikum!"
"Wa-alaikum-salaam!"

There's a big cheer, and the guards look nervous, and the Muslims and the other blacks close in around Kirk. I feel suddenly alone, as foolish as a school kid, and start to walk away. I pass Kirk. He points up at the guards, the blacks all look, and then he turns to me for a second and winks.

In the laundry, a week later, Elizabeth Taylor made his move.

"I've been watching you," he said.

"I know."

"You're a good-looking man."

"That so?"

"Irish, right?"

"Is a pig's pussy pork?"

He stood beside me, leaning on the edge of the washing machine. His arms were shaved and he smelled of lilacs. I finished loading a bag of fresh-washed laundry and slung it over my shoulder.

"You don't *have* to work here, you know."

"Where am I gonna work? Boomingdale's?"

"I could get you something easier."

"No thanks."

"You should wise up, boy." He was blocking my way.

"Wise up to what? I'm not a fag, pal. It's as simple as that."

He smiled. "Is it? Let me tell you something, boy. Some heavy reality. You are what is known as a white fuck. A white fuck don't ever do easy time. You can be a duke or a dip, a fuck boy or a jailhouse punk. Hear?"

He smiled again, his eyes as old as tombs.

"You can do your time in Segregation or you can leave here in a pine box, boy. You keep goin' the way you're goin' and that'll happen, too. You can bet on it." He eased a pack of king-sized Benson & Hedges out of his shirt pocket. "Or you can do easier time, boy. You don't have to be no dead white fuck."

"You mean I can be a live white fuck. *Your* white fuck."

He dragged deeply on a cigarette. "I've been here

a long time, Fallon. I'm gonna be here a lot longer.
Like eleven years longer. And I've seen them come and
I've seen them go."

"I bet you seen more of them come than go," I
said.

He didn't laugh. "When they first come in, they
talk a lot about their *wives* and their *girl* friends and
how much they *love* them. They cry in their bunks at
night and in the yard they talk about their girls' *skin*
and their *hair* and their *breasts*. Their great big beautiful *breasts*. But in a couple of weeks they ain't cryin'
at night no more and in the yard they talkin' 'bout
their *tits*. A month later, they talkin' 'bout beatin' their
skulls in." He took another long drag, without looking
at me. His voice came from far away: "You know
somethin'? I didn't realize how soft a hard-on was until
the first time I had one in my mouth."

He put a hand on my shoulder. It lay there like a
soft hairless animal sniffing for danger. I bent away
under the hand.

"Get lost," I said.

"Don't be a dumb white fuck."

I started to move around past him but he moved
with me. Dampness rose from the giant spin driers.
There was nobody around. I put down the laundry
bag.

Why not? I thought. *Why the fuck not?* They
were sucking and fucking each other all over the goddam prison, in all the cells, in the latrines and the
showers and the laundry rooms, sticking it in any available hole. What difference would it make? Who *cared*
if I let someone suck my pop?

Not a soul. Just me.

I smiled at Elizabeth Taylor and took his face in
my hands, very gently. His eyelashes fluttered. I
pulled his head forward, as if I was about to kiss him.

Then I bit his nose. I bit deep and hard, grinding
my teeth into flesh and cartilage as a scream worked

its way out of the big man's chest. Finally I let go and he lurched back, holding his face, looking terrified.

A screw rushed over, followed by a couple of cons.

"What the hell happened?" the screw shouted. "What the hell is going on wid you two bastids?"

I lifted the laundry bag. "I didn't realize how soft a nose was," I said, "until I had one in my mouth."

They put me in Segregation for forty-eight hours. In the yard, when I got out, Kirk made a circle with his thumb and forefinger but stayed with his crowd of shaved-head Muslims. Elizabeth Taylor leaned against the wall, his nose covered by a tinfoil sunshade, avoiding my look. His boys didn't go near me.

5

TWO DAYS AFTER I GET OUT OF SEGREGATION, a screw
comes to see me. Ernie Thompson. I never took much
notice of him before. All screws look the same when
you're in prison. It must be the uniforms. They move
around on the walls, in the guard towers, in the commissary. But pretty soon you divide them into Okay
or Asshole. An Okay screw realizes you're trying to
get by, just like him, and he doesn't hassle you. An
Asshole is always using his edge. He lives by the book,
knows all the rules and uses them to remind you how
big he is compared to you. He stops you for a search in
the yard. He counts your money and if you're holding
too much he makes you say why. He makes you take
the pictures off the walls of your cell or clear the top of
your bunk. And every once in a while he makes you
strip down for a body search and looks up your ass
for machine guns. He knows this is a waste of time. He
knows it makes you hate him even more than you

normally would. But he doesn't care. It makes life mean something for him, I guess.

Ernie Thompson is Okay. He arrives in my life during the second yard period. I'm in my spot, halfway between the white clique and the black clique, doing push-ups. I'm up to two hundred push-ups a day and I love the feeling it gives me, of grinding and hurting, of fat burning, of my chest swelling. The push-ups are followed by jogging, the muscles bunching and stretching in my legs, my lungs screaming. It's what I do to stay apart. Or to keep from jerking off too much.

I'm on my seventy-fifth push-up when I see his shoes. I stop and look up at a sleepy-eyed guy, maybe fifty, with a mustache.

"Yeah?"

He watches me while I turn around to a sitting position. "You're Fallon, right?"

"That's right. So what?"

"Bobby Fallon?"

"Sometimes they call me 127654-G. What do you want?"

"I hear you're a fighter."

"You do, huh?"

"I hear you did in old Elizabeth Taylor. Over in the laundry. I hear you belted out a couple of cops before you got here."

"You hear a lot of things."

I stand up. Over in the black clique I see Kirk doing his Muslim rap but keeping his eyes on me.

"Why do you want to know?"

"I want to see if you're as smart as you think you are."

"I don't get it."

"There's a saying in jail, Fallon. They say there's hard time and there's easy time. And easy time is better."

"That's what my man Elizabeth was saying."

"There's some guys think *that's* easy time, but

you don't sleep too good when it's over." His eyes drift up at the walls. "Maybe that's the hardest time there is."

"Listen, you're giving me a bad rep just talking to me here. Certain parties are liable to think I'm a stool pigeon or something."

"To hell with what those jerks think," he says in a tough voice. Then: "I run the boxing program here. Not because I think it does any real good. When these bums get out, they'll go right back to raping old ladies and stealing cars and shooting dope. But I figure if a con wears himself out hitting a bag, then he won't try hitting any guards."

"You want my man here to box?"

It's Kirk, moving in. Suddenly crossing the color line. Thompson looks annoyed but nods yes to him.

"I guess you gonna tell him that's easy time," Kirk says.

"You get the brass monkey, pal."

"Just what's he got to do?"

"Fight," Thompson says. "If he can."

"If he can? Why this pretty little blue-eyed devil fights better'n anyone in this joint," Kirk says. "Gotta be a little nigger in him, I always say."

"Who is this potato?" Thompson asks me.

"I am the messenger of Herbert Muhammad," says Kirk, "and as you know he is the manager of Muhammad Ali, the greatest prizefighter in the history of creation. And this poor devil is in my charge. It is through his friendship with me, under the protection of the benevolent Allah, that he has grown to his current ascendency."

Thompson says, "Does this cupcake speak for you?"

"I don't know. When he stops saying fuck and shit, he loses me."

"Well, lemme ask *you,* Fallon. Do you want to fight or what?"

"Of course he does," Kirk says.

"Wait a minute," I say. "What makes either one of you think I want to fight *anyone?* I mean, if it's easy time I'm after, maybe I could sing in the choir."

Thompson's eyes shift to Kirk. "Do you write his material, too?"

"Well, he's only eighteen, you see. And I mean, he *is* Irish. And . . ."

Kirk starts talking faster, gesturing all over the place. When he comes on hard with one of his raps, he can weave a hundred pounds of steel wool into a stove.

"Listen, you have to understand. On the outside —that is to say, when we are out there in *America,* when we are *together,* dig—I am this young man's manager, *mentor,* guardian, friend and trainer. I am his Herbert Muhammad. When he sleeps, I sleep. When he works, I work. I understand this boy. I know what makes him tick. I keep him from feelin' bad and he does the same for me, dig?"

"Is that why you both got locked up the same night?"

"Aw, you've been lookin' at records."

"That was a severe misunderstanding, what happened that night," Kirk says.

"I guess it was," Thompson says. "Some poor son of a bitch ended up in a hospital. For a week."

"He should've ended up in a cemetery," I say.

"You know where I'm comin' from, right?" Kirk says.

The bells ring and the cons start lining up to go back to the cell blocks.

"Be at the gym tomorrow," Thompson says. "Three o'clock sharp." He looks at Kirk and then at me. "The both of you."

When you got back to the cell, you were alone again. Roy was packed and gone, every trace of him, and admit it: you missed him. The way he seemed to fill the cell, the wet, staring eyes as familiar as the walls and the bunks. The case of nerves he gave you every night. The worry as you tried to anticipate his strategies. His availability. And now he had vanished.

Alone, you did more push-ups. Four. Five. Thinking of her. Six. And why her letters had tailed off. Eight. None today. None yesterday. Eleven. Goddam her. I'll tell her to stop writing altogether, to live her life as if I didn't even exist. Sixteen. Just tell her to forget it. Eighteen. And now they're trying to get me to fight. To be a prizefighter. With gloves and trunks and boxing shoes. Twenty. What the hell is Kirk's angle, anyway? One week he's a Muslim, full of all that stomp whitey bullshit, and now he's my manager. Twenty-three. Sometimes it's hard to know what's real. This screw Thompson wants me to fight, but there has to be some scam there and Kirk probably figured it out before I did. I mean, I know I can fight. But I've never been in a gym in my life. Not even in high school. We were never anywhere long enough. Twenty-eight. Ma showed me all that jazz on TV. In the motel that time. In Arizona. Or New Mexico. Somewhere out there, on the way to California. The Coke machine was white from the sun. Thirty. Showing me left hooks and right crosses, saying the words like she knew what they meant. She must've learned them from him. They went to the fights together. Him in a velvet-collared coat, her all made up and smelling like flowers, and the place filled. Thirty-five. They want me to be a fighter. Kirk and Thompson. Shit, I've never even been to the fights. They don't have them in New York anymore. Forty. They used to have them at Eastern Parkway and at Sunnyside Gardens out there in Queens and at the St. Nick's. I remember that from the TV. Forty-three. I was ten and we were in that motel. She washed herself with the door open and I could see her breasts in the mirror, and her body all tan, and the thick V of hair when she turned around for a towel. Smiling at herself. Fifty. The fights came from the St. Nick's and there was a black guy fighting a Puerto Rican and the Puerto Rican held his hands up high to his face like he was looking over a fence and then threw a lot of punches and the black guy was on his back. Ma said, "He throws combinations, this kid. He's good, this kid." I had her say the word over and over again. Combinations. Combinations. Fifty-seven. Thompson must have moved Roy out. Just to show what he can do for me if I fight. Fifty-eight. Make it easy. Fifty-nine. Easy time. Sixty. If you can't do the time, don't do the crime. That's what they say on the yard. Sixty-one. Muhammad Ali is a fighter. They say he's over the hill but I like his black ass. Wise fucker. Doesn't give a goddam. Sixty-five. Maybe I really could be a fighter. A real fighter. I can punch. I know I can punch. But what happens when they hit me back? What happens when I hit a guy who doesn't have a bag of beer in him? Seventy-one. Combinations. He must have taught her the word. When they went to the fights. In the big cars, and the coat with the velvet collar, and dinner at Toots Shor's. Eighty. Why didn't I run across the street that time? Why didn't I go up to them and say I wanted them to come back together, and make everything the way it was before that night when he wrecked the kitchen and made her cry and stood looking at his cards and smoking a Lucky? Eighty-five. Why didn't I ask her about it? At least find out why she never brought it up. Why she lied. Eighty-six. What is she doing anyway? Right now? Right this goddam minute? Cruising the bars in the neighborhood? Gone off again somewhere, across the country, staying in motels? Why doesn't she write more often? I'll tell her to forget it. Live her own goddam life. Don't write to me. Ninety. A fighter. Why not? I like the way it sounds. He's a fighter. With combinations. I saw her in the mirror in the~motel. With beads of water in the black curly V. Ninety-seven. A fighter. Ninety-eight. In the papers, maybe. Ninety-nine. He would read the papers. And then he'd know. A hundred. The son of a bitch.

Fifty gyms later, and a lot of towns, and too many motels, there was really only one gym for me, that first one in the prison in the upstate hills. Narrow and dark, with high ceilings and barred windows, smelling of damp concrete. The biggest thing in the room was the ring, with its thin stained canvas. And that first day Thompson didn't waste time. He handed me some worn Everlast trunks and a pair of low-cut tennis shoes, and gave Kirk the headgear and told him to lace it up for me when it was time to box. I looked at the other fighters while I changed clothes: six or seven of them, shuffling, moving, hitting the bags. Nobody was boxing. A Spanish guy was trying to skip rope. Thompson told me to hold out my hands and started wrapping tape around them.

"I'm gonna do this for you once," he said, "but after today you do it yourself."

He slipped the loop over my thumb and pulled the tape over the top of my right hand and then between my fingers, pulling it around and over very fast, until there was no more tape, only a couple of dangling strings. He tied them in a tight bow and then did it all over again on the other hand. And while he tied the left hand, I flexed the right. I never used the right hand. I wrote with the left hand. I punched people with the left hand. But now, with the tape wrapped around, the right hand felt strange, new, powerful, tremendous. I thought: I can punch holes through walls with this hand.

By the time Thompson finished, I wanted to fight. To break things. To hurt someone. I was moving around, jittery, anxious, snorting.

Thompson said, "Hey! Calm down. You're not

fighting this guy. At least you better not. You're just gonna *move* with him."

"What guy?"

Thompson pointed over his shoulder at a tall, powerful-looking black man, his head shaved in the Muslim style, his eyes blank and cool. He stood alone against the ropes, dressed in a clean white T-shirt and old satin Everlast trunks. His shoes were professional boxing shoes. He didn't bother with headgear.

"That's Harry Shaw," Thompson said. "He had twenty-one pro fights and nineteen knockouts. Then he shot up a saloon and killed four guys. That means he's doing life four times, so he doesn't give a shit what he does. Don't get fresh."

I got into the ring with Kirk. I could almost feel his nervousness. Harry Shaw leaned on the top strand, his back to us. He didn't even look over at me, but a couple of the other fighters did. The Spanish guy who couldn't skip rope smiled as if he already knew what was going to happen.

"Just *move*, you hear, Bobby?" Kirk whispered. "This is a *bad* nigger. So none of that Irish bullshit."

"You know this guy?"

"He's a Muslim. But I don't know him. Nobody does."

Kirk held the leather headgear in front of him, his face screwing into a question, and then leaned forward and shoved it onto my head.

I couldn't see a thing.

"Jesus, not *that* way!" Thompson said. "That's backwards."

He lifted the headgear off me and I could see again. Thompson shook his head and Kirk rolled his eyes, like a guy who'd just been found out but hoped nobody noticed.

"*This* way, schmuck," Thompson said. He put it on right. "Now tie the strings under his chin. Not too tight or they'll dig into him. Then give him that mouth-piece over there."

Kirk was chuckling drily as he tied the string un-der my chin. The headgear slipped over my eyes and I nudged it back with the thumb of a glove. Then he slipped the hard rubber mouthpiece past my lips. I never had one in my mouth before, and it felt smooth and slimy. I was adjusting it with my tongue when Thompson banged three times on the bottom of a bucket.

"Time!"

Shaw turned around as if he knew exactly where I was, touched gloves without a word to me and started to move. He moved beautifully. Smooth and strong, the jab snaking out—*pap*—easy—*pap*—nice—*pap*. He bent and tapped a light hook to my ribs, then brought it up to the side of the headgear—*pap*—and moved again. He wasn't punching at full force, but he made me feel clumsy and fat and young. That day, Harry Shaw was like a woodcutter sizing up a tree.

I was jabbing with the right hand and holding the power in the left, and that made it even harder for me to get at him. Once, I reached his forehead with the jab, but by the time I threw the left he was gone. I heaved a bunch of punches, getting more and more angry, mostly at myself, and all of them missed. I thought: Some fighter I am. Over my head. Sloppy and floundering and feeling stupid. And tight and tense and maybe scared.

And I stopped thinking, calmed down and started to fight. I knew I would have to stop Shaw from mov-ing before I could hit him, so when he moved left be-hind the jab I moved to the right, cutting off the ring. Near the end of the round, I popped him with a cou-ple of jabs. The guy was a fighter and a killer, but he wasn't Superman. My legs felt more springy and I lost the nervousness.

"Time!" Thompson yelled.

We stopped and I came over to the corner.

"Shit! I was just getting started."

"Who says you're finished?"

"Stay cool," Kirk said. He washed the mouthpiece from an old taped Coke bottle, letting the water splash on the floor. "Nice and easy, nice and cool."

"You could try keeping your hands up," Thompson said.

He took the bottle from Kirk and went over to wash off Shaw's mouthpiece. Shaw stood on the far side of the ring, his back to all of us, staring at the wall.

Halfway through the second round, I figured it all out. I flicked with the right hand, slid in quickly on the right foot, shortening the distance, and slammed the left hand home. Shaw was pulling away and the punch hit him on the neck. He made a little gurgling sound and coughed. Something skittery moved in his eyes and I thought: I hurt him. I hurt this bastard. And then it happened. The thing, the scream from the belly, started coming up from inside me and a kind of craziness was on me. I hit Shaw a right hand under the heart and brought up the hook, but I don't remember too much about the rest. Kirk told me later that I was doubling the hooks, pounding at Shaw, piling all over him, with the banshee scream coming from my throat, when Thompson jumped in the ring. Shaw dribbled down the ropes while I hammered at him, my arms pumping like a machine and my eyes all wild.

"Stop it, goddammit, stop it!" Thompson was yelling, and then I was punching at him, too, with Kirk wrapping his arms around me, hugging me, smothering the craziness. "Easy, babe. Easy, now, easy, it's all over. All done. Easy."

When I came out of it, everything in the gym had stopped cold. The speed bags, the skip ropes, the heavy bags. I walked around the ring, kicking at the canvas, pissed off at myself for going berserk.

Thompson was helping Shaw to his feet. "Don't ever do that again," he said to me, his voice like ice. "This is a gymnasium. It's not the street or the yard."

I walked over to Shaw. "Listen, I'm sorry, Harry. I . . . shit, I don't know . . . something *snapped*."

"Forget it," Shaw said, stepping out through the ropes, heading for the shower. The speed bags began to drum again.

"Go back to your cell," Thompson said to me.

"I guess I blew it, huh?"

He turned away, disgusted. "Just be back here to-morrow."

In the shower room next to the gym, Shaw sat on a bench, naked, slowly drying himself with a big terry cloth towel. He didn't look up when I came in. I stepped past him into the shower. The water fell weakly and I could hear Kirk's voice.

"What do you think, brother?"

"He's a banger," Shaw said.

Then Thompson's voice: "Banger? He's a god-dam killer."

"He's got the instinck," Shaw said. "Can't fight but he got the instinck."

6

AND SO I BEGAN TO DO EASY TIME. The next day, Kirk
moved to my cell, bringing his Muslim books, which
he never read again, and the shoes and candy bars that
he had promoted in the yard. He told me the story he
had made up for his Muslim friends: about how he
had dreamed of a visit from the Messenger himself,
and how the Messenger told him that he must become
the new Herbert Muhammad for this poor heathen
white boy, namely me, how he would use this blue-
eyed devil as an instrument of Allah's will, to remind
the people of the Lost-Found Nation that they would
continue to be tested through all of eternity and how
Allah must control the terms of the test.

He told me this like he was rehearsing a part in a
play, going over details, asking for advice on the weak-
er parts, chuckling at his own bullshit. Then he went
out and sold his routine to the Muslims, while the shin-

ing heads nodded in the sun and I went to my spot to exercise.

Elizabeth Taylor and the Fagola Army stayed away. Fuentes came over one day from the Puerto Rican clique and talked about the trip we all took together up here and said he was proud to know me. When I jogged in the yard, guys from the white clique shouted my name. Some of them sent over salami and provolone, which Kirk immediately grabbed. Suddenly I was known. I was no longer a number. No longer a fish. I was respected. I was the man who had knocked out Harry Shaw.

Thompson got permission to set up a series of fights on Sunday afternoons, with the ring pitched outside in the yard. Fighters began to show up at the gym from every clique and cell block. I even met a gay welterweight, a narrow-shouldered Puerto Rican who was a knife artist on the outside. "I'm not a fag," he said. "I'm gay." He fought on three cards, scored three knockouts and was released on parole.

My weight fell, to one eighty-two from one ninety-four, most of it beer from the saloons in Brooklyn. And I started to love boxing: hitting people, making them miss, seeing them fall. And it wasn't just the fighting. I began to love the rest of it: the sweating, the rope skipping, the smell of damp concrete in the gym, the sound of the other fighters grunting when they dug punches into the heavy bags. Harry Shaw boxed with me every day. He showed me the basics, which Thompson didn't really understand. The jab, hook, right hand. He said I should stay a southpaw, because there weren't too many southpaws in jail, or anywhere else, and I would have an extra advantage. I was never able to hurt him again after that first day. And I didn't want to.

In the first six months of tournaments, I had twenty fights and won them all. They were five-round fights, with three-minute rounds, and I fought fast Puerto Ricans, big blacks with scary eyes, guys who were tough back home on the streets but didn't know what to do when someone started to hit them back. I didn't even mind getting hit myself. It became a kind of proof after a while. That I could take punishment and keep coming on.

The funny thing about getting hit was that I didn't really feel it. The world just went blank, as if I was watching a movie with a piece of the film cut out. I'd be boxing, and get hit, and then I'd be boxing again but in some other part of the ring. I wasn't hurt. I just lost some time. And losing a few seconds of time was not the worst thing that could happen when it was time I was doing.

Kirk started to work as hard at being a trainer as I was working as a fighter. Shaw got him to pound my gut with a medicine ball. To get you used to da shock, he said. And Kirk did it until his own arms hung down in weariness and my gut was turning to iron. Once in a while, I caught an odd look in Kirk's eyes: the yellow glints becoming suddenly quiet as he looked at me coolly, like a man studying a new car. In those moments, he seemed like a stranger. But most of the time he was a cheerleader. They gotta bring ass to get ass. He said it and I said it. The slogan. The code word between us. They gotta bring ass to get ass, and they just ain't gonna *get* ass. Kirk was always there, laughing, joking, swabbing my face with a towel, cutting the adhesive on the hand tapes, lacing the gloves and the headgear, and throwing in a good word for Allah whenever blacks were around.

I began to look different. I had never been cut, but the skin over my eyes was thicker. The nose flattened out a little at the bridge. And my body seemed to shift, a fine mesh of muscle appearing over my legs when I did sit-ups, my arms lean and taut. I looked at myself in the mirror and thought: I'm beginning to look like a bad-ass. I went to the barber and got a crew cut, and it made me look even tougher. I was becoming a fighter.

The weekend fights became a major event in the prison. The warden started to attend, and sometimes he brought along outsiders. Men in gray suits, with oatmeal faces and bellies hanging over their belts. They listened to the warden, and I watched Thompson hang around close to them, faking shyness, kicking a rock or two, kissing ass. They would nod and applaud and try to get with it, as if they were watching naughty children at a charity camp putting on a show for the local aristocracy. I knew, without hearing, what they were saying to each other: how this was wonderful for morale, and how it was the most wonderful way to rehabilitate the men, and it was good clean wonderful sport. Before they all went home to their wives and children and fireplaces and barbecues and night clubs and movie houses and department stores and streets and cars and buses and subways. I hated those bastards, all of them.

What I always knew was that this was still jail. I also knew why the fights had become the big thing with the prisoners. Not because of sport, or rehabilitation, but because of gambling. Every week, the gambling was bigger and bigger. For money or cigarettes, for fuck books or comic books, for food or underwear or even blow jobs. On the day of one of the fights, the little hood with the Nestle's Crunch bars came over and said: "You better kick this dinge's ass, Fallon, or half of us are gonna be eatin' black dong tonight." I laughed and walked away, and thought seriously of throwing the fight, just to see what happened. I didn't, of course, because as I beat opponent after opponent, I built up more and more pride. There were some things I just would not do. If I fought a guy and lost, then I wanted it to be because he was better than me. Not because I fooled around. Not because I lost on purpose. Some things you did not do.

And so I made every fight a war. I decided real early that I was in the ring for one single reason: to kill the man I was fighting. To put him in a goddam grave. I knew that someone would always stop me, that Thompson would jump in shouting or the other guy would quit. But while I was in there, my job was to kill him. Because if he killed me, if he beat me, if I lost or was disgraced, I was in terrible trouble. I would become nothing again. It was different for the other fighters. They were all blacks or Puerto Ricans, and in some crazy way they had each other. But I was white. Being unbeatable was my only edge. I was a winner, in their eyes, because I woke up on day one as a white man. Now I would have to stay that way. A winner. And prove it over and over again, until the day I left.

After eight months, there was no one left to fight. I was a heavyweight, I had to fight anyone a hundred and seventy-five pounds and up, and I had beaten them all. Thompson said there was only one solution: to start bringing in teams from outside. Amateurs, from Massachusetts and New York and maybe even Canada. I liked the idea. Fine, I said. Bring 'em on. Anyone. All of them.

What I didn't know then, and didn't learn until a long time later, was that I still didn't know how to fight.

The lights are out.

I'm awake in the cell. Kirk's hand dangles from the top bunk, holding a cigarette, flicking ashes to the floor. He doesn't smoke in the yard. Smoking is against the teachings of the Muslims.

"What time is it, you figure?"

"Prison time. No time. Forget it, Bobby." His voice sounds down and flat.

"Hey . . . what's up, Kirk?"

"Nothin'. Just doin' time," he said. "It's like it don't end, does it?"

"Like we been here all our lives." I sit up, on the edge of the bunk. "You never think about it on the outside. Time, I mean . . ."

"Just piss it away." He grinds the cigarette out on the wall and flips the butt into a corner bucket. "What'd you do on the outside, Bobby? I mean, when you weren't at the factory or havin' a payday drink?"

"Fucked around."

"You can't do that anymore, you know."

"Yeah. I know."

"You have a steady girl?"

"No."

"How come?"

"We moved around too much." I get up and do a knee bend. "Every time we got settled long enough for me to figure out which girls were loose, my mother would move again."

A couple of half-remembered faces shove their way into my head and I shove them back.

"What'd you *really* do on the outside, Kirk?"

"Fucked around."

We both laugh.

"We were made for each other," I say.

"We were both made for the fuckin' can."

Yeah. Two of us, sitting in a third-floor cage.

"What are you gonna do when you get out?" I ask him.

"Breathe," he says. He looks out the barred window. "Bury my face in some good green grass and breathe. Pick up a flower and eat it. Walk through a park and breathe. Go to Prospect Park, and watch some kids play softball, and eat the fuckin' grass like

I was Elsie the Cow. And breathe." He shrugs. "You know . . ."

I know. Flowers. She smelled like flowers. And there were beads of water in her curly black hair.

"What about you, Bobby? What *you* gonna do?"

"I don't know. Lotsa things."

"You better start thinkin', babe. We got seven months left."

"I figure a year."

"You kiddin'? All them boiled shirts comin' aroun' here for the fights—that's the *Parole Board,* man. They ain't gonna hold us for the full bit. No way!"

It's cold. The night smells are drifting around the cell. What am I going to do? On the outside . . .

"I guess . . . I guess I'd like to make a phone call, man," I say. "Just be free to do that. Walk into a phone booth somewhere and dial someone. And get a voice on the other end who knows me. Just that."

"Yeah," says Kirk. "Then what?"

"Then get me a suit. A good suit, with a shirt and a tie, and shoes shining. And an overcoat with a velvet collar." He had heart. He was good with his hands. "And go to a saloon. A New York place, with a headwaiter. A guy in a tuxedo who takes you to the table if you want to eat, or heads you to the bar. The bartenders have little red vests and starchy white aprons, and the glasses are all frosted 'cause they keep them in a refrigerator. They have free peanuts in silver bowls in front of everybody. There's a trio playing, a piano player . . ."

"Teddy Wilson."

"*Any* piano player."

"And women."

"Women."

"Fancy women. With straight black hair."

"Blond."

"And tan skin."

"Pink," I say, afraid of tan.

"With little pearls stuck in their ear lobes."

"And rings on their fingers."

"And great sweet healthy luscious succulent asses."

I laugh. "Big tits."

"And good teeth."

"Perfect teeth."

"And nice big soft lips."

"Yeah," I say. "All that ordinary stuff."

Kirk laughs. "Take a ton of money, Bobby boy."

"Ton and a half."

"You could get it, you know."

In the pale light from the window, I can't see the yellow glint moving in the con man's eyes but I know it's there.

"Where am I gonna get a ton and a half of money?"

"*Hey, knock it off, you motherfuckers! We tryin' to sleep here!*"

"Knock *this* off!"

"Son of a bitches, talkin' all fuggin' night . . ."

Kirk whispers: "First you gotta think you *want* it, Bobby."

"Hell, yes. I want it. Don't everybody?"

"Well, what would you do with it if you had it? I mean, after you finished with booze and pussy and clothes?"

"Shit . . . I don't *know*."

"Say it, babe."

"I guess . . . I'd probably get a place for my mother. A house, maybe. Something like that."

He lights another cigarette. "You really like that lady, don't you?"

"She's something else."

"She'd like a house, huh?"

"Hell, I don't know. I never asked her about it. I never even thought about it until right now. She just . . . never had anything like that."

"What's she do?"

"Everything. After my old man split, we moved through all kinds of crummy towns and Ma took work where she found it. She slung hash. She tended bar. She sold tickets in a movie house and worked in a hospital and a factory. She even took in typing at home, with a typewriter she bought one time. Any goddam thing she could get. Just to hold it together. Hold *us* together, I guess. She won't take welfare. Too proud, or something. I hope she's okay. Haven't heard from her in months."

Someone shouts: "If you don't shut that *mouth,* man, I'll come over there and shove something *in* it!"

Kirk yells back: "I seen that thing of yours in the shower, Willis, and you couldn't fill a *thimble* with it!"

"It'd fill your *shit chute,* man!"

A door opens. Heels clack on metal, then stop. If the screw is an Asshole, he can wake everybody up and turn us out and search each cell. The block goes silent. The footsteps tap away and the door clangs shut again. Bodies turn over in the dark, scrambling for sleep.

"We better hit the sack," I say.

"Wait, man. We ain't finished."

"I am."

"You ain't finished with what you were sayin', Bobby. About the dream."

"What dream? I never said anything about a dream."

"The cars, the clothes, the pussy and . . . you know, uh, the house."

"Don't fill me up with bullshit, Kirk. That's jailhouse talk. You know it."

"In this country you *buy* your dreams, man."

"Ten dollars down. Easy terms."

"That's the key, man. Money buys the dreams. Money makes the dream come true."

"I thought Allah did all that stuff."

He moves right on: "And the bigger the dream, the more of the large you'll need."

"What are you driving at, Kirk?"

He's off the bunk now, fidgety with schemes, his blanket pulled tight over his shoulders. "You're what, nineteen years old?"

"Almost."

"And you're an eighty-two-pounder, right?" He's picked up on fighter talk, dropping the hundred off the weight. "That means you still got time to *grow,* boy. You're gonna be *bigger* than an eighty-two pounder." He pauses dramatically. "You're gonna be a *heavyweight.*"

"So what?"

I know what he's driving at, all right. I just want to hear him say it.

"That means you kin buy that dream, man. You kin buy the biggest dream of all . . . You punch like a motherfucker with the left hand. The right hand is like a mule kickin' downhill. You're gonna be big enough. You got chin. You got guts. But most of all, babe, most of all, my blue-eyed blond-haired devil, most of all, *you are white!* Dig? You know what that means, Bobby boy? You know what the hell that means? It means you kin be the next white hope! The white fuckin' hope of the West! Do you dig it? The white boy who gets the crown back from all the wise-ass jitterbug niggers of the earth! The white hope! Champeen of the world! Champeen of the universe!"

His voice is a whisper now. He can hear the crowds, see the posters, the lights on the marquees. There are cars and headlines and women, shots on the Carson show, clothes by the rack. Champion of the world. Champion of the universe. Only words. But as I climb back into the bunk, they're spinning in my head. Maybe it could happen. Maybe I could get it all.

"Let me think about all that," I say.

"There's nuthin' to think about. All you gotta do is *do* it."

7

THE VOLKSWAGEN BUS, painted sky-blue, rolled slowly through the outer gates, all shiny in the sun. From where we stood, Kirk and I could see Thompson and some other guards signing papers and nodding, and then the doors opening, and young guys coming out of the bus and one of the guards counting to make sure more visitors didn't leave than showed up. The young guys were all wearing green satin jackets with IMPERIAL S.C. on the back and a pair of velvet gloves stitched over the heart.

Kirk smiled. "Amateurs," he said. "Kids. Strictly amateurs."

And compared to the cons they *were* kids, but kids who walked with a lot of confidence, springy, slope-shouldered, carrying little leather bags with their gear. All of them were either black or Spanish, and they looked around at the walls and the towers like tourists at the Statue of Liberty, laughing, joking, making big-eyed expressions and laughing some more.

The last one out of the bus was an older man. He was middle-aged, heavyset but not fat, with a back like a ramrod. He had a crew cut, and in the sunlight each hair looked as if it had been nailed into his scalp. He squinted like a man who should wear glasses but doesn't. His skin was shaved as close as razors can get. His clothes were clean but old, baggy, worn like a large Fuck You to the world. He walked on the balls of his feet. Right away, I knew he was someone special.

"This is Gus Caputo," Thompson said. "He runs the Imperial Sporting Club."

"Hello, fellas."

Gus shook hands with me and Kirk while Thompson kept talking.

"This is Kirk, he's a trainer, and Bobby Fallon, our eighty-two pounder."

"I guess you'll fight Muñoz," Gus said.

"Suits me," I said.

Thompson asked, "Which one's Muñoz?"

"Over there," Gus said, pointing at a tall Puerto Rican made even taller by a pair of platform shoes.

"Muñoz," Kirk said. "Muñoz . . ." He stroked his chin. "The Muñoz from the Gloves last year?"

"That's right," Gus said. "Last year he won the one-sixty-five-pound Sub-Novice. This year, the one-seventy-five-pound Open. He wants to turn pro but I'm saving him for the Olympics."

I looked at Muñoz and then at Gus. "Trying to psych me out?" I said. "Well, it ain't gonna work, pal."

"Want some lunch?" Thompson said to Gus, stepping in front of me.

"Nah, not now," Gus said, squinting at me past Thompson. "After the fights, maybe we'll grab a bite." Then he said to me, in a soft voice: "I wasn't trying to psych you, kid. I was answering a question."

Thompson walked ahead and we followed him. Gus was staring up at the walls. He had the kind of face that told you walls didn't matter. If he was a con, he would go over them. Or through them.

He turned to Thompson: "Where's the ring?"

"Out here in the yard."

Thompson cut through the passageway beside the commissary, leading the way. Gus fell in beside me. Looking straight ahead, he whispered:

"What are *you* doin' here?"

"Time," I said.

It's noon and the yard is like Yankee Stadium on the night of a title fight. I'm dressed in a hospital bathrobe, sitting on a bench. Two bantamweights are banging each other, the kid from Imperial outpointing our guy, a little former junkie from the Bronx named Teddy Negron. Somebody figures out the Imperial kid is a Cuban, so the Puerto Ricans lead the charge for our guy. I see Fuentes jumping up and down on a seat. Fuentes, who came up in the van with Kirk and me a hundred years ago. He's happy. The Puerto Ricans are almost always happy. They like each other. They like the blacks. They even like the whites. They like everybody in the world except Cubans and they're cheering like a fuck for Negron. The problem is, Negron can't fight.

Kirk comes over and sits down beside me.

I say, "Hey, these kids know how to fight."

"Yeah? So do you."

"They make these fast little moves. Real cute. They're all in shape. And they don't get hit a lot, either."

I look past Kirk at the other Imperial kids, sitting on a bench against the far wall, in real trunks, real robes and real boxing shoes. Most of our guys are wearing bathing suits and sneakers. Muñoz is up and talking, shouting advice to the Cuban kid above the roar of the crowd, bubbling and happy and young.

"He looks like he's here on a picnic," I say.

"Well, give 'im the main course," Kirk says, laughing. "Hit 'im with the steak 'n' potatoes."

The Cuban bends away under a right hand, throws the hook and knocks our guy down. The Puerto Ricans shout encouragement, but when Negron gets up he has nothing left. The Cuban drops him again, and Thompson, who is refereeing, stops it. The cons don't protest. The Cuban bows to the audience, gets a round of applause and leaves the ring. Negron shrugs an apology.

The rest of the card shows how far behind we are as fighters. Their guys are trained for speed and power, and most of our guys are trained to hit and hope. My stomach starts jumping around. For months I've been thinking I'm hot shit. Now I'm not so sure.

Two light-heavyweights are working hard, and I'm next. Harry Shaw comes over. They didn't let him fight because he had been a pro on the outside, and Gus remembered him. So all day he's been drifting through the crowd, half watching the bouts. He doesn't look disappointed; he looks like he doesn't care one way or another.

"Watch for right hands," Shaw says. "You a southpaw, Gus gonna tell him throw right hands. Watch faum. Hear?"

"Yeah, Harry. Thanks."

Their guy knocks down our light-heavyweight three times and wins a decision, so when I get in the ring the yard is pretty quiet. The amateurs have been kicking the shit out of the jailbirds.

Muñoz takes off his robe and he's beautifully built, with skin the color of honey. But he has the face of a spoiled kid who's had it too easy, who's got so much talent he doesn't have to work too hard. And his neck is very thin. Looking at him up close, I'm not nervous. Kirk is in the corner alone, putting the mouthpiece in, whispering in my ear: "Just bust him up is all. Just bust his fuckin' ass in half." Shaw comes around and squats down at the foot of the ring behind my corner. He puts a finger to his eye and then to his right hand. I look at Muñoz as Thompson brings us to the center of the ring for the usual bullshit instructions. Muñoz is smiling at me like I'm some kind of fake. Or a victim. Or a meal he's about to eat.

"Have a good fight," he says, like he's pitying me.

"Fuck you, pal. I'm gonna break you in half."

"Knock it off," Thompson says. "This is an exhibition."

"Fuck you too, Ernie."

Then Muñoz dances out, moving at me behind the jab. He's in the Ali style, straight up, head up, hands down, letting the legs do the work, and then popping the punches. Go ahead. Dance, you bastard, but I ain't gonna follow. And I don't. I stay small and bunched up, letting the jabs hit the top of my head or the gloves, as he moves around me in a circle. I start a hook and he bangs me with the right hand. Not hard. But very fast. And proving to himself he can hit me when he wants to. I try to jab with him but he has reach and speed, a great stinging long-armed jab, and those legs carrying him where he wants to go. I move in.

And he hits me a hell of a right hand.

Everything goes white. And I'm standing there, flatfooted, and he throws two more. Right hands, leading with them, snapping my head back, and then dances away and does the Ali Shuffle. This brings the crowd to its feet, roaring, and he throws another right hand lead, and the bell rings.

"Come on, baby," Kirk says. "Get *off!*"

"I'm all right."

"You're letting him do his *number,* man,"

"It's *okay,* Kirk. Shut up."

I look around and the crowd is in a tumult, exchanging bills, gesturing like they're making bets and predictions, and then the Puerto Ricans start to chant: MOON-YOZ! MOON-YOZ! MOON-YOZ! And some of the blacks join in, and even a few of the white guys, the kind of guys that like to see everybody lose. Muñoz is standing up, his back to me, waving at the crowd, getting them hopped up, just like Ali. I see Gus try to get him to sit down, but he pulls his arm away and shakes his right hand at the crowd, and they roar.

I'm really pissed off. At myself, for not staying cooler. But mostly at this spoiled fucking kid.

Then Harry Shaw is beside me, poking his head in through the ropes, ignoring Kirk.

"Forget all this shit, heah? He ain't Ali. He's a fuckin' amatcha. Bend when he jab, and then hook."

He's gone before I can say anything.

At the bell, I come out with a jab and he beats it. He dances more now, jabbing, jabbing, his mouthpiece white behind the sneer. I wait and watch. But he's dancing, listening to the crowd. MOON-YOZ! MOON-YOZ! MOON-YOZ! Popping the jab.

Then he starts the Shuffle.

And I nail him with an overhand left that hits him smack on the bridge of the nose.

Blood bursts out of both nostrils. He reels away, flicking at the blood with the thumb of his glove, and when he faces me again we both know the nose is broken.

And I go after him.

He tries to hold, but I push him and go underneath, rippling punches into the sleek smooth honey-colored belly, and I hear the scream coming up out of me. I club a right hand to his nose. He puts his hand up and I club him again. He angles away, his eyes bleary, and I start the right hand, stop and rip the hook to his jaw.

He falls straight back, his head bouncing hard on the canvas, his legs shuddering.

And twenty-six hundred cheering, yelling cons go apeshit. Wild and happy and full of victory. I look up and see one of the guards put a hand on his machine gun.

The fight is over.

I walk around as Kirk spatters me with water from a sponge and tries to get the bathrobe over my shoulders.

"He hadda bring ass to get ass, and you got his ass, baby!"

Gus is working over Muñoz, and Thompson is leaning down, and I see one of the doctors from the infirmary coming through the crowd.

"Shit! *Shit!*"

"What shit?" Kirk says.

"I was just gettin' warmed *up!* Shit! Bastard goes out like *that!* Shit!"

He shakes his head and finally drapes the robe over me. "Oh boy. Oh boy. You a bad-ass, man. Some kinda *bad-ass.*"

They get Muñoz up, his legs unsteady, his eyes glazed. Gus has a wounded look on his face, as if he knows his fighter is ruined. Thompson waves me to come over, to go through that you're-a-great-fighter act with Muñoz, but I ignore him. Kirk holds the ropes open and I step out.

Most of the cons in the joint seem to be at the foot of the ring, shouting "Right on" and "You're beautiful" and "You're smokin', baby." Fuentes is beaming. "Hey, man, I win six bucks on you!" Even Elizabeth Taylor and his gang are standing and clapping in the back. And for the first time, in all those fights in the can, I think I've done something big. Muñoz was as close to Muhammad Ali as most of these guys would ever get. And I had knocked him on his ass. Me. A con like them. It was like all of us, for that round and a half, had gone over that fucking wall.

As I move through the crowd, heading for the gym to change clothes, Harry Shaw comes close.

"Don't shake so many hands," he says. "Them hands is your tools."

"Okay, Harry. And Harry? Thanks, man."

Something like a smile moves in his face. He's doing life four times and he doesn't smile very much. I made him smile.

When I stepped out of the shower, Gus was standing there, his face ashen and grim.

"That was a good fighter you beat out there."

"Not as good as me."

"You're not as good as you think, kid."

"Who knocked him out? God?"

"He did it to himself. Because he's dumb. He was performing out there, not fighting."

"When I hit him on the chin, he went out."

"You're a mean little prick, aren't you?"

"Sometimes. Sometimes butter melts in my mouth."

"What are you gonna do when you get out?"

"Have about three hundred beers and two dozen women."

"I thought so."

"What're you tryin' to say?"

"That you're as dumb as every other Irishman I ever met."

He took a wallet out of his wrinkled trousers, removed a card and handed it to me. The card was printed: IMPERIAL GYM—BOXING INSTRUCTION. GUS CAPUTO—MANAGER AND TRAINER. There was an address on 14th Street and a phone number.

"If you want to be a fighter, look me up," he said. "You ain't much of a human being, but who knows?"

He gave me one last look, then left without saying goodbye.

You lay there that night: The prison feeling somehow empty: the amateurs back in the city, walking the streets: the bets all paid off: the cuts all stitched: the night smell of prison driving away the smells of hard sweat and arnica: Kirk asleep: dreams floating in the air so real and possible you can almost touch them: thinking of Ma.

You wish she'd been there. You've been in jail for fourteen months now, and for three months you haven't heard a word. You knew it was your fault. You sent that dumb letter. You told her not to write. You told her you knew it was a hassle to write and she should forget it, just write when there was real news. You wrote to her coldly, almost brutally, because you couldn't stand not hearing from her all the time, couldn't stand the daily worry over mail or the anger at night. It was better knowing you wouldn't hear from her at all. As if she didn't even exist. As if she were as dead as everything else on the outside.

But that night you wished she'd been there. To see you handle that fresh-ass kid. That Muhammad Ali of the road. You wish she'd seen you after you got hit. She would have been forced to say, Hey, you got *heart*, boy.

Good with his hands,
That Bobby Fallon.
He's got a lot of heart.

The gym is packed when I walk in, but Thompson isn't around.

"Where's the big man?"

"Got a phone call," Kirk says. "He'll be back."

I'm suiting up when Thompson comes in. He has his hands in his pockets, and he comes straight over to us.

"I got some news."

"They're making Kirk the warden."

"No, they're letting you out."

Out.

"Well, I'll be goddamned," Kirk says.

"The Parole Board granted the application," Thompson says. "Both of you."

Out.

"Oh shit. Oh sweet shit," Kirk says.

"It'll take a couple of days."

"I'll be damned," Kirk says. "I'll be god-damned."

"You don't have to work today," Thompson says. "You can go back and lay dead."

"Oh shit," Kirk says. "Oh sweet shit."

Just like that. No preliminaries. No warning. It's almost over. Going home. To streets. Cities. Flowers. Telephone booths and the D train. Rivers and ferries and gas stations. Women.

Just like that.

Out.

BOOK
TWO

8

ACROSS ALL THOSE MONTHS, I'd dreamed of release on a morning of sunshine and summer. The two years would be finished. I would have paid what I owed. And she'd be there waiting on that summer morning, in a lime-green dress, with the sun picking up the red highlights in her hair. She'd have a rented car and a fresh suit of clothes for me, and she'd smile, and I'd run to her from the walls, leaving behind the iron and the bars, the loneliness, and I'd get in beside her and drive out onto the highway, with the window open to the smell of summer fields. I'd listen to the new music on the car radio, and we'd stop in a roadside restaurant and eat shrimps and steak and have cold beers. And talk about nothing. And tell dumb jokes.

So the day I got the news from Thompson I wrote her a hurried note, telling her where and when I'd get out, addressing it to the place where she'd lived when I last heard from her. The house in Brooklyn.

On Prospect Avenue. On the top floor right. The words were quick and rushed, but I asked her to come meet me if she could. Even though it was autumn, and summer was gone, I hoped she would come and that the sun would pick up the highlights in her hair.

But there was no sun on the day we got out. Fog rolled in from the mountains. The walls of the prison were damp and cold. Thompson walked us to the main gate. We heard voices shouting at us from C Block, and we passed some fresh fish checking in. Then we turned in our uniforms, and they gave us the street clothes we wore when we arrived. Eight other guys were getting out, and Kirk and I were last on line. At the main gate, Thompson stood with us for a while.

"Well," he said, "I hope I don't see either of you bastards again."

"Hey, come *on,* Ernie," Kirk said. "That's what they say in *all* them prison movies. You gotta get some new *lines,* man. Some *words.* Some *juice.*"

"That's from hanging around you bastards," Thompson said. "You bastards are a bad movie."

"Who's the hero of this movie?"

"Allah," I said. "Who else?"

Kirk laughed and Thompson smiled. I looked out through the gates but I couldn't see anything: not grass or streets. Only the rolling fog.

"Well," Thompson said. "Have a good trip."

"Yeah," Kirk said.

"And stay out of jams."

"We'll try our best," I said.

Thompson shook Kirk's hand and then mine.

"So long, Ernie," I said, and we turned around to freedom.

Beyond the gate, there's a double row of thirty-foot wire fences. The cons used to say the fences were electrified, but looking at them now they look like plain old wire fences.

It's seven in the morning and we have to move across three hundred yards of foggy ground to clear the second fence.

"Smell it, Kirk. Smell that free air."

"Let's just get through that fence, man, 'fore these suckers change their mind."

I start to jog. Slowly at first. Wondering if Ma is out there. Wondering if she got the letter. If she's there in the lime-green dress. Wondering if someone will stop us and tell us the papers were a mistake. That it was two other guys, we don't have the parole, we owe them time, we have to turn around, go back, take off the clothes again, get searched, photographed, fingerprinted. Jogging slowly. Then faster. Then running flat out, with Kirk beside me, his face almost frantic with happiness and tears streaming down his face as we reach that last gate.

The gatehouse is shrouded in fog, the guard looking ghostly as we hand him the papers. If we're going to be stopped, this is the place where they'll do it. The guard looks at the papers, then at me. And he smiles.

"Hey, Fallon. Good luck, fella."

"Thanks."

"You gonna turn pro?"

"Who knows?"

I peer into the fog. There are parked cars. A kid riding a bike. A bus waiting at a bus stop and some cons getting on, carrying little bags. But no Ma.

Kirk sprints another twenty yards and dives straight out on the grass. Face down. The way he said he would when he got out. Face down in the damp grass. Crying his ass off, arms stretched out, fingers digging into the dirt.

"Son of a bitch," he says. "Son of a bitch. Son of a bitch. Son of a bitch."

We hear a hiss; the doors of the bus close and it pulls away quickly.

We're alone in the fog.

I hear a car horn. Some bells ring in the prison, which I can no longer see. Kirk sits up slowly. I squat and put my arm around him.

"It's all over," I say. "We finished it. It's over, man."

He shakes his head, wiping the tears with his sleeve. The car horn beeps again. I can see yellow fog lights but only the dim outline of a car.

"Who the hell *is* that?" Kirk says.

I get up, hurrying toward the yellow lights. The car is a battered blue Chevy. The window near the curb is rolled down. Behind the wheel is Gus Caputo.

Not Ma. Gus Caputo, in a windbreaker zippered to the neck.

"Good morning," he says.

"Whaddya say."

"It's kind of warm for October," he says, as if he spends most of his time hanging around prison gates. "That's what causes the fog. The ground's cold, a lot of winter in it, but the air's warm. Presto. Fog."

"Yeah."

"Hello, Kirk," he says.

"I'll be damned," Kirk says, coming up slow through the fog. His eyes are dry. "Mr. Caputo."

"I figured you guys'd need a ride."

"Kirk," I say, "do we need a ride?"

"I mean, you can't have a hell of a lot of money."

"I got ninety bucks in cash," I tell him. "They pay you up here, you know. Thirty cents an hour."

"Well, you still might need a ride."

Kirk says: " 'Pends where you going."

"I'm going to Brooklyn," I say. If she still lives there. If she hasn't run off.

"Me, too," Kirk says. "Bed-Stuy."

Gus sits listening to us run this game on him, and I can see he's losing his patience.

Finally he says: "Get in."

Kirk opens the back door and slides in.

I hold back.

"Listen, Mr. Caputo, I—"

"Wait a minute," he says, the temper snapping. "I didn't come up here for a negotiation. I came up to get you two bastards to New York without an arrest. You got questions? Okay. One, I ain't a cop. Two, I ain't a fag. Three, I . . . There ain't any three."

"If you ain't a cop or a fag, what are you, then?" I say.

He stares hard at me. "I'm a sucker," he says. "For kids who can punch with the left hand."

I get in.

9

MOST OF THE WAY, Gus said nothing and neither
did I. Kirk fiddled with the knobs of the radio. We
went through Jersey and then across the George Wash-
ington Bridge. Gus drove jerkily, bouncing from one
lane to another like a man who hated driving. We
went down the West Side Drive. Near the entrance to
the Brooklyn Battery Tunnel, a cabdriver screamed,
"Hey, whyn't you learn howda drive dat ting?" and
I knew I was home.

"You got any schooling?" Gus said, as we
moved into the tunnel.

"Three years of high school."

"Why didn't you finish?"

"I didn't like it."

"What do you mean, you didn't like it?"

"Too many assholes in suits, playing teacher."

"So you decided to be a bigger asshole?"

"Well, you had to be there."

Gus paid the toll, took the Brooklyn-Queens Expressway to Atlantic Avenue, got off and headed out to Classon Avenue in Bed-Stuy.

"Hey, you really *know* this place," Kirk said.

"I drove a cab years ago. When I need money, I still do. I know a lot of places."

"New York changed a lot, huh?"

"Everything changes, Kirk. Babe Ruth don't play for the Yankees anymore and Fiorello LaGuardia ain't the Mayor. There ain't an Ebbetts Field or a Brooklyn Eagle. It's been a long time since anyone liked the President of the United States. It all changes. Usually for the worst."

We were going up Atlantic to Flatbush when I saw a department store open and asked Gus to stop.

"What for?"

"I want to buy something."

"What kind of a something?"

"A present. For my mother."

He pulled into a bus stop and I got out.

The store felt weird and crowded. There were women everywhere, fat and skinny, old and young, examining tablecloths and underwear and blouses, and I could smell their perfume, their skin, their softness. They made me feel rough and brutal. Like an ox who had escaped from a zoo. I wanted to get her something but didn't know what. I looked at perfume for sixty bucks a smash, and checked out some clothes but didn't know her sizes, and it seemed stupid to get her a box of candy, and even more stupid to get a bottle of booze. I went up some escalators and passed right through the book department, knowing that if I bought her a book she'd be pleased and happy and smile a lot and never open it again. I found myself in the fur coat department. There were statues of women, all thin and without hair, made of pink plastic and the furs draped all over them, and I wandered through them, touching the fur. A woman wearing a badge came up.

"Yes?"

"Hello."

She was the first woman I'd talked to in seventeen months. She had soft rambling gray hair and murky eyes the color of a cup of bad coffee.

"Do you want something?" she said in a snotty way.

"Yeah. You."

"What?"

"I'd like you to get into one of those fur coats, and then I'd like to bang you."

"What?"

I turned and walked away fast, certain she would call the police and charge me with something. Felonious bad-mouthing. Something. I hurried down the escalators but never heard a thing.

On the first floor, I went back to the perfume counter. They had a lot of different blue bottles called "Evening in Paris" that went for forty dollars a set. The woman who took care of me made a sad face, like she felt sorry for me. I gave her the money and asked her to gift-wrap the box. She breathed out hard, as if all of life was a pain in the ass.

By the time I got back to the car, it was dark. Gus gave me a look, but didn't say anything. Kirk was stretched out stiffly in the back, lost in thought.

"Sorry I took so long."

"It's okay."

"It's hard getting used to."

"What is?"

"Being out. People. Women."

"Well, don't get too used to it."

When we reached Kirk's block, I knew why Kirk was so quiet. The street looked like Purgatory. A lot of buildings were gone, with scorch marks on the walls of those that were still standing. About fifteen men were shooting craps under a streetlight. Kids were everywhere, playing in the piles of garbage, broken furniture and burned mattresses. Small wiry black kids, with eyes that stared at us as Gus moved slowly through the street. They all looked like the kid brothers of the guys we'd just left behind us.

"Holy Christ," I said.

"Somethin', ain't it?" Kirk said softly.

The guys in the crap game looked up and stiffened. Kirk gave them a small wave and they relaxed, but they still looked like a group of cons hanging near the west wall in the Big Cube.

"You live here?" Gus said.

"My sister does."

We went past a saloon called Rodney's, a dark evil-looking place with bricked-over windows.

"Anywhere here is okay," Kirk said.

Gus pulled over and I could hear Kirk breathe deeply.

"I can find you a place to stay if you want," Gus said. "Over in New York."

"No. Thanks, Gus. You know . . ."

"I understand."

Kirk got out, holding his little bag, and I opened the door in the front. A few blacks stepped out of the door of Rodney's, dressed in bellbottoms, shades and high-heeled shoes, their hair all tightly braided. Kirk's shaved head gleamed in the streetlight. He nodded at the men from Rodney's and then shook my hand.

"Well, you better go on out of here, Bobby."

"Yeah, well, I'll see you, Kirk. Maybe in a couple of days. You got a phone here?"

"No. What about you?"

"I don't know the number. We . . ."

He laughed. "I know, you moved around a lot."

"Fallon. It's in the book. I guess."

"Yeah."

Kirk gazed around, at the block, then at Gus, and back to me. Something twitched in his face.

"Well, maybe I'll call you at that gym. What is it again?"

"The Imperial. But jeez, Kirk, I don't know if I . . . you know, whether I'm gonna do that."

Quickly, with some embarrassment, he hugged me.

"Hey, no matter what, you dream a big dream, hear?"

Then he turned and walked across the street and up the stoop of one of the tenements.

I got back in the car.

Gus drives slowly through Prospect Park, staying quiet, as if he's giving me time to talk. But I don't want to talk. Prospect Park was my yard when I was a small kid, the place where I played after school and in the summers when we weren't on the road. I want to see it.

"Go all the way around, could you?"

"Sure."

"Down to the Coney Island Avenue exit."

We pass some kids scrambling through piles of leaves at the foot of the cemetery. I remember a time when I was really small and some actor died, and they buried him in that cemetery because he was related to some people who fought in the Revolutionary War and all their descendants have the right to be buried there, and we went up to watch the big limousines that in the end couldn't get up to the cemetery and the coffin had to be carried there by hand.

He was still at home then.

Yeah. I remember coming home to the place on Seventh Avenue and telling him about it, and he said, Well, it only proves that even if you're rich and famous and in the movies, you still end up dead.

Jack Fallon.

You still end up dead.

Gus stops at a light near the Seeley Street playground. A young guy is walking through the playground with his arm around a girl. Outside the fence, a woman pushes a baby carriage, hurrying along. When I was a kid, I loved this season. The parkies would make great piles of the leaves and set them on fire, and the smell would drift all through the park, and we would sit on the hills or move along the section called the Indian War Path and talk about what we would do when the snow came. I don't remember who the other kids were, but I wasn't alone.

The light changes and Gus drives on, around the curve beside the Big Lake. That's where I first saw a dead man. One spring, when we all ran to the park from school, we saw the cop cars around the edge of the lake, and the cops were all looking at this green pile on the shore, and when we came close they waved us away, and there was a group of big people standing over to the side, and then some more cop cars came, and we made believe we were going away, and then I ran over to see what it was, and it was a man.

All green and moldy. Like snot.

The back of his head was gone.

And the next day in the *Daily News* there was a story about the body that was found in the Prospect Park lake and the cops were trying to identify him and they thought it was what they always called a gangland slaying. I was a kid and I wanted to know where Gangland was. This new strange country that wasn't in the geography books.

But he was already gone then. Jack Fallon. He would have known but he was gone, and I didn't know how to ask Ma.

We're at the exit and I think about telling Gus to just let me out there. So I can run back to the park, and lie down in the grass the way Kirk did, and go down to the place beside the lake where they found the body that day. And maybe sleep on a hill or watch the stars.

But I don't. I let Gus drive me home, up to Tenth Avenue and left over to Prospect Avenue, along Prospect Avenue past Holy Name Church, where the lights are shining on the plaster statue of Our Lady of Fatima, and then down the hill into the neighborhood. Down to the neighborhood where we always, always ended up, no matter how far we had traveled. A different apartment, and sometimes different furniture, but always the neighborhood.

It looks darker, and I can see there are even fewer stores now, and I remember all the talk among the older people about how the neighborhood was all changing and how it used to be.

How there used to be seven movie houses, playing two movies and three cartoons and a newsreel and a chapter, and it was 12 cents to get in before noon on a Saturday and they gave you a free dish on Saturday night. How the avenues were filled with grocery stores and fish stores and butchers; stores for stuff they called notions, which meant thread and scissors and tubes of glue; candy stores and bakeries and drugstores; stores that sold old comic books; pet shops, barbershops, poolrooms. And saloons. Dozens of saloons. Sometimes two facing each other on the same corner. Saloons where the ironworkers and dock-wallopers drank; Irish saloons and Italian saloons; saloons where women were barred and saloons with jukeboxes and backrooms where the women danced on Saturday night. That kind of neighborhood. Where an Italian with a monkey played the organ on Saturday mornings; where a truck came around once every two weeks and sharpened knives; where they played stickball in money games beside the 14th Street Armory, and the tough guys were in a gang called The Tigers and their girls were the Tigerettes and the younger guys were the Juniors, and school hours were spent making zip guns. A neighborhood of pigeon coops and V.F.W. clambakes and card games that started on Wednesday and ended on Sunday.

The neighborhood where Jack Fallon was famous.

And the place that was always different every time we came back. Always smaller. Always emptier. Until most of the stores were gone, and the movie houses had closed, and the old-timers who stayed behind hid up in the apartments and watched TV. Their children all moved away, to the Island or Jersey or California. That's why there was always a place for us to stay whenever we came back. All the rest of them were moving, and the vans would be parked in front of the buildings, and people would throw farewell parties in the saloons and everybody would get drunk and cry when the furniture and the clothes were all loaded away, and then they would be gone. And the kids who went with me to the park would be gone. The kids whose names I could never remember.

Jack Fallon moved away, too, but he didn't take his family with him.

"Lulu Perez lived around here," Gus says.

We're stopped at another light, on Eighth Avenue and Prospect. A block from the house. The last house. The last place Katey Fallon came home to.

"Who's Lulu Perez?"

"Hell of a little featherweight at one time," he says. "Came out of the amateurs around '56. Boxed in some P.A.L. around here."

"Loew Center, on Eighth Street?"

"That's it. That's the place."

"It's closed now."

"Anyway, Lulu was a good boxer, a good Golden Glover, a fair puncher. He won about twenty fights in a row after he turned pro, against mostly ordinary guys, and kept improving. Every once in a while he even knocked a guy out. Then they made him with

Willie Pep in the Garden. In the second round, Willie went down three times, and when someone asked me what I thought of the fight, I said they oughtta give out an Academy Award."

"Right over here," I say.

"The three-story building?"

"Yeah, next to the fruit store."

"Anyway, Lulu got the win, and made a name for himself that night, but it was the end of him. He was a good kid and I guess he was real proud of himself, knocking out a great fighter. But a couple of days later, the Commission suspended Willie Pep for life. They said it was for medical reasons, because Willie was falling down from punches that wouldn't harm a nun. But the suspension seemed to hurt Lulu more than it hurt Willie Pep. The kid lost his confidence. He lost his belief. Willie Pep kept going for years, all over the place, fighting stiffolas. But Lulu never got it back."

I look up to the top floor. I can't see any lights.

"That's a sad story," I say.

"It sure is."

"Who was Willie Pep?"

He looks at me. "You really are young, aren't you?"

The fruit store is different, the windows dirty, the inside dark and empty. A FOR RENT sign is on the door.

Gus says, "Well?"

"Well, thanks for the ride."

"I'll see you, kid."

"Maybe."

"What are you gonna do?"

"I don't know. I blew the last job."

"If you want to work there's always jobs around."

"Doing what?"

"Ironworking. The docks. You can drive a cab like I do when I'm busted."

"I thought you wanted me to be a fighter."

"What *I* want you to be doesn't matter. It's what *you* want to be."

He has this funny distant look in his face, like a priest who's heard everything too many times. He turns off the lights and the engine. He wants to talk some more.

"How come you went up there to meet us?" I say. "What's the angle?"

"No angle. It was just something to do with my hands."

I smile. "You're a sarcastic bastard."

"Sometimes."

"You got a cigarette?"

"I don't smoke."

"Very pure, huh?"

"No. Just smart."

I lift the gift-wrapped perfume and put it on my lap. "What do you want from me, anyway?"

"You don't have to ask that question, and you know it."

"To make me a fighter? I already am a fighter."

Suddenly his voice heats up and he faces me: "You're not a fighter. You're a bum. An Irish bum." He pauses, lets the words sink in. "Guys who fight in saloons are bums and you got saloon written all over your face, wise guy. I don't even know why I'm interested, because I know someday you'll break my goddam heart." Another pause. "But I can make you a fighter. If you got the character, if you got the heart, I might even make you a champion. That part I don't know yet. You might have a ton of dog in you. Maybe you got a weak left tit. Maybe you're too much of a bum and can't change. But if not, I'll make you a champion."

He leans over and turns the handle of the door, opening it.

"Good night, kid."

I get out, close the door and lean back in. He starts the engine and turns on the lights.

"I'll let you know. I still got that card you gave me in jail."

"Don't do me any big favors, kid."

He puts the car in gear and drives away, steady and fast.

10

HOME.

Up the stairs, two at a time on the first flight, then slowing. The old warm hallway smell, made of garbage and backed-up sewers, and babies and beer, the smell of all the other places in the neighborhood. Past doors that had become people in my head. The second floor left, where Aggie the Pet Shop Lady lived with ten dogs and seventeen cats until the day they carted her off to Kings County. Across the hall the battling Greens, who finally got married after eleven years of beating up on each other and then lived happily ever after. The smell follows me all the way to the top floor. The linoleum is still sticky. The light still comes from these little twenty-watt bulbs. But it all seems smaller, dirtier, more stale. I'm used to other smells.

I stop on the landing at the top floor and fumble in my pockets for the key.

I try the door.

The key doesn't fit.

I step back and look again, peering down the hall, looking up to the skylight on the roof. Maybe I went into the wrong house. Maybe it's the wrong door. No, it's the right door but she must have changed the lock.

Damn.

Or maybe she moved.

Maybe she got my letter that time, the one where I told her not to write, and she took it harder than I meant her to take it and decided to hell with it, she had nothing to stay around for, no real job, a kid in the can, no old man, and maybe she just took off, left, did el splitto, went on the duck. Maybe she . . .

I press the buzzer.

I hear movement deep in the apartment but nobody comes to the door.

I buzz again and this time add a pretty healthy rap—bop ba bop bop.

I hear the lock turn and then the door pulls back about six inches. There's a chain pulled tight across the narrow space and a guy standing behind it who I'd never seen before, wearing a frayed brown bathrobe. *She moved.* His face is thick, flushed, half-shaved. He has yellow eyes. Past him I see the furniture. It's our furniture.

"Who the hell are *you?*" I whisper.

"Who the hell are *you?*" he whispers back, trying to sound tough but not really making it.

His yellow eyes blink, the chain is taut, and I'm thinking I'll have to knock this door down, when I hear a voice from inside the apartment. Muffled, tired. Ma.

"Holy cow! Holy Jesus!" Then: "Open the door, dummy, that's my son!"

The yellow eyes shift, and he fumbles at the latch, mumbling, "Oh. *Oh!* Yeah, Katey, sure."

The door opens and there she is.

"Oh my God."

We stand there, looking at each other. Her hair in curlers, dressed in a thin cotton bathrobe.

"Ma . . ."

And she rushes me, throwing her arms around me, pressing her body up against mine, kissing me on the face, the neck, the eyes. And I can't help it. I start to get a hard-on. She has to know, but she's hugging me, rubbing against me. And all the time, this man with the yellow eyes is standing there watching us.

"Why didn't you tell me you were coming?" she says, "Why didn't you say something? Write me a letter? Some goddam thing?"

"I did, Ma, I . . ."

"Is this for me?"

"Yeah. Hope you like it, I . . ."

She pulls back and starts tearing away the gift-wrapping, and opens the box and sees this set of Evening in Paris, and her face falls a little, and then brightens again, and she says, "It's beautiful, Bobby," but I know she doesn't like it. I know it's not her brand, or she thinks it's cheap or something. I just know it. She squeezes the box against her breasts but I don't believe her.

"Sit," she says, and takes my hand and pushes me to a chair. She puts the perfume on the table and flips a Marlboro out of a box. The guy with the yellow eyes leans in and lights it for her with a book match. "We want to talk, Charlie," she says. He picks up the *Daily News* and shuffles away through the rooms. I watch him so I don't have to look at her, with the gown open too much in the front. A TV set glows in the darkness at the other end of the flat, with the sound turned very low. He stands in front of it, turns the sound up a little and sits somewhere in the dark.

"Charlie's all right," she says, reaching into the bottom of a cabinet for a frying pan. "He works nights at Harry Dillon's up on Eighth Avenue. He doesn't bother anyone, including me." She looks at him. "He goes to work in half an hour."

She puts butter, eggs and bacon on the side of the stove, smoking the Marlboro, her back to me as I sit down at the table.

"What's his story?"

"He loves me, that's his story," she says. "He loves me for my teeth. Says all his life he only knew these Irish ladies with teeth like chalk, so he sees my Indian choppers and falls in love. I tell him I'm part Irish, so maybe the teeth will go bad, sooner or later, but he doesn't care. He's in love."

"You in love with him?"

"Don't be ridiculous. Fried or scrambled?"

"Scrambled. When does he wash?"

"Fridays. He washes, I dry."

She laughs. When I was small, we had a joke about the way we did the dishes in the places where we went. She washed, I dried.

"He has some talent," she says. "He knows the first line of every song ever written in the history of the world. Sometimes even the first *two* lines. But after that he's in trouble. He ends up going diddle-de-diddle-de-diddle-de-diddle, like a sick bagpipe."

"Maybe we can get him on TV."

She drops the bacon in the hot pan. "You look good, Bobby."

"I worked out a lot up there."

The bacon sizzles and she whips the eggs in a bowl, using a fork. She turns to look at me.

"What happened to your face?"

"What about it?"

"It's . . . I don't know, *different*."

"I've been boxing."

"Boxing?"

"Yeah."

"Is that so? Boxing . . ." She pokes at the bacon.

There are some letters on top of the refrigerator, and I go over and start looking through them.

"I did write you a note about getting out, Ma."

"I never got it, Bobby. I swear."

"You got the other one, where I told you not to write?"

The bacon is fried now and she lays it out to dry on paper towels. Her voice drops.

"Yes, I got that one. I understood what you meant."

There's an envelope with my name written on it. Also two letters from the draft board. I drop them in the garbage and hold the one with the name Bobby on it.

"This for me?"

"What? Oh, *that*. Yes, that's yours."

I open it and there's money inside.

She says, "A check came from the plant while you were away. It must have been for the last week you worked, before the trouble. I cashed it for you. One forty-three and change. I kept the change."

I riffle the bills, all fives and ones to make the roll look fatter.

"You should've given this to that lawyer . . ."

"He was lucky I didn't give him a knuckle sandwich, the way he walked out of court that day."

She drops the eggs in the pan and they make a bubbling sound.

"Well, I'll pay you back for all that, Ma. I promise."

"Forget it. You need money. Just don't waste it."

I hear a cough and Charlie comes through, dressed in shirt and trousers. He goes to the door of the bathroom and closes it behind him. Ma picks up the eggs with a spatula and lays them on a shining white plate in front of me at the table. I hear water running, and the cough again. *He lathered me and then he lathered her*. She puts some buttered toast down next to the eggs, then takes a bottle of Canadian Club out of a cabinet and pours herself a stiff drink.

"He sleeps on the couch," she whispers.

"I didn't ask, Ma."

"I want you to know." A pause. "He's what I did because of the loneliness."

"It's okay, Ma. I didn't ask."

She gives me a big smile and raises her glass. "Welcome home."

Her eyes start to get wet and she looks as if she wants to say something. But there's a flushing sound and more coughing, and Charlie comes out, his face shining. In the full light of the kitchen, the yellow eyes are more like hazel, and they're gentle, and uncomfortable.

"Well, I'll see you later, Kate," he says. "I gotta go up to work, you know."

"Stay out of trouble, Charlie," she says, her eyes drying.

The eggs are delicious. I'm starting to think Charlie might be kind of a nice guy.

"Pleased to meet you, Bobby," he says, shaking my hand.

I shake back but don't get up.

"I heard a lot about you," he says.

"Nice to meet you, Charlie."

I go to the door and turn the lock behind him.

"Leave the chain off," she says, sipping the Canadian, leaning against the sink. "If you put the chain on, he won't be able to get in."

In the room off the kitchen, I see a chair and a typewriter on a folding metal stand. Where my bed used to be.

"What's this?"

"A typewriter, silly. I went back to night school and brushed up. I did all right while you were gone."

"I wish you'd written to me, Ma."

"You told me not to."

"I know. I still wish you'd written."

She pours another cup of coffee for me. "If I wrote all the time, it would've been worse. You'd be reminded and miss the outside. I didn't want to make you want to come home."

She's on the other side of the table now, with one elbow in front of her. The front of her gown is open slightly. When she moves, I can see her breasts, tan and full.

"Did you think of me much?" she says.

"A lot."

"What did you think?"

"Oh, how you were getting on and how things were with you."

"Did you think of the times we used to have?"

"Sure."

"We went a lot of places."

"We did."

"And always came back."

"Back to the neighborhood."

"It's changing fast now, Bobby. Faster than before, even."

"Well, Babe Ruth doesn't play for the Yankees anymore."

"What does that mean?"

"A guy said that to me today. The guy who drove me home."

"You drove?"

"Yeah, this guy met us up there. He wants me to be a fighter."

"A professional?"

She looks suspicious. Her glass stops short of her lips and she clunks the cubes around.

"He thinks I could be a champion."

"Oh, Bobby . . ."

"I mean it, Ma. He's a manager and that's what he said."

"Who is he?"

"Gus Caputo. He runs a gym over in New York."

"I never heard of him."

I laugh. "And I never heard of *me*."

She sips the drink and gets up and opens the refrigerator, pops a few more cubes in the glass and splashes some more Canadian over them. She closes her robe, pushing one flap inside the other. Then she moves behind me and touches my hair and kisses me on top of the head. Her breasts push softly against my back.

"I'm gonna run you a bath," she says.

"It's okay, Ma. You don't have to do that."

"Are you kidding? You just came home, boy."

I sit there, staring at my hands. They look too small for a fighter. I hear the water start to pour and then gurgle as it gets deeper.

"Come on," she says.

I get up and she's standing at the door of the bathroom, a drink in one hand, the other hand against the door frame.

"Your bath, sir," she says with a big wide smile.

"Thank you, ma'am."

She touches my shoulder as I pass her. The smile fades.

"I missed you," she says. "I missed hell out of you." She sips the drink. "You're all I've got."

I closed the door behind me and turned off the brass handle on the tub and undressed in the narrow space. There was a clean towel and face cloth on the sink. The bath was frothy with bubbles. I opened the medicine cabinet above the sink and saw Charlie's razor and his can of Rise, neat on the glass shelf where she had put them, along with small brown bottles half filled with pills, and little disks of eyeshadow, and deodorants, and a hair rinse for brunettes. Maybe she's gray, I thought, and I don't really know it. I picked up one of the disks, held it in my hand, imagined how many times she'd held it across the months when I was gone. I lifted a can of deodorant and sprayed it in the air, just to smell it in the hot closed space of the bathroom. The walls were blistering with sweat. I felt a fine glaze on my back, and I was certain that even here, in this room with its smell of soap and lime and its woman's smell of deodorant, even here, in this place, this home, the smell of prison touched everything.

I put one foot in the bath, the water scalding, held it there until I could move it without feeling burned, then stepped in with the other foot and squatted down, the bubbles rising around me, the water hot and full and enclosing. I stretched out the length of the tub, keeping just my head above the water line, and lay there very still. Remembering the shower stalls in jail, bodies moving in clouds of steam, the scummy surface of raw concrete under my feet. You were never alone in jail. And now I was in a place from before that time, lying very still. A few drops from the tap made the only sound except for Ma in the kitchen and the sighing wind outside. My eyes moved to all the objects: the blue flannel of the face cloth, the chunky whiteness of the bar of soap, the bottle of Johnson's Baby Shampoo wedged between the tub and the wall. The shampoo was like soft gold. I ran a hand through my hair, thinking: This hair came from him. And his people. From the Irish side, not the Indians.

Above me, on the towel rack, I saw a bra. White, and hooked at the back to form a loop around the rack, where she'd left it to dry. I could see through most of it. I stared for a long time, then reached out and touched it. Prison and showers and cells and fighting drifted away from me, and I felt warm and safe as I held it more tightly. And then I unhooked it and held it to my face.

It's the middle of the night. After two, from the sounds in the street. I don't know where I am. It's certainly not jail. Then I smell the house. The bedroom smell. I'm home.

Someone is pressing against me in the bed.

I remember a bath. Feeling tired and drained. Saying good night. Turning off the TV. Undressing in the dark and falling into the big bed, where she said I should sleep. No couch for Bobby. Not tonight. Not the day he gets out of jail. Before sleep, seeing her in the bright light of the kitchen. Holding her drink. Then looking at the perfume. Lifting the blue bottle to the light. Smiling. Shaking her head. That smile. She doesn't like it. It's not her brand. It's cheap. It's not right. Like it, Ma. Please like it. Don't smile like that.

Peering through the rooms, before sleep, and she was alone in the kitchen. When I was born, she was my age now. The light picked out the red in her hair. Sipping the Canadian. Then clearing dishes. The sound of plates and forks against each other in a sink. Water flowing. You wash and I dry.

Someone is pressing against me in the bed.

It's her.

Wearing a nightgown, silky and soft against my skin. Deep in sleep. Breathing against the back of my neck. Warm and thick and musky in the darkness.

I'm on my side, my legs drawn up slightly, and she follows the curve of my body with hers. There is a fine sweat where her breasts spread against my naked back. Her thighs are cooler and damp against the back of my legs. She's almost as big as I am.

I'm getting hard. Think of something else. The sounds of traffic: a lone car moving away towards 9th Street, the rumble of a Seventh Avenue bus. Muñoz, and making him miss and nailing him with the hook.

She stirs, her arm moves, her hand holds the front of my shoulder, she snuggles closer against me. I'm afraid but she doesn't move again. She's deep in a thick sleep. And after a while I relax and stretch out in the bed, her body following mine. I let the drowsiness flow through me as it did on nights long ago, when I always felt close and safe and loved.

11

YOU LEFT IN THE MORNING. Furtive, ashamed, though you had done nothing. You woke up afraid. You: the container of fear, the skin wrapped around your cowardice, even your bones infected by it. Charlie lay face down on the couch, fully dressed, one hand bent at the wrist on the linoleum floor. You heard his breath: thick, clogged, the breath of hangover, full of phlegm, cigarettes, saloon lies.

You were on your belly, too. Your erection was under you, pressed between the mattress and your stomach: hard against hard. Your cock engorged, packed, strained, crazy for relief. Your head was in the pillow. You reached over, tentative and afraid. She wasn't there.

So you listened for her, through Charlie's hangover wheeze. She had spent a night with her breasts and legs and belly up against you. And you did nothing and finally slept. And then on this first morning home you lay there, with your cock throbbing and hard, afraid to move. Afraid to get out of bed. Afraid that Charlie would wake up and see. Afraid she would see and smile that teasing, welcoming smile.

You turned on your side, your back to Charlie, and listened to the sounds of traffic again. You invented patterns of movement: cars moving around buses, and buses moving around trucks, and trucks unloading carpets at the factory across the street. You created winter: steamy windows, drifts deep in the yards, clotheslines iced and stiff, the great open whiteness of Prospect Park. You dug tunnels through mountains of snow on the corners. You shoveled sidewalks. You ran errands. And soon you could get up.

You pulled on trousers, socks and shoes, and walked through the rooms.

You found her standing near the sink in a blouse and skirt and flat shoes. That was when you could have told her you wanted Charlie out, that you wanted to stay, that you wanted her to close the door on everything out there. You could have told her that you wanted her. But you were mute.

She smiled, her clear, luminous skin free of make-up.

You smiled back and went into the bathroom. You pissed, lathered, shaved, and went to the bureau and found a fresh shirt. You ate. Then you packed.

You can stay, she said. You don't have to go.

It's better this way, Ma.

Suit yourself.

You wanted her to plead with you, to beg you to stay. You wanted her to go in and shake Charlie out of his silence and hurl him to the streets. But you stood at the door, with your clothes in the suitcase, and lied about needing to be on your own and couldn't avoid looking at her breasts, moving softly, without a bra, dark-nippled under the thin white blouse.

You let her kiss you on the cheek. You whispered goodbye.

You went to Diamond's on the corner of Ninth Street, with its long mahogany bar, its old men squashed in stools, its smell of Clorox and pretzels. You had a couple of beers, then left the bag behind the bar and went looking for a room.

There was one for rent beside the synagogue. You paid the tiny, bent-backed landlady $22 for a week and went back to the bar. You had six more beers.

You been away? the bartender asked.

Yeah, California.

I hear its great out there.

Yeah, it's great. Sunny. Lots of oranges.

Well, this ain't so great around here anymore. We're up to our ass in spics and niggers.

So I heard.

You left him a quarter tip and went to the room.

Everything was gray. You opened the greasy shades as far as they would go but the windows were streaked. You put on all the lights but the room stayed dark and it was only noon. You unpacked the suit, the two sport jackets, the three pairs of trousers and put them in a big standing closet with mirrors on the doors. The hangers were wire, with paper advertising the Sanjak Cleaners 24 Hour Service and Kent Cleaners, which had both been closed for six years, and Peerless Cleaners, closed for two.

You thought: I should call Gus Caputo right now. I should go up the block to the subway and go over to New York and go to the gym and get started.

But you didn't call and you knew why. You were afraid. Alone, you felt fear pounding against your rib cage: fear that you would have to do something yourself, you would have to fight against people who could fight, you would do something to shame yourself.

Fear that Gus would make you someone you weren't ready to be.

Until, lying in the gray room, you couldn't think about it any longer, and you counted your money, saw that you had almost $180 and went out drinking.

One bar moved into another, one day into the next. You didn't care. You had money for the beer and that was all that mattered. Twice you tried to get Kirk on the phone, but there was no Nelson Kirk on Classon Avenue, no Nelson Kirk at all, not in Brooklyn, or any of the five boroughs. Once, you took a cab back to the neighborhood where you last saw him, you and the driver both scared, but when you got to the place you didn't get out. You even called the gym to see if he'd been there, taking the number off the card, but you hung up before anyone could answer.

At first, you called Kate Fallon twice a day. She was friendly or cool or busy with her typing jobs. She didn't ask you to come over. Then once you called drunk, and she was annoyed and snapped at you, telling you it was time to get a job. She wanted to know if you were eating right and how the room was. But mostly she wanted you to get a job. You hung up and went back to the bar, and later ate runny eggs in the Greek's before taking the sad emptying streets to the gray room with its dwarf landlady peering through the curtains when you came in.

And you knew you weren't him.

I stood at the end of the bar in the Metropolis on Broadway, drinking a two-dollar bottle of Heineken's and watching the go-go dancers. There were three of them. One was a Spanish girl with shiny black hair and heavy thighs. Wisps of hair jutted from the sides of her G-string and ran in a curly line to her navel. The music was Ike and Tina Turner, and when she started a grind her breasts moved with her. Beside her, a white girl with stringy bleached hair chewed gum to the rhythm but didn't move as well on her thin legs, and I thought her nipples looked sore. The third one was Lana.

Lana was black. She had a helmet of silver hair, long thin legs, lips that pulled taut as she mimicked the words of the record, and an ass that stuck out like a pair of pillows. Her eyes moved around the room, peering through the smoke, glancing out at the street, checking the mounds of change on the bar, until she stopped at me. The music turned into "Body and Soul," and then she looked the other way, and the music changed again and she stared back at me, at the goddam blond hair and the blue eyes, and she held the stare while she eased into a slow drugged dance and I looked at the skin so black that it was blue in the lights of the bar, held it when four sailors down near the men's room started arguing loudly with some college guys in raincoats, held it until we were on our way around the corner together to the Hotel Scott. She made me feel as if she'd never been with a white man before, and we went into the lobby with its high bright fluorescent lights and past the bellhop in a stained jacket, paid the Spanish guy at the desk $12 in advance and went up to the fourth floor.

She knew the way, all right. She led me into the room, reached automatically for the light switch, closed the door behind us and told me to undress. I put a pint of Carstairs on the bureau. She unzippered her dress and kicked off her shoes and turned back the cover of the narrow bed, and then took my cock in her hands and went to work.

While she was dressing, I gave her twenty dollars. She smiled and said she had one more session at the Metropolis and she would see me around.

I thought: Your eyes are the color of bone.

The door closed, and I lay there for a long time, drinking from the pint of Carstairs and remembering nights in jail. Nights when I would invent tremendous women who would wash it all away, get rid of the fags and the dust of the yard and the jerking off and the loneliness.

And now I had fucked my first woman since leaving jail, and she was gone, and I was left in this room with people's hand prints on the windows and an orange stain in the sink where a tap kept leaking, and I started to cry.

I thought of Rosie Towbell. I was fifteen, she was a year older, and we sat on the couch in a basement apartment on Ovington Avenue in Bay Ridge: her parents away: my hand between her legs, and her all wet. I was afraid then, too. Afraid I'd do it wrong, put it in the wrong hole, because out on the street they said there were two, one for piss and one for puss. Her wetness made me want more, and she was fumbling with my fly, and I was afraid the zipper would tear my cock but she was careful, and then she reached into my shorts and it popped out, springy and hard, and she held it in her small hand.

I let her hold it, and she started to move her hand, and I was afraid I would come and make a mess, and I started to peel her panties down, first one side, then the other, over her bare legs, her hand moving slowly, and she folded her legs and wiggled and they were off.

I remembered that night. Her hand guiding me, and the wetness, and the silky feel of her pubic hair, and her pink freckled boobs, and prodding and probing and pushing until I drove into the deepest darkest wetness of all.

Rosie, I said out loud. Sipping the Carstairs.

The last time I heard, you had a couple of kids and one in the oven.

Rosie.

I didn't give you twenty dollars. I didn't cry when it was over.

Bless me father for I have sinned.

12

WHEN I WENT OUT, an army of hookers huddled in the doorways, their coats too short for the wind off the river, and I passed them and went into the Xochtl on 46th Street and ate enchiladas and drank three bottles of Carta Blanca beer and then went back outside. I had $60 left. It was time to take the subway to Brooklyn.

I moved through the train, looking for a seat, the other passengers indifferent to me. I bumped one of them, excused myself, bumped another. I was telling them I was there. But even the bumping didn't matter. They didn't see me. They were almost all black or Puerto Rican, heading off across the river, or coming from a day at the zoo or a relative's house. I found a single seat in a corner, and as the train pushed on to Brooklyn the cars began to empty. Across the aisle, a large black woman in a nurse's uniform sat with her legs apart, too tired from a long day to make the effort of closing them. I imagined her fat black tits and her fat clit, quivering above the entrance to the cave, and I wondered when she got home whether some poor dude would have to climb wearily on top of her to add to the city's endless supply of come.

Then I dozed off, and dreamed of the sea, where I saw a man on a horse riding on a pier that had no railings. The man was naked. The horse galloped until it went off the pier, carrying the rider with him, and I was moving sluggishly through the surf towards the horse. I was trying to rescue the rider, but as I came closer I saw that the rider was me.

When I woke up, the nurse was gone and a cop was standing against the nearest door, staring at me. A black cop, in a leather coat with a fur collar. The night stick hanging at his side. The badge shining.

He watched me, and I waited for him to make a move. I realized it had been a long time between stops. I wondered where I was. Without looking directly at him, I saw the cop unbutton the leather jacket. I could see the gun. He was getting ready. I stared at the floor.

"Hey," he said, "could I look at your *Daily News,* man?"

He had a half-smile on his face. I handed him the paper.

"Sure, take it," I said. "I'm finished."

He turned to the sports section, opened it to the race results.

"Shit," he said. "Some people hit the number six times a year. I never hit it yet."

"Me neither," I said.

The train slowed down and my stomach loosened. I saw 15 STREET-PROSPECT PARK WEST on the walls of the station. I had gone two stops past my own. This was where you got off to see Katey Fallon. Not to go to the gray furnished room.

I got up, nodded goodbye to the cop and went out. Everything was loose now. My stomach. My guts.

Standing there on the platform, unsure, fear ran through me so that I had to shit, thought I would shit right there, in my pants, on that platform.

I moved quickly up the stairs and came out onto Bartel-Pritchard Square. I never understood why they called it a square, because it was round and everybody knew it as The Circle. If you crossed The Circle and kept walking up the hill, past Farrell's and the Pride of Brooklyn barbership and Ebinger's bakery and the hardware store and the candy stores and the florists, you would get to the church. And if you took a right at the church and walked down Prospect Avenue, you would get to Katey Fallon. And I wanted to do that, to go home. But I was afraid.

I crossed the street to Lewnes' soda fountain. I passed kids in the booths who were having the last Cokes and banana splits of the night, moved up the steps leading to the bar and went into the men's room. It was very hot. I took off my raincoat and hung it on a hook. Then I lifted the edges of my sport jacket, as if it were a skirt, and the shit came in a rush. Shitting out all the fear, shitting my disgust. I sat there for a long time, feeling my body relax, shrink, grow still. I wondered whether I had picked up the crabs from Lana. If I had, I was giving them to someone right then. Afterwards, at the sink, I washed my hands very hard, scraping with my nails at the skin.

A dozen men were at the bar, watching a football game. I ordered a bottle of Schlitz and a glass, poured for myself, slipped a five across the counter. The beer tasted good. I looked up at the game. The customers were shouting at Joe Namath, asking him to do something he couldn't get done, but I wasn't interested. Football lost me. There were too many teams and too many players, and the announcers and the sportswriters all used a language of their own. Red-dogging. Blitzing. The secondary. The one time I played it, in Buffalo when I was ten, it was much simpler: You-

hit - the - Polack - and - I'll - hit - the - Guinea - and - everybody - go - out - for - a - long - one. Now it was all too
complicated. I understood the right hand behind the jab,
the hook off the jab, the feint, but almost everything
else was too complicated.

The men at the bar didn't know me but they
knew my face. It was a neighborhood face, a face that
drifted in and out of their time and place but never got
completely identified. They weren't hostile, they just
didn't care. I wondered what they would think about
the evening I'd just spent. The Metropolis, the Scott
Hotel, Lana. They'd talk about black pussy. They
talked a lot about black pussy. Here and up the avenue
in Farrell's and down on Seventh Avenue and in Fitz-
gerald's and Diamond's and McCauley's. I had heard
the cops and the firemen talk about the black pussy
they'd had in Bed-Stuy and Harlem and the South
Bronx. About how big the pussies were, how wet and
grinding and sucking they were. But now I'd had my
own black pussy and it made me cry when it was over.

A guy in a sharkskin suit came in, with thinning
hair, a red face, unshined shoes, and I heard them welcome him. Hey, Harry, howza boy? Howza family?
Whatsa score? Shit, these fucking guys . . . They got no
line . . . Can't put Joe out there with nobody in front
of him . . . The bartender automatically put a shot and
a beer in front of this guy named Harry and I envied
him. He was known here, he had a place to come to
where they asked him how he was and how his family
was. I envied his kids, who had a father who went out
at night for a paper and a beer and stood at the bar
and talked to his friends and watched the football
game and then came home. Here's to you, Harry. You
know a guy named Harry Shaw, Harry? Nice guy.
Doing life four times. Taught me how to fight a little.

I was halfway through the third beer when I
thought of calling Kate Fallon. I played with a dime,
and thought about her, thick and warm against my

back. Did Charlie share the big bed, or was he just a piece of furniture, part of the couch, someone to talk to? I could find out. Just walk up the hill to the place where Charlie worked, take him aside, tell him the honeymoon was over and I wanted him out in the morning, and if he didn't like it I'd break both his legs. But I'd never do that. Not because of him. Because of her.

I had a flash of them in bed and then pushed it away. It was her business, not mine. I said that to myself a dozen times in a few seconds: her business, not mine, her business, not mine . . . I remembered the water beaded in her hair. I wondered if her nipples got hard under the touch of a tongue.

I piled the change for the bartender, drained the rest of the beer and went out again, through the empty soda fountain, and walked along the parkside. Newspapers blew along the avenue and I saw a few garbage cans overturned in front of the buildings that faced the park. The lights of the buildings were all out. It was a neighborhood where people woke up early and went to work or school or to shop. Even the guys in the bars woke up early. I looked up at the blank dark windows and wondered if anyone behind them had ever heard of me. Some of them knew Jack Fallon but they'd probably never heard of me. Not one of them.

I turned at Ninth Street, passing the statue of the Marquis de Lafayette. Someone had stuck a small tree branch between his legs. There were names scrawled all over the statue with spray paint. One of them said that Murphy's Sister Sucks. My name was not there.

I hurried up the stoop of the house with the gray room. I turned on the light, undressed, brushed my teeth and went to bed.

Tomorrow, I said to myself, I'll go to the gym.

13

I'M STANDING IN FRONT OF KLEIN'S, on the Fourth Avenue corner of 14th Street. The sidewalks are jammed with Christmas shoppers and the sky is dark with the threat of snow. I have $7 left in my pocket. And I'm searching for a sign that says *Imperial Gym*. I see Luchow's and a Flame Steak joint and the Academy of Music and Con Ed across the street. A half-dozen shoe stores. I don't see a gym.

Two rummies stare out the window of the White Rose as I pass. They have boozy faces and scoured eyes, and they gaze out at the shoppers and the Christmas decorations. I turn away from them and my eyes roam around the upper stories across the street. Finally, high above the sidewalk, I see the gym. The lights are on and fighters are moving like shadows. The entrance is nowhere in sight and I figure it must be behind a small open-air candy store next to the Flame Steak joint. But I don't cross the street. Instead, I duck into the White Rose.

The rummies don't move. I put a dollar on the counter and order a beer. The bartender has a thick neck and papery indoor skin. The beer is sour.

I have another one and try to get up the nerve to cross the street, which has suddenly become the widest street in New York. The buses are the biggest, the traffic the most scary. The stoplight doesn't work. I'm conning myself, of course, but I don't really know if I have the talent to be a fighter or if I can live the life. I don't know whether I can work with Gus, who thinks I'm an Irish bum. Maybe I am. I don't know.

A half-hour later, I finish a third beer and pick up my change and cross the street to find out.

The sign is there, right beside the candy store. IMPERIAL GYM. BOXING INSTRUCTION AVAILABLE. It sounds formal as hell, and I picture a lot of English kids in knickers, standing in military rows with their hands up in front of them, turned in at the wrist. I pull the door open and go in.

The stairs are right inside the door, rising high up into the building. It's very dark. I wait a second at the bottom, thinking I can always go right back out and forget it. But I start up. Past the twenty-watt bulbs and the dusty walls. A small black kid bounces past me, carrying a gym bag, heading for the street.

A landing, a turn, another flight. I hear the gym before I get to the door. Speed bags rattling. Ropes skipping. Noise and grunting and a bell ringing. I step inside, trying to look casual, like a guy who came in out of the cold.

The gym takes up the whole third floor, from front to back, and it's crowded.

A small Spanish guy is turning a speed bag into a blur. A chubby black heavyweight is punching one of the three heavy bags, each smack deliberate, as if he were driving nails. Some of the fighters can't be more than fourteen. Off to the right, against the three large windows, is a raised platform, with funeral parlor folding chairs on it and two Puerto Rican women sitting there stiffly, like the women you see around courtrooms. Standing behind them are two middle-aged guys in black overcoats, smoking cigars. The women are watching the ring. So are the guys with the cigars.

In the ring, wearing headgear, is Muñoz, boxing with a lanky black heavyweight. Leaning over the top strand of the ropes is Gus, shouting instructions, his face all squinched up.

I edge along the wall, past the speed-bag rigs, and stand beside the cigars on the visitor's platform. At the far end of the gym are another dozen fighters, skipping rope, shadowboxing in front of a large cracked mirror, doing sit-ups on exercise tables. Four fighters are seated on a bench behind the ring, waiting their turn to box. Gus is shouting over the noise.

"Now *bend,* Willie! After you punch, *bend!*"

Muñoz punches but doesn't bend. He dances and drifts, even more skittery now than he was that day in the can.

"Bend!"

Muñoz looks at Gus, eyes scared, tries to punch and then bend. But his style is to peck and peck and peck and then bang you coming in. The black guy starts to press, and Muñoz moves, sliding away before he can finish his combination, and the black guy comes in, hits him on the shoulder with a wild right hand and breaks the rhythm. The two cigars exchange glances. The women are stiff with tension. Muñoz gets mad, throws a right-hand lead, which surprises the black guy, and then moves in with a blizzard of punches. His hands are very fast, but if he throws that right-hand lead at a left hooker he's dead.

"Underneath!" Gus yells. "Underneath! Underneath, goddammit! *Al cuerpo,* Willie . . . No! Not yet!"

One of the cigars says: "Ole Gus never gives up, does he?"

The other cigar says: "This kid couldn't punch to the body if the body was nailed to a cross."

Beyond the ring, beside the waiting fighters, is an open door leading to a small room. I can see a cot, an easy chair, a shelf of books, a TV set and a German shepherd lying with his head on his paws.

The automatic bell rings, ending the round. Gus climbs into the ring and talks rapidly to Muñoz. The two Puerto Rican women chatter in Spanish, one smiling and full of admiration, the other more tense. I figure the tense one must be Muñoz's girl friend.

The first cigar says: "What happened to this kid, anyway?"

"Who knows?"

"He was a hell of a prospect once. I thought if anyone could make him a puncher, it was Gus."

"It's a ticker problem."

"Sure looks that way."

"No left tit."

"Could be."

Gus is working with Muñoz, throwing a straight jab, then bending at the knees to avoid the counter. He shows him how if he bends at the waist, instead of the knees, he can't see the opponent anymore, he can only see the floor. Then the bell rings and Gus steps out through the ropes.

That's when he sees me.

He just stands there, squinting, as Muñoz starts to box behind him. His eyes look at me so hard I feel as if he's trying to bore a hole through me. He glances back at Muñoz, then motions to a little guy with a squashed nose who's over to the side, helping another fighter get ready to box. The little guy nods and climbs up to the apron as Gus gets down and walks over to me.

"What do you want?" Gus says, his voice cold.

"I want to be a fighter."

"Get out of here."

"What?"

"You heard me. Beat it. I don't want you here."

"Well, kiss my ass."

"Four weeks ago, I made you an offer. You waited about three weeks and six days too long, buster."

"I had things to do."

"I'll bet. You look like a toilet and you smell worse. Get lost, bum."

"I've been trying to get a job."

"Doing what? Humping elephants?"

"I'm sorry, I . . ."

"Hey, listen, Fallon, don't try that sorry crap on me. You ain't sorry. You got no obligation to me anyway, bum. I made you an offer and you took a hike. Now take another hike, before you give these kids here the Ethiopian rot."

He turns, crosses the gym and goes up the steps to the ring apron, where he talks steadily to Muñoz. He's wasted me. And I'm sure everybody in the gym heard every word. I look over at the cigars and the Puerto Rican women, but they're a blur. You son of a bitch, Gus. You lousy son of a bitch. Nobody's made me cry in front of anyone since I was six. Not a cop, not a screw, not Ma. Nobody. Except you. You son of a bitch.

I start to leave, and then turn, my legs taking me back across the gym. I reach up and grab Gus by the arm.

"Hey, Gus!" I yell. "Hey, bastard!"

He looks at my face, his eyes wary, and at my hand on his arm. He focuses on the hand until I let go. Then, very carefully, he steps down off the apron. The bell rings. I can feel bodies moving around behind me, setting themselves for trouble. The flat-nosed old guy puts his bucket down and angles over. The gym is quiet.

"Yeah?" Gus says.

I spit the words out. "I came here to become a fighter. You're gonna let me become a fighter or you'll have to carry me out of here for trying."

Gus stares at me. Fuck you, Gus. You're not gonna stare me down. I stare back, holding it: twenty, thirty, maybe forty seconds, my eyes sore from hangover, and the bell rings starting the next round, and I don't blink, I'm giving him the stare I gave Kingsize in the bar in Brooklyn, trying to hit him with it, hurt him, break him. He just bores in.

Until he hears Muñoz grunt in the ring, starting to box his third round, and he turns to watch him. Doesn't like what he sees. Doesn't like Muñoz covering up with his hands in front of his face or the shudder in his thin legs. And looks back at me, as if he's just found something he's been looking for.

"Come on," he says.

I follow him to the locker room. Twenty-four green metal lockers are along the wall, with benches in front of them, and there are two stall showers and sinks and mirrors for shaving. A door leads into the small office I'd seen from outside and the German shepherd pokes his head around the corner to look. An older black fighter is in the shower, his head hanging, tired, letting the water do all the work.

Gus gestures at my clothes.

"Get them off."

"I don't have any boxing stuff."

"Hey, I told you to get the clothes off."

I start to undress as he yells at the guy in the shower: "Smitty, you got any clean trunks?"

"Top shelf. Thirty-one. It's open."

Gus goes to the locker, takes out a jock, a pair of worn boxing shoes and some clean white socks.

"These are tens but they oughtta do for now."

"Thanks."

"Get that stuff off and take a shower first."

"If I'm gonna work out, why don't I take it after?"

"Now." His voice softens a little. "You got a job?"

"I told you, I tried, but . . ."

"You got one Monday at the Cortelyou Hotel. That's four blocks up Irving Place. Irving Place is right across the street. You get sixty bucks a week, plus tips, plus a room."

"Doing what?"

"Doing whatever the hell they tell you to do."

I start to go into the shower. He touches my arm.

"And the next time you come here smelling like this, forget it. It'll be your last."

He turns on his heel and leaves.

"Fuck you," I mumble.

But I don't really mean it.

14

GUS WAS WAITING FOR ME at one of the heavy bags.
Muñoz had finished boxing and was skipping rope
now at the far end. His girl sat nervously with her
friend on the little raised bench. The two white men
with the cigars were still there, and one of them nudged
the other when he saw me in gym clothes. Gus had
hand tapes draped over his neck. He whipped them
off in a quick, little movement and walked over to me.

"You know how to put these on?"

"Sure."

He stood there, hands on hips, watching me bandage the left hand the way I had learned to do it in jail.
His face wrinkled, and he stopped me and unwound
the bandage.

"Lesson number one," he said. "Don't say you can
do something if you can't. Wrap a bandage that way
and some night you'll break your wrist. If you don't
know what you're doing, ask me. That's why I'm here."

He started wrapping the hand, over, under, through the fingers, around the wrist. When he finished, I flexed the left hand, making a fist that felt like a mace. I had to laugh.

"Try the right hand."

I tried and botched it, and Gus had to do it all over again. Then he had me unwrap both tapes and wrap them again. Once. Twice. Three times. If I was off a quarter-inch, he made me start again.

"In this gym, you do everything over until you do it right."

"What is this, school?"

"Yeah, and you're in kindergarten. Now put these bag gloves on and work three rounds on the heavy bag."

"I want to fight one of these guys."

"Yeah?"

"I always start a workout with boxing."

"You won't box for a while."

"Why not?" I said.

"You're gonna walk before you run, bum. That's why not. You think you know something about boxing, but you got more to unlearn before you can learn to do anything right."

"Okay."

The simple word of agreement seemed to surprise him. He scratched the side of his chin.

"Hit that heavy bag."

So I started to bang the heavy bag, smashing it with left after left, the hook making a sound like an ax socking oak. I could feel Gus watching me, and some others moving over to take a peek. I shifted position and saw myself in one of the mirrors, looking like a kid, with the goddam choirboy face, the blond hair lifting up when I punched, my legs too thin and my skin too white. And I was hitting the bag like I hated it, piling into it, digging hooks where the belly would be, bringing them up to where the head was, then steadying the bag with the right hand, pushing it off and smashing it when it swung back. The bell rang and I spun away. I could see the little man with the pail raise his eyes in approval. But Gus's face was blank.

"All right," he said. "Let's start from scratch."

"Meaning what?"

"First, we're gonna turn you around."

The men in overcoats had taken the cigars out of their mouths and were looking closely at us. They just stood there, not saying a word, silhouetted against the night glow from the street.

"You're a southpaw," Gus said. "Nobody wants to fight southpaws, so you could be the best fighter in the gym and never get a fight. You're gonna learn you own a right hand. Freddie, give me some of that tape."

Freddie, the man with the pail, came over with tape and scissors, and Gus cut off some strips and very methodically taped my left arm to my hip. When I tried to move the arm, the tape pulled at my hair.

"What's this?"

"Your hands are your guns," Freddie said. "He's gonna give you two guns."

"For the next couple of weeks," Gus said, "forget you have two hands. I want you to hit that bag with the right hand and the right hand only. I want you doing one-hand push-ups with that hand. When you walk down a street, you're gonna squeeze a handball with that hand."

The bell rang and two fighters started boxing in the ring. Gus ignored them.

"You're gonna cut steak with that hand and ring doorbells with that hand and pick your nose with that hand. Now face me."

I turned and faced him, the left arm dead at my side.

"Take one step forward on the left foot. That's it. Bounce on both feet. Feel comfortable? Good. Now take that right hand and put it up to the side of your head. That's it. Now touch your jaw right there under the ear where it curves away. With your thumb. That's it. No, don't make a fist. Never make a fist unless you're punching or you'll tire out all the muscles in your arm."

He took a fighter's position, facing me, and opened his left hand flat out.

"Now, hit my hand with the right hand."

I threw the right hand in a looping arc. Gus made a disgusted face.

"No, throw it straight. Like this."

He whipped a right hand into the air, on a straight line from his right shoulder, his body twisting at the waist, his left leg extended and serving as a fulcrum. I tried it, and the punch was straighter but still looked feeble as it hit Gus's open palm. I tried it again and it felt better, and then I started to move as I punched, circling with the left foot forward, throwing the right hand, trying to make it as straight as it looked when Gus showed it to me. And all the time Gus was talking, now tough, now irritated, now gentle, once even pleased. Talking all the time: "That's it. Straight, keep it straight. Turn the hand just before it lands, so you hit with the whole hand. Freddie, give me that big hand mitt. In the office. Straight, straight. That's it, again now. Now twist at the waist, so you get shoulder in it, and some snap. Now bring it right back to your chin, so the guy can't hook over it after you punch. Faster. That's it. *Faster*. Straight, twist it, back to the chin."

The bell rang again.

"Walk around, hand on your waist, take deep breaths."

I walked around, breathing deeply, the sweat streaming down my face. I saw Muñoz doing the same, nodded to him and kept going without noticing whether he nodded back. Gus was pulling on a glove, ribbed with leather, that looked like a large flat catcher's mitt. Freddie came over. There was no broken bone in his nose. There was no bone at all. He dried my face with a clean towel.

"Yer doin' okay," he said.

The bell rang and he walked away. Gus came over and held up the catcher's mitt.

"Okay, let's do it again."

I threw the right hand.

And so Gus put me through a full tough endless workout. Banging the heavy bag. Trying to get the skip rope going. Sit-ups on the exercise table. Halfway through, I felt as if my shoes were filled with water. My throat hurt. I got a stitch in my side during the session with the skip rope. Finally Gus removed the tapes and let me shadowbox, and I watched myself in the cracked mirror, my hands slow, moving clumsily. I was mad at myself for getting tired, and when I stood beside a little bantamweight for a round and tried to imitate his moves, I got angrier and even more tired. By the time Gus came back, I could hardly walk.

"Okay, take a shower," he said. "And see me before you leave."

I went into the locker room, slumped on a bench and picked at the laces of the borrowed shoes. I tried to count up the number of three-minute rounds I had worked. Close to twenty. Goddam. Months since I'd been in a gym and I worked twenty rounds the first day. Goddam.

Then I saw a pair of polished dark blue two-decker shoes in front of me and pale blue slacks, and when I looked up Muñoz was standing over me. Oh, wow. This is all I need. I can barely breathe, never mind fight. And what if he has a knife, what if he . . .

Muñoz held out his hand and smiled. I got up and we shook hands.

"Anything you need, just ask."

"Oh. Yeah. Thanks, man."

"They call me Willie."

"Bobby. Glad to see you again, Willie."

"You gonna run tomorrow, we meet at the reservoir around six-thirty. Some of the guys from Clancy's Gym come, too."

"The reservoir?"

"In the park. Central Park, you know?"

"Oh, yeah. Six-thirty, huh? Well, maybe I'll see you there. So long, Willie."

He tapped me on the shoulder and went out.

I sat back down and finished unlacing the shoes and unpeeled the socks and took off the trunks and then walked into the shower. I let the water pour down, as hot as I could make it, boiling my sore, aching body, flexing and unflexing my new right hand.

Later, I found Gus jammed in a small worn easy chair in a corner of the room he called The Office. The place was crowded and tiny: a couch with pillows, the chair, a table covered with newspapers, a shelf overflowing with books, a rug with a big S on it, a television set. The walls were covered with pictures, not all of them fighters; at least one of them looked like some guy from the Civil War.

"Sit down," he said, motioning me to the couch. Then, without waiting: "I want you to start running."

"I talked to Willie Muñoz. They run at the reservoir in the morning."

"Run a mile, walk a mile, run a mile. For now. Then we can up it. I want to get the crap out of your lungs."

"You gonna be there?"

"Hell, no. I'm not the fighter. You are. No more drinking, either."

His eyes were on the dog at the foot of the couch. The dog's head was resting on his paws and he was looking at me the way a judge would.

"You live here?" I said.

"Sometimes."

I felt uncomfortable and started to get up.

"Wait," he said.

The dog's ears stood straight up.

"I want you to know this ain't gonna be easy. You're gonna live like a priest. You got a girl?"

"No."

"What about family?"

"My mother lives in Brooklyn. Where you dropped me off that night."

"What about your father?"

"He took off. A long time ago. I was only six, so I never got to know him too good."

"Lots of kids in this gym have it worse. At least you had him till you were six. Some of them never saw a father at all."

He removed the lid from a bowl, grabbed a handful of jellybeans and popped a few in his mouth.

"Where you living?" he said.

I told him and he frowned.

"Get out of there this weekend. Go up to the Cortelyou. Ask for George MacDonald. He'll be expecting you. Do you read?"

"Sure."

"What?"

"I dunno. Magazines."

"Read something good," he said, squinting at the bookshelf. He took down a book about Robert E. Lee. "Read this."

I looked at the cover; it showed the same bearded man whose picture was on the wall.

"Robert E. Lee? Hey, I'm not interested in that kind of stuff."

"It's about boxing."

"Robert E. Lee?"

"You'll find out lots of things are about boxing. In the gym, you'll learn weapons and tactics. Read books like this and you learn about strategy."

"I'd rather knock people out."

"A fight is like a war. You have to figure the other guy's strength and weaknesses. You avoid his strength and attack his weaknesses. You study what the guy did in the past, to figure out what he's gonna do in the future. You *always* respect him. So I want you to stop reading crap and study some fighters."

He stood up and tucked the book under my arm. Class was over.

"Next week, I'll start showing you fight movies. I want you to study them the way a lawyer studies lawbooks. Not to imitate the old guys. But to see styles, to get used to guys who fight ways that are different than yours."

"Could that Willie Pep beat Robert E. Lee?"

"No, but Ho Chi Minh woulda known exactly what Willie was doing."

He walked me to the door through the empty gym. The lights of 14th Street glowed beyond the windows. The silence was eerie, as if a hundred people had just left the room.

"I forgot to tell you. Your friend Kirk from the can called a couple times."

"Did he leave a number?"

"No. He said he moved to Newark and didn't have a phone."

"What did you tell him?"

"I told him you hadn't been around yet, but keep trying. You would be."

I came out into the street feeling strong and sore and clean. Puerto Rican women hurried along in the cold, heading for the tenements to the east, and there was a feeling of bustle and excitement in the air. Then one of the cigar smokers slid out of a parked car. His face was very pink, and he had eyes so blue they didn't seem to have dots in the middle. Like Orphan Annie.

"Hey, kid!" he shouted.

I stopped and waited for him to come over.

"Hey, how are you? I'm Irv Pleskes."

"Whaddya you say."

"You want to be a fighter, right?"

"Who wants to know?"

"I'm a manager."

"I got a manager."

"Who? Gus?"

"Yeah."

"Come on, kid. Everybody knows Gus is crazy."

"He don't look crazy to me."

"Ask anyone in boxing."

"I guess it depends on what you mean by crazy."

"He . . . well, he won't play ball. If Gus don't like a match, he don't take it for his fighter. I don't know . . . he's crazy, if you ask me."

"I didn't ask."

"Well, if you need a manager, I'll be around."

He went back to the car, shaking his head in disgust as he got in. The other cigar was behind the wheel, and there were fight posters, yellow and black and red, on the ledge behind the back seat. The car pulled away.

I walked to Fourth Avenue with the book about Robert E. Lee under my arm and bought some chestnuts from an old man in the doorway of a bank, then took the stairs down into the subway. I considered calling Ma. But I was about to become a fighter and I didn't want to talk to anyone about permission.

15

Yes, it was something like that. That's the way it would have come out if Red Smith had written it, or you had told it to Dave Anderson, sitting outside at a table in Greenwood Lake while the tape recorder purred.

But you would leave out what happened that Sunday, when the gym was closed and there was nowhere for you to go. The day before you were to begin everything for real.

You had called Kate in the afternoon to invite yourself to dinner in the apartment. You could tell her all your plans, tell her about Gus and the job you would have, and what it was like running those first few mornings in the gray dawn of Central Park. You could tell her how you would become a professional. You would become famous. You would become a champion of the world. And in the telling, you would erase the memory of Jack Fallon.

But when you got her on the phone, her voice was cold. She asked how you were. You asked how she was. You were both all right. She said she was going out to a movie. You asked about Charlie. She said he was all right. Everything was all right, even the lies. And you decided then, standing at the pay phone in the cigar store on Sheridan Square, that you would go no further. You would suggest no dinner. You would not plead. She asked if you had money. You said you were all right, and then you said goodbye and softly hung up the phone, waiting a moment before you left the booth.

You sat on a bench in the little park. Near one of the exits, two winos moved in a slow, ambling dance, their arms lazily pawing the air, their legs melting under them but never completely giving way. One of them had the White Rose look: the Army greatcoat, the scoured eyes. The other guy had a wine bottle in his hand. And you suddenly realized that the dance was a fight, and that the two men were trying to hit each other. A move, a collision, the bottle splintered on the ground. The man who had held the bottle turned to see where it went, and then he was hit, more a push than a punch, and fell. In a sitting position on the broken bottle. He made no sound. He simply rolled over, and you could see the blood staining the bottom of his chinos.

You walked out of the park, pursued by phantoms: somewhere, out in America, was Jack Fallon. And he might be fighting in scummy little parks, under the eyes of bronzed dead generals. You thought that, babe. Not in those words, maybe. But the pictures were in your head. And in some of the pictures it was you in the greatcoat, with the empty bottle of muscatel.

Across the street was a bar called the Lion's Head and you went down the three small steps to the entrance. Inside, it was warm and dark and close, with steam gathering in the corners of the windows, and a small group of men playing darts, and another half-dozen scattered along the bar. There were a few Christmas decorations on the walls. You put a ten on the bar. You would have one beer. Maybe two. A Sunday reward. Then you would go over to Riker's and eat, and then you would go back to the room to pack.

You turned your back to the single barred window, so you couldn't see the park, and tried to figure out the bar. It wasn't easy. Some of the men wore thick wool sweaters, caps pulled over boozer's faces, rough pants; they looked like longshoremen, but their hands were pink and their nails were clean. Standing beside them, deep in conversation, were men dressed more conservatively, sport jackets and an occasional tie, except that their hands were harder, more callused. Businessmen in expensive suits, wearing vests on a Sunday, talked with the men in the tweed caps. A fat blond woman with bad teeth and thick harlequin glasses was the center of a group at one end of the bar. A thin girl with a limp came in, said nothing to anybody, climbed a stool, ordered straight bourbon and threw it down like she was in the habit of getting paralyzed drunk, often, and fast. You ordered another beer. Nobody talked to you, but you didn't feel out of place. It was a strange crowd, and a good saloon. A dense, warm harbor. A refuge against the newspapers that were scattering down the streets before the cold river wind.

The walls in the men's room were covered with graffiti. In pencil and pen, in felt-tips, ball-points and Magic Markers, hundreds of words, in English and Spanish, in Greek and Latin. Someone had written, I'm eight inches long and four inches around, call 783-5462. And someone else had written alongside it, That's swell, how big is your prick? Over to the right was the sentence: I'd like to suck what you have in your hand. And the answer below was: You'd suck a wrench? I'm the plumber. You had to laugh. It was like the things they yelled at each other in the night in prison.

A girl was sitting in your place when you went back to the bar. She was about twenty-five, with dark brown hair streaming down the back of her leather jacket. Her legs were long, one of them hooked in the bottom rung of the stool, the other extended, the curves and muscles encased in tight white dungarees. Over her shoulder, hanging from a strap, she had a tape recorder. You looked at her face in the mirror as you came up behind her for your drink: oval head, dark trimmed eyebrows, a longish nose, wide brown eyes, good lips.

There was a man beside her, in a sharply cut blue suit, with that fake-hip white hair that you see on TV anchormen and the crinkly eyes of an actor. She wasn't talking to him. Her eyes were moving around the bar, soaking up faces and details, listening to fragments of conversation.

You reached in and picked up your beer and moved your change to the side.

Oh, have I taken your stool?

It's all right, keep it.

No, it's your stool and—

It's all right, I'd rather stand.

You smiled at her. Risking that. Risking a reply you might not like. The white-haired man looked bored.

She said, suddenly: Why do you come here?

You were surprised. Oh, to drink beer, you said. Or kill time.

She seemed disappointed.

What about you?

This is my first time. We're doing a story about the new swinging bars, and this is up there on the list.

Story?

Yes, I'm Michelle Gordon from Channel 5 News.

You smiled again, feeling foolish. She had introduced herself as if you should know her name, but you hadn't looked at television news for almost two years.

Hi, you said. I'm Bobby Fallon.

Hi, Bobby. What do you do?

You were embarrassed. She hadn't asked you who you were, but what you did. Maybe, you thought, they were the same thing.

Well . . . I'm a fighter.

A prizefighter?

That's right.

How *marvelous!*

Yeah . . .

But you're *drinking!*

I'm between fights. You know . . .

Paul, he's a *prizefighter!* Paul Stuart, Bobby Fallon.

Hello, Bobby Fallon.

He gave you a deep voice and one of those Hifella-I'm-as-strong-as-you-are handshakes that you later came to hate.

Michelle said: How *marvelous!* Prizefighters and newspapermen and poets and carpenters and merchant mariners! All in the same place. I hear Dylan was in here the other night, singing with the Clancy Brothers.

Yeah? I didn't hear that.

You look like the kind of guy who keeps to himself.

I guess you could say that.

Excuse me, she said.

And got up to greet a tall man in an Anzac hat, a gray wiry beard, rimless glasses. He was soaked. The gusty day had turned to rain.

Are you Joel Oppenheimer, the poet? she said.

Well, *yeah*, he said, pleased to be recognized, showing tobacco-stained teeth when he smiled. She took his arm, holding the tape recorder steady with her other hand, and moved with him to the backroom.

You could see the muscles moving under the white dungarees. They fit her like a tattoo.

You could have left then, couldn't you, babe? You could have picked up the change and gone home to pack. But you had seen muscles rippling under her dungarees. And you had found a warm place on a cold Sunday.

Stuart turned to you and said: Would you like another beer?

No, I'm okay.

What did you say your name was?

Fallon. Bobby Fallon.

Well, you know, I handle all the sports specials at the station and I don't think I ever saw you fight.

I haven't turned pro yet.

Aha.

I will, pretty soon. It's up to my manager.

Who's that?

Gus Caputo.

Oh, yeah, I know Gus. Crazy bastard, but honest. At least that's what they say.

What do you mean, crazy?

Oh, just a little weird. He lives there in that gym, doesn't he? With a dog.

It's his way.

He had a couple of good fighters years ago, when I was at the *Telegram*. They always got away from him.

That was their loss.

Some good fighters trained in that gym. Floyd Patterson. Jose Torres. I haven't been there in years.

You oughtta come around.

You know something, Fallon? You're right. We could do a hell of a piece. The Kid's First Fight. That kind of thing. And Jesus, you must be one of the few *white* fighters around.

I'm just a fighter.

Yeah, but it's all blacks and Puerto Ricans now, isn't it. You Irish?

Yeah.

The Last Irish Fighter. Jesus, it would make a hell of a piece. The Last Irish Fighter . . .

Remember, babe? Remember how you listened? How you took his card when he handed it to you? His name was larger than the name of the station. You listened to him. Until you heard singing from the back, and you lifted your beer and your change and moved that way, the card in your pocket. You saw Michelle sitting at a small table beside the door to the kitchen, finishing with Oppenheimer. The archway leading to the back room was to her left. You looked at her through the smoke and the crowd, and once your eyes connected but she didn't really see you. The singing ended, and you decided you'd have one more and go. You went to the end of the bar, where the bartender refilled the mug and rapped on the counter, indicating that it was the house's round. You would have to stay for one more after that, because you couldn't leave on a free drink. The rain was pounding down now and your head was beginning to glow from the beers, and then you heard a guitar begin to strum and again voices starting to sing.

> *Look at the widow,*
> *A bloody great female,*
> *Isn't it grand, boys,*
> *To be bloody well dead . . .*

People left the bar, a few at a time, and went to the back. You saw Michelle's eyes change, dead now to Oppenheimer, and look into the back.

> *Let's not have a sniffle,*
> *Let's have a bloody good cry . . .*

She got up, leaning one shoulder against the wall, fiddling with the tape recorder.

> *And always remember,*
> *The longer you'll live,*
> *The sooner you'll bloody well die . . .*

The place seemed strange now, and you felt more alone than ever. You went to the pay phone on the wall, asked the operator for the area code for Newark, fed quarters into the slot, tried to get a number for Nelson Kirk. But there was no number. There was no Kirk. There was the singing from the back, the girl with the long brown hair and the muscled legs, the mellow buzz, the warmth, the dampness, the dart players, the thick woolen sweaters, the pounding of the rain.

Stuart was talking to the girl with the limp. You went to the end of the bar, drained the beer, ordered another. Just one more. Michelle was leaning on the pastry case in the back room, listening to the singing. A new song:

> *It's not the leaving of Liverpool*
> *That grieves me,*
> *But my darling,*
> *When I think of thee . . .*

Oppenheimer came over to her with a young man who was losing his hair. She recognized his name and shook hands and smiled. They moved away from the pastry case and stood beside the coatrack. You went to the pastry case. The singers were grouped around a huge oaken table, covered with beer mugs, their backs against the bare brick walls, and there were others at the smaller tables, facing the red-faced, capped, heavy-sweatered singers, joining in all the choruses. A tall thin man was beside you at the pastry case and you asked him who they were.

Clancy Brothers. Great Irish group. Just great. Wonderful gusto.

You thought: This guy must be English.

And said: They play here all the time?

Play here all the time, he said. Play Carnegie Hall, places like that, for money. Big money. Great guys. Wonderful gusto. Bob Dylan was in the other night, to sing with them.

And so you listened. The youngest one was singing about a girl named Eileen Aroon. All about how castles were sacked in war but truth is a fixed star. And it touched you in some dark way. You had never really felt Irish. You hated St. Patrick's Day with all the beer bellies puking their guts out on Third Avenue. You hated the Galway Bay bullshit you heard in the Brooklyn saloons. You had never heard anything Irish around the house. Even from Kate. She was Irish, or part Irish, but she was Indian, too, and Southern, and probably a couple of other things. She didn't sing Danny Boy late at night. This was different. The strange old haunting sound, the wailing harmonica, the strum of the guitars. You remembered what it was like in jail, lying there at night, separated from everything, looking out through the barred window at the endless sky.

Then you smelled a light perfume. And saw Michelle. She was standing next to you, holding a pink drink in her hand.

You said: You're beautiful.

She gave you a cold smile and started to move past you. Who the hell were you to call her beautiful? You were a nobody, babe. A fighter without a name. A kid without a rep. You grabbed her arm.

I said you were beautiful.

Her body tensed, and for an instant she seemed like a small girl expecting to be hit. Then she looked annoyed.

That hurts, she said.

You let go of her arm. Ashamed of yourself. You

had grabbed her the way you had grabbed Gus except that she was smaller, she was a woman, she wouldn't hit back. A bum, he called you. A saloon bum.

You said: I'm sorry.

She studied your face and must have seen something in your eyes.

She said: Are you all right?

Yeah.

Maybe you shouldn't drink.

Maybe.

Maybe you have to train for drinking the way you train for boxing.

She smiled more warmly at you, then started to walk into the back room. The music had changed, again, to a rousing song about the D-Day Dodgers. You stayed with her.

You said: Please talk to me.

You said it with all the hurt that was in you then, with the lonesome phantoms moving through you, full of the need to make contact, to hear a voice, to touch a hand.

She cut it short. I'm working right now, Fallon. It's been nice meeting you. Keep punching or whatever it is you do.

She moved away quickly, over to the fireplace beside the round table. One of the Clancy Brothers smiled and pulled her into the table, where she sat on his lap.

You pushed your way out through the bar, up the steps and into the rain.

You hit a few more bars. Then you were in a place on 23rd Street. A woman sat on a plastic stool near the end of the bar. There was no dense packed warmth. No singing. Just a jukebox and TV playing at the same time and the faint smell of disinfectant rising off dirty tile floors.

You took the woman to a room with dirty ochre walls in an Eighth Avenue hotel. She chewed gum as she undressed. Her skin was the color of ivory and she looked at you with hot eyes. She must have been fifty. Her breasts flowed over the tops of her black bra. She shuddered as she stepped out of her black panties. Her pubic hair was gray. Her skin was damp.

She said: What do you want me to do?

Love me, you said.

Love you? she said, her crooked mouth moving sideways.

She came forward, pressing her damp body against you, pinning you with her weight against the dresser.

Love you? I'll love you, boy. I'll sit on your fucking face and smother you, boy. I'll love you.

She started biting your neck and shoulders.

I'll fuck your prick off, you little mutt.

She moved down your body, biting at your stomach and the skin around your hips. She made smacking sounds with her lips. Then she turned you, moving you to the bed.

You never talked about any of that. You kept it inside, kept it there as a reminder, as fuel. Because that was the last of it for a long time, wasn't it? The bars and the booze. The remorse. The hangover dawns and the strange women in chilly rooms. That was it. That afternoon made you a fighter.

16

THE WEEKS BEFORE CHRISTMAS were a beautiful time.
I'd wake up early in the small room on the fourth floor
of the hotel, the streets still dark, and dress alone and
head up to the park. The other fighters would be waiting
in the clean cold dark, their breath making little puffs of
steam, stamping their feet and shaking their bodies and
shadowboxing to stay warm.

Most of them wore sweat pants and shirts under
their street clothes and heavy bridgeman's shoes so their
feet and legs would feel lighter when they boxed, and
they carried apples or oranges in their pockets to eat
later. One big light-heavyweight wore a rubber suit under the sweat clothes, trying to make weight for a Janu-
ary fight in Holyoke. The smaller guys, most of them
Puerto Ricans, were hardening themselves for the Golden Gloves, which started after the holidays, and they
would ask me whether I was entering this year, and what
division would I be in, and what did I weigh, and I

would shrug and say I didn't know, it was all up to Gus.

And with it all up to Gus, I could run without thought, talking and living and breathing fights when we slowed down or walked, but silent as we went off around the reservoir in the dark, breaking into twos and threes, moving at a jog, then bursting into sudden speed, flicking punches at the air, reversing, jogging backwards on the straight sections of the path, moving through wire brambles, groves of blasted city trees, pounding over iron-cold earth, nobody mad at anybody, nobody afraid of anybody else there or in the whole big world around us.

Then, the run over, the city bright with winter morning, we would walk down to 59th Street and have ham and bacon and sausage and eggs in the cafeteria at Eighth Avenue, looking at the *Daily News* for fight results, talking about Ali and Mantequilla Napoles, the welterweight champion of the world, and then reading from back to front and discussing a good rape on page 4, the blaze that killed so many firemen, the bits and pieces of the night's bad news.

The Spanish guys talked away in their own language and I'd try to understand, but it was like listening to a machine gun. Sometimes they would stop, explain in English, and be off again: the Puerto Ricans telling the Cubans they talked Spanish like monkeys, and the Dominicans abusing both for being *estúpidos,* while the blacks looked at me and rolled their eyes, wondering out loud where all these crazy spics came from anyway. Then the Puerto Ricans would tell me not to listen to these goddam niggers, and remember never to hit a nigger in the head or you'll break your fucking hands, man.

"They got heads like rocks," Muñoz said one morning, and Smitty, the black who had loaned me the trunks that first day, laughed and said, "And don't hit no Porto in the dick, either, man. They *always* hard."

It would go on like that for an hour, until we had finished eating, and had our tea, and exhausted the news, and it was time to scatter around the city. None of the others lived off boxing, because there weren't many fights around New York anymore, unless you were a champion or well-connected to a manager who had a champion. So most of them worked as stockboys, or hospital orderlies, or messengers; some were still in high school; all of them were dreaming of the big score, about the dues they were paying for the score that was bound to come, the break into the ratings, the drive for the championship, the one great beautiful and complete and perfect fight that would make them famous all over the world.

I would take the subway downtown and go over to the Cortelyou, where George MacDonald was waiting. He was the hotel manager, a pale, sallow man with rheumatic hands and a shuffling walk, who loved Gus and loved fighters.

"Three champions worked here, boy," he said one day. "Three champions, and seven fighters who fought for the championship. Sent here just like Gus sent you."

"I didn't know Gus managed any champions."

"Well," MacDonald said slowly, "they wasn't Gus's fighters when they became champions. People robbed them from Gus. But he made them fighters. He made them the champions and they would've been champions a lot longer if they stood with Gus."

"Who were they?"

"Don't matter. Don't matter."

He'd send me up to the fifth floor to take Mr. Schiele out for his walk in Gramercy Park, or to go shopping with Mrs. Collins, who lived on Social Security, or to pick up the cleaning for Harry Rose, who'd been in the army with George MacDonald in the First World War.

I ate for free in the coffee shop and MacDonald paid me every Monday, which was what he did with all of Gus's fighters, on the theory that a fighter was less liable to get in trouble with money in his pocket on a Monday than he would on a Friday. MacDonald had a suite of his own on the top floor, but none of the people who worked in the hotel ever saw it except for Bess, the Lithuanian lady who went up there twice a week to clean. "It very neat," she said. "Very empty. Very neat."

For an hour after lunch, I would go uptown to see Jerry Jensen, who had a big collection of fight movies, and I would sit with Gus and study the old fighters in this little screening room on 48th Street. "Only an hour, no more," Gus said. "After an hour you stop seeing the moves and you're just looking at a movie." I watched all the heavyweight champions first, from Jack Johnson, who I thought would have been a preliminary boy nowadays, to Ali. Louis was really good, a methodical, devastating puncher, but easy to hit with a right hand. "Watch the patterns, watch the patterns," Gus said. And I would watch carefully, quietly, filing away the moves and the patterns. "Now, what would you hit him with?" Gus asked one day as we watched Louis with Max Baer. "A right hand behind the jab," I said. Gus raised his eyebrows and asked Jensen to put on the Schmeling fight. "The first one." And there was Schmeling, a tough-looking German, punching with the right hand behind the jab, just tipping Louis with the jab, snapping him off balance, and punching with the right hand before Louis could throw the hook. Gus didn't show me the second Louis-Schmeling fight for months.

In the gym, in the afternoons, Gus brought me along slowly. I held my chin too high, he said, so he made me clamp a bag glove under the chin and hit the heavy bag with the right hand, round after round after round, without dropping the bag glove. At first, I dropped the glove every time I threw a punch. But after a week I was doing it better, dropping it less fre-

quently, and sometimes not at all. When he thought I
was ready, Gus took the tape off my left arm and let
me punch with both hands. I felt wild and happy, and I
threw dozens of punches at the heavy bag, trying to
remember the sequences I'd seen Louis throw. At
Jensen's office, we were still on the heavyweights. I still
hadn't seen Willie Pep.

A couple of days before Christmas, Gus waved me over
to the side of the ring. He was holding headgear.

"Merry Christmas," Gus said. "You're boxing
Valdes."

Valdes was from Brazil and spoke Portuguese
instead of Spanish, so he always looked lonesome. He
was black, with a touch of Indian in his high cheekbones and round hooked nose. His manager, who
owned a restaurant uptown and found him on the docks
in Rio during a vacation, had asked Gus to watch over
him. I saw him standing in the corner of the ring,
looking out into the afternoon, and the high cheekbones
reminded me in some odd way of my mother.

Gus slipped the mouthpiece in, slapped some
Vaseline on my face, pulled on the headgear, tied it under my chin, and put tapes over the loose lace ends on
the gloves. Freddie called Valdes over and taped his
laces down, too.

"One of them gets loose," Gus said, "you could
blow a lamp."

The bell rang, and I touched gloves with Valdes
and started to box. He had a long straight jab that
came like a pole and he kept his hands up high, covering his chin. We moved and jabbed, moved and jabbed,
but nothing much was happening. "Let him come
to you!" Gus shouted, and I did. I jabbed and waited.
Valdes jabbed and waited. I thought: If we were in an
arena, the customers would be throwing chairs by now.
We jabbed and waited some more, and the bell rang
and I went back to Gus.

"He's a cutie," I said. "For a big bastard, he's a cutie."

"No, he's a counterpuncher. He wants you to come in, and then he'll bang you coming in. Think about it."

The bell rang again and I stepped in more aggressively. I doubled the jab and threw a right hand to the heart and *bing!* Valdes hit me with the right hand. The punch was high and bounced off the fat leather brow of my headgear, but the son of a bitch had hit me. I jabbed again and Valdes threw the right hand. He was a thumping puncher, too musclebound to be a real sharp banger, but he stunned me. That made two times.

I backed away, flicking the jab and thinking: The guy is moving to my right, away from my hook, which he knows is my power hand, so I have to change the pattern. I started a jab, bent suddenly to the side and slammed the hook into the kidneys. Valdes made a little wheezing sound and started a right hand, but by the time it arrived I was gone. Then I tried the same move from the other side, first jabbing, then feinting the right hand, which brought Valdes's left up to protect his chin. I bent and slammed the right to his kidneys. All this as fast as I could make it happen. Then I went inside, chin down, punching freely in a volley to his belly, finishing with the hook to the jaw as the bell rang. Valdes looked confused and more lonesome than ever and I felt like a king. I went to the corner, smiling as Gus pried out the mouthpiece and washed it.

"You see it, Gus?" I said. "You see what I did?"

"Yeah," he said. "It was all right. But you lift your chin up like that when you're hooking and you'll get flattened." He untied the gloves and turned to Muñoz. "Okay, Willie, do three rounds with Valdes."

"Let me go another round, Gus," I said.

"Maybe tomorrow." He was pulling the gloves off now.

"Come on, Gus."

"I told you, two rounds is enough. Go work the heavy bag. And watch that chin."

He started tending Muñoz, saying things to him that I couldn't hear. I went over and started hitting the heavy bag, repeating some of the moves I had used against Valdes, polishing them, refining them, while a welterweight named Larry Barker worked the speed-bag rig and Smitty skipped rope and Muñoz danced around the ring, flicking out his jab at Valdes. I felt good being there in the hot sweaty gym, among friends, among people who didn't care who I was or where I came from, and I felt sorry for all those lonesome people down on 14th Street, and the ones lying around on steel bunks in all the prisons, or downing beers in all the saloons. Christmas was almost here and at last I had something I could do.

I looked up at the ring and saw Valdes's eyes begin to widen, watching something beyond the ring, and beyond the gym itself, and then he was gesturing, no longer fighting.

It was the snow, falling in great white globs past the windows. Valdes climbed out of the ring, yelling something in Portuguese, while Muñoz strolled around the ring with his hands on his hips. Gus came down off the apron and passed me on his way to Valdes.

"Crazy bastard never saw *snow* before," he said.

Now Valdes was trying to open one of the windows with the big training gloves still on his hands, and the other fighters were all joining him, abandoning the bags, the ropes, the exercise tables.

"Hey, what *is* this!" Gus shouted.

"Snow," Barker was saying to Valdes, pointing outside. "Say *snow*."

"Snow," Valdes said, tapping Barker on the chest. "Snow."

"Come on, get back to work, let's go!"

"Scrooge Caputo," Barker said.

"Snow," Valdes said.

I move through the crowds on 14th Street, my body
aching with a good soreness. The snow is gathering on
the parked cars, in the hair of the passing girls. I love
the look of Spanish faces made red by the snow. The
color of cinnamon.

I need a Christmas present for my mother.

Not the perfume. Not the Evening in Paris again.
Something you'll like, Ma. Something that'll please you,
this time. Please let me please you.

The first floor of Klein's is jammed, everyone wet
with the snow, the red faces tinged with blue from the
high fluorescent lights in the ceiling. I'm trying to think
of something for Ma. It's been weeks now since we
talked. I never know what to say, what to tell her. I
never know if Charlie will answer. No. That's not it. I
don't care about Charlie. Why should I? Who the hell
is Charlie? Some old guy from the bar who came in out
of the rain. Like some dog she found shivering in a
doorway. That's all. Maybe a bathrobe. Some nice kind
of bathrobe. What the hell size is she, anyway? Or
some kind of nightgown. Something soft and frilly. She
lay beside me, with my heart thumping in the night.
No, some kind of book. One of those big fat cook-
books. Betty Crocker or Fanny Farmer or whoever the
hell they are. She'll think I don't like her cooking, that
I'm giving her some kind of hint. Some book with a lot
of fancy pictures in it, then. A real art book. Nah. Shit.
Ma doesn't read. Ma goes to movies and cries at the
sad parts. When John Wayne rides away. I used to cry
with her. Jack Fallon, riding into the sunset. Maybe a
nice pair of gloves. They all look too small. How big
is her hand? She was bigger than I thought she was.
Her legs longer, damp against mine. Or nylons. A doz-
en pairs of nylons. I could ask one of these girls about
sizes. This black girl with the taut lips and the coal

black eyes and the bushy Afro. She looks like Larry
Barker, from the gym. If Larry Barker was a girl and
wore an Afro. Brassieres, panties, stockings, slips. Soft.
Silky. She'll wear them close to her skin. The skin
damp. No. A bathrobe. Big and thick, warm in the
cold night on Prospect Avenue. I can get one of these
girls to try it on.

I buy a plaid bathrobe and it takes them half an
hour to gift-wrap it. Then I go back outside, to walk
to the hotel.

The snow is coming down thick and heavy. The
flakes are the size of half-dollars. Away from Klein's,
the streets are quiet and muffled. I look up at the windows of the gym on the corner of Irving Place. There's
a dim light leaking from the back. Gus is still up,
watching TV with the dog, or reading, or just sitting
there, adding up the day. Gotta get him something, too.
A book. For him a book is good. A Civil War book.
Not a sex book. Not for Gus. A memory of a crooked
mouth and gray pubic hair scribbles through my head.
No. I'm through with that. That's gone. That's behind
me. But I feel like there are some things I can't scrub
away with a wire brush. Someday I'll call that other
one. The one with the brown hair. The tape recorder.
Someday I'll be famous, too. She'll want to talk to me.
She'll come around for an interview and I'll ask her
why she didn't talk to me that night when I was un-
known and lonesome. Then I can tell her to kiss my
ass. Yeah. I'll tell her to meet me in the Lion's Head,
and all the sportswriters will want to talk to me, and
they'll ask me to sit at the round table and sing with
the Clancy Brothers. And she'll want to interview me
and I'll tell her to kiss my ass. Yeah. The rain will be
coming down outside and I'll be drinking ginger ale and
she'll come in and I'll blink and try to remember her
face, and she'll introduce herself and I'll say, Oh yes,
yes, I forgot what you looked like. And I'll give her an
interview with a lot of yes and no, and cool quiet

grunts, so she won't have any interview, she'll only have this tape that doesn't mean anything. They'll be talking in excited tones at the bar, because they know I'm in the back, and I'm not just a singer or some bearded poet, I'm not just some jerk from a TV station, I'm Bobby Fallon, the heavyweight champion of the world.

Against the wall at the corner of Irving Place, an old blind man leans out of the snow. He's holding a cane, tapping at the ground. I go over to him.

"Want to cross the street, pal?"

"Oh, yes. That's kind. That's very kind."

I give him my hand. "Let's go."

"It's the snow, you know. It changes all the sounds."

"It really does, doesn't it?"

"Yes, it does. You're very kind."

We cross the street and he releases his grip.

"You going to be all right?"

"Yes. From here it's all right. You're very kind. Merry Christmas."

"Merry Christmas to you."

I watch him move along, the cane in the right hand, the left elbow brushing the walls and windows of the Con Ed building. I wonder where Jack Fallon is.

17

THE NEXT DAY, the gym was emptier. A lot of the Puerto Rican guys had left for holidays back home and there were no guests sitting on the little platform. One of the fighters had drawn some words and faces in the steam that covered the windows over the radiators. HELP. And GOODBYE AMERICA. And a picture of a squinting man who looked like Gus. I was on the exercise tables, doing sit-ups, when Freddie said there was a phone call for me. I waited until the bell and then ran over.

"How are you, babe?" a voice said.

"Kirk!"

"I tracked you down, ole buddy."

"Where the hell are you?"

" 'Cross the street in the Automat."

"Well, shit! Come on over!"

He came in the door a few minutes later. The

clothes were cleaner, sharper, but the face was the same. We hugged each other.

"I tried to find you," I said. "I called and called. Brooklyn, Newark. I even went out to Bed-Stuy one night."

"There was *nuthin'* left out there, man. Not a thing. Unbelievable. Houses burned out. Guys I know gone off to the can or dead with needles in the arm. Nuthin', man. My sister was moved out to that Newark, so I stayed out there till I could get on the unemployment."

He was drinking it all in, breathing the smell of sweat and arnica, listening to the chatter of the speed bags.

"Man oh man."

"It's something, isn't it?"

"Now, this is a *place*," Kirk said. "Here you could boil out that jail smell."

"The jail smell's gone, Kirk."

He gave me a look that I understood. The look that said, Hey, man, say anything you want, but once you've been there you never get out.

"You can smoke down there," I said. "Where the chairs are. I'll be through in ten minutes."

"I want to see you hit somebody," he said, giving me a wide white grin.

"I already boxed. And the gym closes tomorrow for a three-day holiday."

"You mean I can't see you box?"

"Stick around a couple of years."

After the workout, after the introductions and goodbyes to Gus and the other fighters, we picked our way through the black 14th Street slush and hills of filth-splattered snow to the Automat. I got myself some hot tea and an apple. Kirk broke a dollar for nickles and bought a dinner roll, the macaroni tray and a cup of coffee. I watched him move glumly from machine to machine.

"You're not working, huh?" I said as we sat down at a table near the window.

"Maybe after the holidays things'll open up. You know, people wait for that Christmas bonus before they make a move. What about you?"

I told him about the job at the Cortelyou.

"Hey, that's great, man."

"It's a way to eat."

"But listen . . . when you gonna start making *real* bread?"

"I don't know."

"How come?"

"I haven't asked Gus yet."

"It's up to him?"

"Yeah."

"He gonna put you in the Gloves?"

"I guess so, but he didn't say yet."

Kirk wolfed down the macaroni. "You should go in the Gloves and turn pro right after."

"It's up to him."

He wiped the macaroni tray with the dinner roll, then dropped two sugars into the coffee. He glanced out at the darkened street. Then his face brightened.

"Hey, you want to go to a party?"

"I'm in training, Kirk."

"Come on, man. I heard you tell them cats you'd see them in three days."

"I got things to do. I gotta get Gus a gift or something."

"How long's that gonna take? Twenty minutes?"

"I've had it with parties and that jazz, Kirk."

"So don't drink. Just look around at the friendly faces."

He laughed out loud, and I laughed with him.

"Give yissef a break, Bobby. It's Christmas."

"I feel good the way I am. Clean and good."

Kirk tried to look shocked. *"Clean and good?* Well, that just ain't the Bobby Fallon I knew and loved."

I felt embarrassed, as if I'd been caught in a Cub Scout uniform.

Kirk said, "Look, you wanna keep in shape, right? So you go with me and you *dance.* Skippin' rope, runnin', dancin', it's all the same, right?"

"I don't have any clothes for *parties,* Kirk."

"Go like *that!* Nobody expects a fighter, an *Irish* fighter, to come in lookin' like a nigger dude pimpo beauty, man."

"Nah, really, Kirk, I . . ."

"Ain't they got a union in that hotel? Don't you get no days off? Shee-it."

I looked out at the street. "It's today."

"The day off?"

"Yeah."

"Let's get uptown, man."

You went to a place called Chez Jose on 79th Street, and there was no party. No private party in someone's house. Just some people Kirk knew, jammed into a huge crowded downstairs place with two bands, one black and one Spanish. You wanted to leave. You wanted your own room and the quiet. But you went instead to the dance floor, to dance with two thin Spanish girls, Kirk alongside you, the girls good dancers, the floor throbbing from a half a thousand people doing a mambo, and you danced as if you were in front of the mirror in the gym: thumbs at the cheekbones, chin down on the chest, moving with the music, your legs strong. The girls were intense and tight and thin, and the old reckless careless Friday night feeling flooded through you. Then the dance ended, and you and Kirk bowed formally as if you were a couple of English dukes and not a pair of tapped-out ex-cons, and you went and stood against the wall as the band shifted into a ballad.

Up on the stage, a girl began to sing. She was a tall solid Latin, with glossy black hair, a strong face,

clean sharp features, hard white teeth. You stared at
her, at the white gown that glittered when the light
picked up the sequins. The white gown that was cut
right above her nipples. Her breasts were lush and
creamy-looking, rising and falling as she breathed to
sing. And you stared at her mouth. It moved with a
whory life of its own, biting and chewing off the words,
her tongue darting in and out, caressing her own lips.

Kirk said: You like that, huh?

Yes.

I know her. Name is Yolanda Chacon.

Where's she from?

From where I'm from in Brooklyn. I know her
since she's a little girl.

She ain't a little girl now.

She wasn't a little girl when she was a little girl.

She started on another song, and the dance floor
filled, and she was singing against the delayed beat,
and you wanted her. You wanted Yolanda Chacon.
Kirk handed you a Coke and nursed a bourbon. And
Yolanda Chacon took the words of the song as if they
meant nothing to her, tearing them, twisting them,
breaking them down and building them up, her breasts
bobbing and her body stretching, sweat pouring off
her, building and building in a stomping writhing
ecstasy of music and throat and sound. The women on
the floor competing with her, grinding at the men,
pressing at them, flicking tongues at their necks and
ears. While Yolanda Chacon built and built and built,
moving herself to someplace beyond that street, that
city, her song broken by pants and grunts and snarls
and glistening sliding notes, until she ended it in one
final tearing scream.

The stage blacked out and the audience cheered
and whistled and called for *mas, chiquita, mas*. But
you saw them take her off the bandstand. Limp and
drained and boneless. She was finished. Spent and
gone.

Kirk said: Jesus Christ.

You wanted to meet her, to have her sing like that in a bed, under you, on top of you. In that white gown, soaked with sweat.

You looked down at your rough pants, the jacket that didn't fit, the scuffed bridgeman's shoes stained from the snow.

And you said: I've gotta go, Kirk. I have to run in the morning.

He said: Hey, I want to introduce ya, man. I know her.

You said: I'll see you after Christmas. At the gym.

You pushed through the crowd and went out, past the black guy with the shining Muslim skull who sat behind the entrance counter like an unfolding switchblade. His eyes moved over your clothes as you left.

The phone woke me at seven o'clock the next morning. It was Gus. I told him to come up, then pulled on trousers and straightened the room. I hadn't touched a drink but I felt hung over. Too many things warring in my head. Gus knocked and I let him in. He was carrying a manila envelope.

"How come you're not running?"

"Gus, it's Christmas Eve. None of the guys are running."

"You're not like the other guys."

"What's that supposed to mean?"

"Never mind. Here. Fill these out." He took some forms out of the envelope. "I'm putting you in the Gloves."

I smiled. "Beautiful."

"I had a hassle with them. One bastard told me ex-cons couldn't go in but I found out that was bullshit. Then some other bastard wanted to count the fights you had in the can as amateur fights, which means you would have had to go in the Open."

"What's the difference? I'll fight anybody."

"Oh, yeah?" he said grimly as I filled out the form. "Listen, make all that stuff accurate or they'll get you for perjury, and you'll be back boxing burglars."

"Why can't I go in the Open?"

"Because the Sub-Novice is for guys who never fought before. If you ever had one fight in an amateur tournament, you go in the Open. That means you could end up fighting some guy with a hundred and twenty-six amateur fights and more experience than Marciano. You're not good enough for that, pal. That's why."

I signed the form and handed it back to Gus. He read it over and nodded to himself and put it in the envelope. The address of the *Daily News* was hand-printed on the outside in big black letters. Gus licked the flap of the envelope and sealed it.

"Well . . . that's it. I'll mail this and you should be ready for the first fight in a couple of weeks." He looked around the room. "Keep this place neat or MacDonald will be breaking my balls."

"Wait," I said as he started for the door. I opened the bottom drawer of the bureau and took out the package I'd picked up in Times Square the night before. "This is for you. Merry Christmas."

"For me?"

"Yeah. Open it up if you want."

He had a doubtful look on his face, like a man used to disappointment. He opened the ribbon very carefully and then took the paper off. It was a book about Field Marshal Rommel.

"Well, I'll be damned."

"I hope you don't have it already. I never saw it over at the gym."

"No. No, I never read this one. You know, this Rommel was a hell of a good fighter, a Robinson. A boxer-puncher. He'd feint you and then whack you.

Or he'd go on the bicycle, backing away, backing away, moving, backing away, on his toes, see? And bang! the hook! bang! the right hand! Too bad he was fighting for the other guys."

"Sugar Ray Robinson?"

"Yeah. I told Jensen not to show you the movies of Robinson. He was so good you might quit in disgust."

He leafed through the book, looking pleased and relaxed.

"Well, why don't you just go down and eat?" he said after a while. "You can run tomorrow."

"I think I'll run."

"Alone?"

"What the hell. I can eat later."

I pulled on a sweat shirt and socks and laced up the bridgeman's shoes. Gus examined a picture of horses that was hanging on the wall.

"What are you gonna do tomorrow?" he said.

"Go over my mother's house, I guess. I gotta call her. What about you?"

"I got things to do."

"Come over with me."

"No, I got some friends. I'll go see them."

He was lying but I didn't press him. I put on an army jacket and we went out together. We walked to 14th Street. A few bums, up from the Bowery for a Christmas Eve score, huddled together in a doorway. A sanitation truck rumbled by with three sleepy Italians in the cab.

"You win the Sub-Novice this year, and next year you can go in the Open and maybe after that the Olympics," Gus said. "You might be able to pull it off. The Olympics, I mean. You got the talent. It depends on your determination. Other things . . ."

I stopped and touched his arm. "Aw, Gus, come *on*. That's . . . it can't be that way."

Gus looked at me, surprised. "What do you mean? I'll decide the way it's gonna be. That's our deal."

"Gus, I'm already nineteen. At that rate, I'll be twenty-two, twenty-three when I turn pro. That means I'll be twenty-six, twenty-seven before I can get the big money."

"Perfect. Irish heavyweights always mature late."

"But I don't want to *wait* that long."

The words hung in the cold air. I felt my face twitch. Finally Gus spoke. Softly.

"Archie Moore boxed seventeen years before he made big money," he said. "Walcott took longer. You can wait, too."

"I want to get to it faster."

Gus stood there, squinting at me.

"Every one of you kids wants to be a star, don't ya?" he said acidly. "Money, cars, clothes, your name in the paper. Instant stars." He took a deep breath, glanced up at the gym, then looked at me.

"Well, why not?" I said. "What's wrong with that?"

"Let me ask you something. Something you gotta ask yourself. Do you want to be famous and rich, or do you want to be *good?*" He paused. "Think about that. Who knows? You might be the best who ever lived. These guys around now, they don't know half of what there is to know and they're on closed-circuit TV in theaters all over the world. Making fortunes. That Muhammad Ali, or Cassius Clay, or whatever the hell he calls himself, he didn't learn how to fight at *all* till *after* he won the championship, and even then it wasn't enough. He never did learn how to fight on the inside, or how to take a guy out with one punch. You might be able to do all of it, if you don't go running too quick after the goddam rainbow. Being a fighter is like being a doctor or a lawyer or a writer or a general. You gotta be a pro. You gotta be a *finished pro*. Anybody can be good, but not just anybody can be *perfect*."

He was talking fast, and quick, and with a lot of feeling, like an artist describing a masterpiece he had planned for years but never had a chance to paint. I took my hands out of my pockets.

"I see what you mean," I said.

"I'm not sure you do. I wish you did. But I'm not sure." He tapped me on the shoulder with the Rommel book. "Merry Christmas," he said. Then, hefting the book: "Thanks for this."

"Merry Christmas."

He walked across the street to the gym, dodging traffic, looking older and thicker and more ordinary than he did up close. He opened the door beside the candy store and disappeared.

There was no one at the reservoir. I ran harder than I had ever run before.

18

You DIDN'T RUN on the morning of Christmas Day. You slept late in the hotel room, coming awake slowly, caught between dream and morning, between the face of a black man with a knife and the thin light that came through the blinds. The black man wore shades and stood in a doorway, the knife a part of his hand, a steel finger, slicing at you, and your feet couldn't move, your shoes were filled with water, your hands were tied, and your stomach suddenly fell out, in red slimy coils, and you couldn't grab it to shove it back where it belonged, and you were awake. Awake with fear moving through you.

You went to Brooklyn, the package under your arm, the train plunging into the tunnel and then rising over the Gowanus Canal. The great piles of coal in the yards were topped with snow, the shovels and cranes frozen for the day, the barges tied to the docks. You got off at your stop and walked up the stairs and out onto Seventh Avenue, and watched the neighborhood grow harder and emptier as you neared Prospect. An abandoned car was up on an icy sidewalk, its hood open like the broken jaw of some defeated animal, the lower jaw filled with snow where the engine should have been.

And as you came closer, you began to feel like a scared kid. You'd been gone for weeks. You hadn't called, afraid the answer would be cold, indifferent, full of accusation. Your hands were damp with sweat, and you dried them on your coat and walked on. At the corner of Prospect Avenue, you saw a lone teenager in the schoolyard of P.S. 10, shooting a new basketball through the iron hoop, dribbling on the wet ground, faking, swerving, dropping hooks. And you stood across the street on the corner, thinking of those boys you saw in the garbage of Bed-Stuy the night you got out of jail: thinking of the guys still up there in the cells, waiting for the Christmas turkey that came from a can.

Until you turned and went in.

The vestibule: the hallway: the sewer smell driven out by the smell of pine needles and fresh roasting turkey. You heard voices murmuring beyond the doors as you went upstairs, heard Frank Sinatra singing Have Yourself a Merry Little Christmas from some phonograph, and glasses clunking, and dogs barking at you. And then you reached your own door. The door on the top floor right, with the new lock, and Kate Fallon on the other side.

You knocked. A tap. Tentative. Tap tap. Heels moving on linoleum. The lock turns, a chain comes off. The door opens.

She said: Well, I'll be goddamned.

Merry Christmas, Ma.

Merry Christmas, stranger. Come on in.

You stepped inside. Sniffed around for some other presence, found none and handed her the package. The smile.

She said: Well, I'll be damned. Two surprises in one day.

You watched her as she opened the package. Her hair was piled in small tight curls, with copper highlights glittering was she moved under the ceiling bulb, burning against the gray day. She had make-up on and her dark Indian face seemed creamier to you, and pinker, with a flush in the cheeks that was either embarrassment or rouge. Her tan dress was pulled tight at the waist and she was wearing old-fashioned high-heeled spikes. Her legs were firm, packed tightly in stockings.

She said: Beautiful! I love it! And this plaid! Did you pick it out yourself?

Sure.

It's terrific, Bobby. You didn't have some little girl helping you?

No, Ma. I picked it out all myself.

She let it flop out long and full, and held it against her body, and opened the bathroom door and looked at herself in the mirror.

Wait a minute, she said.

You watched her drape the robe over a chair and move through the rooms, past the bedroom to the living room, where a small Christmas tree was winking on and off from the top of the TV set. She walked straight ahead, the spikes digging into the linoleum with each step. One leg directly in front of the other. Then she bent at the knees, poked around out of your line of vision, and came back with two packages, wrapped with ribbons.

Merry Christmas, she said, her voice husky.

You took the packages, and she hugged you, the satin of her dress making a sighing sound against your rough plaid jacket.

I wasn't sure you'd be here, she said. But I got them anyway.

She backed away, and you opened the packages, and found a yellow scarf and two multicolored shirts and a dark blue turtleneck sweater.

You said: Hey, these are great.

I hope they're the right size, she said. Hey, you look *great*.

Yeah, they're the right size, look.

You held the turtleneck against your chest and smiled at her and she smiled at you. It was the right size.

She said: It's so dark you can wear it with anything, even with brown, even with plaid. You should look nifty in it, big boy.

You laughed, and took the pins and cardboard out of the shirts, and held them against you for size, and they were right, too. You held them and stretched them, and made a little ritual of it all, because then you wouldn't have to ask any questions, you wouldn't have to move beyond the small scene, you wouldn't have to feel. She said nothing about where you'd been and why you hadn't called. And you were glad. You didn't have answers yet that even you could understand.

She said: Charlie's gone.

Did they make him a judge or something?

No, she said, it was worse than that.

She moved around to put a kettle on the stove, rinsing it, filling it with water.

Would you believe, he wanted to spend Christmas with his *mother*? He's fifty-one years old! That has to make her, what? Eighty-nine, or seventy-two or something? I said to him I wouldn't mind as long as he took me up there with him. So he says, Uh, Kate, uh, listen, Kate, uh, my mother, uh, is one of these Irish ladies from the old country, see, and, uh, you know, she goes to Mass every morning and, uh, well, she wouldn't understand about *us*, Kate. So I said to him, Oh yeah?

Well, listen, Charlie, you no longer have any problems, there is nothing for her to understand, she can go to Mass in peace, because, Charlie boy, you are now out on your ass! Honest to God, Bobby. That's what I told him. And put all his clothes in a shopping bag and dropped them out the window on him. Hey, don't laugh, Bobby! This was a *big* thing, throwing that guy out.

You're murder, Ma.

I called you, she said. I wanted to tell you about it.

You went into the bathroom and took off the jacket and pulled on the turtleneck over your shirt. The door was open. You watched her as she moved around the kitchen. There was no razor on the sink and no lather.

She kept talking: On the way out the door he says to me, Katey, you don't understand, Katey, I want to *marry* you, Katey, I love you, Katey, and I want to get married. And I say to him, Keep going, buster, go back to Momma, go have your quince pie, and besides I *am* married, you jerk!

Something tumbled. You came out of the bathroom and she smoothed the wrinkles from the turtleneck.

You said: You're married?

Of course. To your father. Do you want cream?

You said: No, just black. You mean you never divorced him?

She said: What for? So I could make the same mistake all over again?

You wanted to say, Ma, I saw you that day when you met him at Toots Shor's and went with him to the Hotel Taft. I saw you that day. I know he's somewhere. I saw you with your hand on his arm and his hat pulled tight over his forehead. He was big and smelled of tobacco. You smiled at him, Ma.

Instead you said: You could probably get him declared legally dead, if you wanted.

She said, very softly: That bastard's not dead. It would take a lot of bullets, knives, car crashes, poisons and snakebites to kill that son of a bitch.

You sat at the table and sipped the coffee and smelled the pine from the tree in the other room. And you knew from what she had said, and the way she had said it, that Jack Fallon really was still alive, that he was somewhere out there and that she still saw him. You wanted to ask all about him. You wanted to know who he was and where he came from. And how they met and why he left, and what happened that night in the kitchen when he wrecked the furniture and pulled over the refrigerator and stood there smoking his Luckies. If you knew who he was, then you could find out who you were. But you sipped the coffee and said nothing.

She said: How's the boxing coming along?

I go in the Golden Gloves next month.

Oh, wow.

What, Oh, wow? I have to start somewhere.

She said: You mean you'll be in a ring in some arena in front of all those people?

That's right.

Can I come?

I don't know, Ma. Let me see. Let me get started.

She was staring at you like you were someone else. And you looked away, trying to feel comfortable.

You said: Are you going out? I don't see any turkey.

Yes, she said. *He's* gone, and I wasn't sure about you. I thought I'd go out somewhere later.

Alone?

I did it that way most of my life, Bobby, she said. No sense changing now.

Well, you said. You look beautiful.

You saw her blush. Through the dark skin and the make-up. She smiled and blinked. As if she didn't expect you to say that but was pleased you did.

She said: Well, thanks.

And then started talking, the words rushing out of her, everything coming too fast:

I thought I'd get dressed up. I thought I'd get my hair done and fix my face and put on something pretty and just go out, just go take a walk around the world. I mean, after I threw Charlie out I looked at myself and I looked like hell, Bobby. It happens every time you live with somebody. You'll see. All these pretty little girls, every hair in place, their faces like a painting, you'll see, you live with them six months and they'll look the worst. You start getting careless, and you don't have anything to really dress up for, and nothing to show off for, and nobody around who really cares, because you figure, hell, he loves me, not my clothes or my make-up or my hair, but *me,* and I went down to A&S and bought this dress and some shoes. You know something? You can't get a decent pair of women's shoes anywhere, do you realize that? They make you look either like Carmen Miranda or Frankenstein, these great big clomping heels. It's all these fag designers. Make us all look like the linebackers on the Giants. And I got my hair done, too, in this style. What do you think?

It looks great.

She stared at you again, in that funny way, as if she had never seen you before. She got up and poured you another cup of coffee. You saw the muscles moving under the skin of her bare arms. You watched the solid packed legs, the curve at the ankle. She sat down and tapped a knuckle against her chin. It was very quiet.

She said: Why are you looking at me like that?

And you said: You look pretty great. That's all.

Risking the words. Saying them. Slipping them out, in a casual voice, giving them to her. Like a gift.

And she said: You look pretty good yourself. You lost a lot of weight, didn't you?

About fifteen pounds. I'm one seventy-eight now.

You look great.

You thought: Say it again. Please say it again.

But she got up and went to the refrigerator and took out a tray of ice cubes. She offered you a brandy but you said you were in training, even on Christmas, and she laughed and went to the closet and found the bottle of Canadian Club and poured some into a glass, then clunked in the cubes and put two cubes in a glass for you, filling your glass with club soda and splashing some over her Canadian Club. Then she said you should see the tree, and she could play some music, and you said that would be great and you walked behind her into the other room. The covers of the big bed were mussed on one side. The lights of the tree winked and winked and she went over to the phonograph and put on a record and Frank Sinatra started singing In the Wee Small Hours of the Morning.

She said she couldn't help it, she still liked Sinatra, and she couldn't get with rock 'n' roll, she had tried but she could never make out the words, and they had no feelings in them, no tenderness, and you said you liked some of it, Dylan, and the Stones, and the Beatles when they were together, and then you asked her what kind of music he liked. And her face stopped, she didn't know who you meant, and then she understood.

She said that at first he liked Crosby, because he thought Crosby was Irish and always sang that toora-loora-loora stuff and Galway Bay, and Irish Eyes Are Smiling. But then he got to like Frank, too. At first he thought Frank was a Guinea bastard, and he hated the way the teenagers went crazy for him when he first started, and he used to shout about how the Guinea bastard had ducked the war by making movies in sailor suits. But then the guy went on his ass, his marriage broke up, he was ditched by Ava Gardner, and he came back. He came all the way back, playing this soldier in From Here to Eternity, and he won the Academy Award and made some good records, and *he* liked him for that, *he* respected him, *he* said the Guinea bastard was becoming a man. He said the guy couldn't fight his way out of a chocolate factory but he knew about saloons and loneliness and losing things and people.

She put another cube in her glass and stared at the rim for a while, sitting back on the couch, with you beside her, and you realized she had just told you more about Jack Fallon than you had ever really heard before, and she did it by talking about Frank Sinatra, who was still singing on the phonograph. She asked whether you were really serious about this boxing thing, and you said yes, you were, and she said it would be nice to have a ton of money, to buy anything you wanted and go anywhere you liked, and you said she had done all right without a lot of money, and she said yeah, she probably had, but it would be nice to try it all over again with a ton.

You turned and looked out through the blinds. It was snowing again. She turned, too, and brushed your arm. Well, I'll be goddamned, she said. A White Christmas. Steam hissed in the radiator. The room felt close and warm, and you remembered another room you both lived in once, with a coiled heater that seemed to shrink the walls, sucking everything into its glowing coils, burning the air.

Now, that was a song that Crosby could sing, she said, White Christmas, and you asked her if she had the record, and she said no, she didn't have anything by Crosby anymore. She stared at her glass, one leg crossed over the other, the hand of one arm placed in the crook of the other, her perfume heavy in the close heat, and she asked if you had found yourself a girl. No, you told her, you didn't have a girl, and she asked if you had ever had a girl, and you said yes, you had had a few, and she asked if you had loved them, and you said you probably did at the time and she laughed. It was very hot now, and you pulled the turtleneck over your head and laid it on the arm of the couch, and she said it was a hell of a Christmas, you without a girl and her without a guy.

She touched the biceps of your right arm and said, Wow, it's as hard as a rock, and you told her you were up to two hundred push-ups a day, and she said again how hard it was, and you said fighters don't really need muscles, and she said, Well, what do they need? and you said, They need balance and quickness and talent and heart, and when you said heart she put down her glass and there was a long silence between you.

Then she asked if you remembered the trains she got you that year, and you said sure you remembered them, you really loved those trains, and she asked whether you loved her. Of course, you said. You know that, Ma. And she said she didn't feel loved much anymore, not by anyone, and you said, Hey, come on, Ma, and she asked why you would only say of course, why wouldn't you say it out loud? And you said, I love you, Ma, and she started to hum, Threeeee little words, eightlittleletters, and you told her she should put some more soda in the drink, and she said she didn't want any soda, she wanted to get stoned. You hated the way she looked when she was drinking and you told her so. And she said you had just proved what she felt, that you hated her. And you said, Only when you're drinking too much, and she said no, you hated her, and you told her not to be stupid, it was Christmas.

Oh yeah, she said. It's Christmas, all right. It's snowing and it's Christmas and the kids are all playing with their train sets and the fathers and mothers are

sitting around with the eggnog and they have neckties
and new coats and dresses and everything is new and
it's snowing and they have the eggnog and friends are
coming over and the table is set and they're slicing the
ham and the pineapples and sticking in the cloves and
breaking out the ice and the aunts and uncles and
grandfathers and grandmothers are all on their way and
it's snowing.

You wanted to stop her but she kept going, her
voice sarcastic and bitter and abandoned, singing May
your days be merry and bright and may all your
Christmases be white.

And started to cry.

And leaned into you.

You took the glass from her hand and put it on
the table beside the phonograph.

She cried, full of her pain and loss and loneliness, and you put your arm around her and moved her
so she was facing you, her cheek against your chest and
your arms around her, and she kicked off the shoes and
curled her legs up on the couch, and you realized she
had the feet of a little girl. She cried for a long time.

Until after a while she said you were the only one
in the world who cared for her. With her head buried
in your chest and her voice very small and young.

You told her that lots of people liked her. You
said, It'll be okay, Ma.

Don't call me Ma, she said.

You said it was hard calling her Kate, and she
said you should call her something else.

Call me Mary, she said. We'll play a game. You'll
be Joe. I'll be Mary.

Her mascara was smeared by the tears, but her
face was starting to brighten.

Hi, Mary. When'd you get into this here town?

Wal, she said, ah jess gotta offen this here Grey-
hound. Come all the way from Memphis. Chick-a-ling-
bone come and see . . .

Nice ta meet ya, Mary.

Nice ta meet *you*, Joe. You shore are a good-lookin' fella. Hope you ain't already taken, 'cause I'd be jealous as all git-out.

Hell, I jess ain't found the right gal, Mary.

Listen, what you got that necktie on for, boy? Too darn hot for ties an' formalities. There. That does it. Don't need that tie. And these buttons. What you need this for? Damn, you got smooth skin. And these doo-dads, what you got them for?

The fear came right up to your neck. You mumbled, started to speak.

She said, Hush, now, Joe, you heah? Yore my fella.

She took you by the hand and you moved across the room with her. The way you did long ago. You went where she took you, did what she did.

You shouldn't look, Joe. You should get surprised.

In the mirror, you saw her reach back to unhook the brassiere. The breasts falling slightly. Round. Darker nipples against the dark skin. Pebbled circles.

Nuthin' to worry you, Joe. Door's locked, if that's what's got you. Just nuthin' to worry about. We got these pills now, and that takes care of it. No way to make a baby, Joe. I mean, you won't have to marry me. Less'n you want to.

Yes, Mary. I know. I understand.

It's all right, Joe. Everything is all right. Now and forever.

The snow fell steadily. There were no sounds from the street.

You said: I love you, Ma.

BOOK
THREE

19

IN THE DAYS AFTER CHRISTMAS, I plunged into the life
of the gym, battering my body, burning off the fat,
fighting long gigantic complicated fights in my head.
Gus drilled me with instructions, giving me words and
slogans to remember, and they ran through my mind
like pieces of an old catechism: "Your hands are your
guns, your body is your ammunition. You knock a guy
out with the punch he don't see. And he can't see
punches you throw in combinations. Combinations.
Combinations. Use everything, remember everything.
Never make the same mistake twice. Make the other
guy make mistakes. Take away his weapons. Look for
his strength, neutralize his strength, then use your
strength." He said the words over and over again, and
they stayed with me through the days, and into the
nights. I heard Gus talking while I brushed my teeth,
while I ran in the park, while I did my work at the
hotel. He kept at it while I watched the fight movies

studying McLarnin, Ross, Graziano, Zale, Pep, Louis, Ross, Canzoneri, Conn, Loughran, all the men Gus called the old masters. "Watch what McLarnin does here, he feints Ross with the right shoulder and *then* jabs, but then instead of following with the right hand, which Ross is expecting, he hooks off the jab! Hey, Jerry, run that again, will you?"

And I would try it all, using the lessons in the ring, practicing the moves in the mirror, forcing my body and hands to do what my mind told them to do. I was trying to make my body an arsenal, pushing it past any point it could already reach: four hundred sit-ups, a thousand knee bends, allowing the medicine ball to slam against me for eight rounds a day, building my body into something hard and lean and dangerous. It was what I did so I didn't have to think about her.

Kirk came around that Monday, and Freddie put him to work filling water bottles and emptying pails. A few days later, he was calling himself the assistant trainer, and Freddie said that was all right with him because he liked the idea of having an assistant. In the second week, Gus got him a job in a friend's place in the garment district, working a freight elevator at nights. So Kirk had time to go to the park in the morning, to keep a thermos of hot tea around for when we finished running, to share breakfast with us in the cafeteria, and listen to the fighters.

Once, I saw him talking quietly to Freddie after a session of boxing. He was evasive when I wanted to know what they'd been saying, but finally I pulled it out of him.

"I asked Freddie what he really thought of you," he said. "He says you're an animal in the gym, the best-conditioned fighter he's seen in years. He says you got comas in the left hand. He says the right hand is getting better and better, that you're punching with it, not throwing it. He says you throw combinations better than anyone since Patterson was a kid."

"But?"

"But it depends on what happens when someone fights you back, Freddie says. And he taps his heart, you know. He says it depends if you got the heart. The desire. The left tit. He says to me: Kirk, you and me and Gus don't fight the fights, *he* does. And we don't know that yet. We won't know till somebody hurts him bad."

I stared at him. "So what did *you* say, Kirk?"

He laughed. "I said: Freddie, if you wondrin' whether this boy got heart, well I *know* he does 'cause I *seen* him. I seen him fight big bastards. I seen him fight mean bastards. I *know* what he got."

"And what did Freddie say?"

"You know how Freddie says things. He just gives a little lift of the shoulder and the eyebrows and says, you know, the same thing. We won't know he's a fighter till somebody fights him back."

"He's a smart little bastard, isn't he?"

"What he says don't matter. You just go in there and let them know they gotta bring ass to get ass."

"Maybe there's someone out there who *can* get ass," I said. "Some mean terrible son of a bitch."

"That sucker ain't been born yet."

That night, I talked on the phone to Ma. I told her I'd be fighting the following Monday at Sunnyside Gardens, and that I didn't want her to come because she'd make me nervous. I told her I couldn't see her until after the fight.

"But I want to come," she said.

"Not this one, Ma."

"You don't want me there."

"I do, but I don't."

"Are you ashamed?"

"Stop it, Ma. Have you been drinking?"

"Well, maybe I'll go out that night by myself."

She hung up. I sat on the bed in the hotel room, stared at the phone, then dialed her number.

"I'm sorry," I said. "If you drink, it's none of my business."

"I miss you," she said. "That's all. I'm here alone and I miss you."

"I miss you, too."

"I don't think you do. I think you're afraid."

"I do miss you."

"Can I come over?"

"I'm training, Ma."

"Don't call me Ma."

"I'll come see you after the fight."

"That's four days away."

"I know, but I promise I'll come."

"Okay."

"So let's both get some sleep."

"You're right. Good night. I love you."

I lay back on the bed with my clothes on. In my head, I saw myself walking up the stairs into the warmth and the smell of steam and pine and perfume mixed in the dark.

Then I pushed it all away by inventing an arena. In the arena, life was different. Fighting was tough, but at least there were rules. The rounds were three minutes long with a minute of rest in between. You did not kick, bite or punch in the balls. You did not rabbit-punch or hit a man when he was down. You did not punch after the bell. There were ropes that limited the world, that brought the world down to that twenty-foot square where you fought another man. You used your body and your mind, but there were rules. Not like life.

And then the arena was suddenly populated. In the corner of the ring, calm and still in the roar of the crowd, stood the man who had my number. He was black, muscled, silent as death. He stood alone, without seconds or managers or fans. His head moved once: to spit. He had brought ass to get ass, and I was afraid. I went at him, behind the jab, but my legs were too thick and heavy. I threw the right hand, but he was gone. He was over on the side, the stone face gleaming, the arms pumping like the oiled gun-metal parts of a dark machine. He came to me, full of dazzle and menace and contempt, as I fell over, into sleep.

20

THE FIRST FIGHTER, in the first fight of the Golden
Gloves, isn't black at all. He's a short musclebound
Italian with long, curly hair, a wiry black thicket on
his chest, and a rooting section that seems to fill the
entire end arena. When I get in the ring, in the terry-
cloth robe and Smitty's boxing shoes and a pair of
stained trunks, nobody much notices. I just stand there,
leaning back on the ropes, with Gus, Kirk and Freddie
around me. But when my opponent comes in from
the dressing room, the end arena starts to chant: *"Carmine! Car-mine! Car-mine!"* And I can see his curly
head bobbing, and his shiny blue-trimmed robe, and his
hand waving to the crowd like he's already won the
title, and I think about the movie of Graziano and Zale
and how Graziano heaved the right hand like it was a
sash weight at the end of a chain. *"Car-mine! Carmine! Car-mine!"* They're down around ringside, guys

with shades and sharp-cut suits right out of Barney's and some older guys with pinkie-rings, and one guy gives me the horns and there are a lot of girls with piled-up beehive hairdos behind the guys who are chanting. And all the while I'm fighting Graziano. I'm stepping fast to my own right, away from his power, and hooking to the belly to stop him, then hammering with the right hand and coming back with the hook. These people are screaming for Carmine and I'm knocking out a movie.

Carmine finally makes it through his fans and climbs into the ring. The robe is over his shoulders and he has on brand-new boxing shoes. I'm sitting on the stool, fighting off the fear. Freddie is working the muscles in the back of my neck and upper back, keeping me loose.

I look carefully at Carmine. He has his robe off now. His shoulders are wide and powerful. The muscles in his stomach are like a washboard, his arms and chest packed solid. He does some squats and whirls his arms, and the crowd roars. *"Car-mine! Car-mine! Car-mine!"* My right leg jumps in a steady rhythm. I want to get it on. Then there's an announcer in the center of the ring and a small, slick referee in the neutral corner. My leg moves steadily. Gus faces me, his back to Carmine. His voice is soft and steady.

"Remember to *remember*. Stay cool. See how the guy moves. And throw combinations."

They announce Carmine. Gus slips the mouthpiece in and Kirk winks at me.

". . . and from Brooklyn, weighing one seventy-four and a quarter, Bobby Fallon!" He points at me. "Fallon!"

There are a lot of boos from Carmine's end and some scattered applause from the rest of the audience. I can't see who's out there now because of the glare. All I can see is a smoky haze.

"Okay, fight good," Gus says.

And Carmine and I are facing each other in the center of the ring while the referee rattles off the instructions. I look in Carmine's eyes and I see it: a little hesitation, a little shyness. We tap gloves and I go back to the corner. Freddie takes my robe and hands it to Kirk while Gus climbs out through the ropes.

"Car-mine! Car-mine! Car-mine!"

He's on one knee, blessing himself.

Then the bell rings.

He comes out like a locomotive, his eyes wide, his right hand cocked, and then swings. I step aside and he goes past me into the ropes. I'm right there when he turns around. I hit him with the hook. His eyes blur. I throw the combination: hook to body, up to the jaw, right hand to the face, the hook again. Hard.

He lands with a thump, his right arm straight out, his face on the canvas. The referee starts a count, then waves his arms across his body.

It's over.

The referee looks at my face, his own jaw hanging loose in shock. And then the ring is full. Kirk hugs me, lifts me, drapes the robe over my shoulders, and a doctor is kneeling beside Carmine, turning him over, prying out the mouthpiece, and the seconds are spattering water on his face, and the hall quiets down and Carmine's people crowd around ringside. A thick-necked young guy is the loudest, yelling up at me.

"You're a bum, Fallon! A bum that got lucky! On the street you couldn't wipe Carmine's ass!"

"Up yours, pal!" I shout.

"Come on down here, you Irish bastid! Come down here, I break your fuckin' face."

"Shut up, will you?" Gus whispers to me. "Go over and look at the guy."

"Fuck him."

"He's hurt bad."

"That's what I was trying to *do* to him, Gus!"

"Fake it, then," Gus says. *"Make believe* you care, for Chrissake."

So I go over and lean down. Carmine's eyes are open now. His seconds begin to lift him.

"He's okay," the doctor says. "But I want him at St. Ann's. He might have a minor concussion."

Carmine is standing, supported by his seconds. His massive body seems drained and boneless. He looks at me, his eyes afraid.

"Holy shit," he says, his voice a croak. "Holy shit."

I put my arm around him while one of his seconds drapes a robe over his shoulders. Then I hold his arm up. It's a cheap bit, something I saw in a movie or on TV, but it seems to work. The crowd starts to applaud. It's what they all want, some show of sportsmanship, or whatever the hell they think I'm doing. A minute ago I was an Irish bum who couldn't wipe Carmine's ass in the street. Now they're cheering.

"You're a good fighter, kid," one of Carmine's seconds says. "Real good."

"Thanks," I say. Then, lying: "So is Carmine."

When I came out of the shower, only Kirk was smiling. Freddie was packing the equipment bag in silence. Gus sat on a table. Outside in the arena, the middleweights were boxing and most of the other fighters had gone home.

Kirk wrapped his arms around me. "Twenty-seven seconds, man! It's official."

"You mean it went that long?" I said.

"Shit, man, I thought you knocked him out *forever.*"

"That son of a bitch. Did you see some of those people out there? Animals!"

Gus slid off the table. "They ain't all gonna be that easy," he said quietly.

I looked at him and went on dressing: "Maybe not."

"He was a weightlifter. That kind of a body is for moving refrigerators, not fighting."

"But he *was* there to fight, Gus. And I *fought* the bastard, didn't I?"

"Yeah. You fought him."

"Then what are you so unhappy-looking for?"

"I'm not unhappy."

Kirk laughed to break the tension and gave me my jacket. There was a roar from the arena. Kirk and I turned towards the sound, but Gus and Freddie didn't bother. Kirk handed me a flat longshoreman's cap.

"In the Gloves, the first fights are filled with that type of guy," Gus said. "They're the toughest guy on the block, usually with a great build. They can beat the shit out of the whole schoolyard but they can't fight."

"How'd I look?"

"You looked okay. Considering the guy was a walking heavy bag."

Freddie sat quietly, smoking a cigar, his face sour.

"What'd *you* think, Freddie?" I asked.

"The right hand. In the combination, the right hand was a little high."

Gus turned his head away and smiled.

Kirk said: "Let's go eat."

We went out through the arena. Two out-of-shape heavyweights were mauling each other in the ring. Most of Carmine's crowd was gone. A black guy with a round shiny face reached over from a seat.

"Hey! *You!* You, Fallon!" he said. "You can fight, boy."

"Well, thanks."

"Good luck, y'heah?"

The same thing happened again on the way out: from an usher, from a white man with thick glasses, from one of the special cops. Congratulating me, reaching over to shake hands or slap me on the back. And I liked it. They knew *me*. Three hours earlier, they wouldn't have known me from the guy who drove the Wonder Bread truck. Now they were wishing me luck. I bounced through the lobby. They knew me. In twenty-seven violent seconds I had finally said hello.

"Watch when you're shaking hands," Gus said. "Some of these guys, they give you the bone-crusher. To make you respect them, or show they're tough, too, or something. They could ruin your hands. Your hands—"

"—are your tools. I know, Gus. I even learned that in the can."

We drove out to Queens Boulevard to an Italian restaurant. There was a painting of Naples on the wall, and white cloths on the tables, and candles stuck in Chianti bottles. Sinatra was singing on the jukebox, "Nancy with the Laughing Face." We sat in a booth and a waiter came over and took our orders. *Have you ever heard mission bells ringing? Well, they'll give you a very good sign . . . Betty Grable, Lamour and Turner, she makes my heart a charcoal burner . . .* I got up and went to the john, and on the way back I called her. There was no answer.

"What's the matter with you?" Gus said when I got to the booth.

"Nothing," I said. "I promised my mother I'd call her after the fight. She wasn't home."

"She prob'ly tried calling Sunnyside and couldn't get through, so she went out for a paper. You know. Get the *News*, find out what happened."

"Yeah," I said. "Could be. I'll try her a little later."

"I loved the way you let that cat fly by you," Kirk said. "Jus' like a matador."

"Them weightlifters fight like trains," Freddie said.

"Well, this one got hisself de-*railed* tonight."

We talked about the fight until finally the waiter brought our food. None of us said much while we ate. I chewed at my steak and then ordered some coffee and apple pie with ice cream.

"You fight again Friday night," Gus said.

"Good."

"You don't hafta run tomorrow but I want you at the gym."

"Whatever you say."

I was thinking that Kate probably got fidgety and went down for a drink, just a fast one for the nerves, and I could see her in my mind, up on a stool in a dark neighborhood joint, and she's getting a little loaded and maybe feeling sorry for herself, and a guy buys her a drink and starts to laugh with her, and they have a couple more and go up to the apartment, and I remembered the padding sound her bare feet made on Christmas Day in the afternoon while the snow fell steadily. And then I stopped thinking, and Gus was settling the bill and we all went out into the cold.

"You wanna try her again?" Gus said as he unlocked the car.

"No, by now she's probably sleeping."

"I could drive you over there. It ain't that far from here. I just get on the Brooklyn-Queens Expressway."

"Thanks, Gus. I better get back to the hotel."

Freddie got out somewhere near the Queens side of the 59th Street Bridge, and then we crossed over to the city. Off to the left, the skyline was all lit up and gorgeous. We went down Second Avenue, and Gus stopped at 53rd Street to get the papers. Kirk leaned forward and draped his arms over the front seat.

"How come you so depressed?" he said.

"I don't know."

"You beat the guy, man."

"It wasn't much of a fight."

"That wasn't your fault, man. You hit him. He went."

Gus picked up two *Daily News* and two *Times,* and I watched him hand a dollar into the brightly lit interior of the shack and then squint at his change.

"Friday you'll get another guy," Kirk said.

"I hope he ain't another tomato can."

Gus came towards us slowly, looking at the back page of the *News*. He walked around to the driver's side and handed each of us a copy. I looked at the back page and knew my life was now changed.

21

YOU STARED AT THE PICTURE and let it burn into you.
Imagining it on all the newsstands, in the hands of
thousands, maybe millions of people who hadn't been
there that night to see you destroy Carmine. Across the
top, the main headline said: FALLON STARS IN GG
OPENER. The story on the inside described you as
"Irish" Bobby Fallon, a "savage puncher," with "fast
moves," who "disposed" of his opponent in a record-
breaking 27 seconds, "including the count." But the
words weren't as important as the picture. The picture
filled the entire back page, and it showed Carmine with
his face mashed into the canvas, his body bent into an
A with his ass in the air, the muscles of his arms piled
against each other like grapefruits in a bag, and the
referee frozen in astonishment. And you in the background, looking over your shoulder at Carmine as you
strode to the neutral corner, your hair barely mussed,

your body lean and tense and hard, your eyes full of murder.

Gus said it was a good picture of a bad fight, and Kirk shook his head, saying, Son of a bitch, son of a bitch, and the car kept moving downtown, and Gus left Kirk in the car and walked with you into the lobby of the Cortelyou. Howard, the night desk man, stood up with the newspaper and had you autograph it and put the date under your signature, and he smiled and handed you a couple of messages and said you were going all the way. Gus said he'd see you in the gym tomorrow, but his face told you there was something more on his mind. And you asked:

What is it, Gus?

Nothing.

Come on, somethin's bugging you.

I guess it is.

Well, say it.

Don't let this shit go to your head. That's all.

Okay.

Soon as you lose, the same people who think you're wonderful won't even answer the phones.

You smiled. Who says I'm gonna lose?

Sooner or later in this life, everybody loses. It's part of the deal. Original sin or something. Nobody's perfect. It's part of the deal.

The elevator arrived and you stood there. He jabbed a finger at your shoulder.

You did fine, he said.

Thanks.

And don't worry about losing. Who knows? Maybe you're the one it won't ever happen to.

You got on the elevator, the folded messages in your hand, feeling that somehow you'd been robbed. You'd been cheated by Gus's cranky purity, the mean way he said what he thought. What the hell did he want from you? You'd gone there to do battle and you'd won. What more could you do? Would he have been satisfied if you'd lost? If you'd been hurt and fought back and had still gotten beat?

You went into the room, locked the door and looked at the messages. One was from Muñoz. Short and simple: Congratulations. The other was from Kate Fallon. Just a number and to please call. It wasn't the number of the apartment. You picked up the phone and told Howard you didn't want to take any calls. You were tired and you were going to sleep late. He said: Okay, champ.

She was somewhere else. In some saloon. And with somebody. That was for sure. She wasn't the type to sit by herself for very long. She could never do that. She had to talk and kid around and share a drink. She had to be entertained. So someone was with her, wherever she was, drinking with her, conning her, running his hands over her.

To hell with her.

The picture is scotch-taped to the door of the gym. Muñoz smiles and I thank him for his message the night before. Barker slaps me on the back. Valdes gives me a little wave.

The guys with the cigars are back, looking at me really hard but not coming over to talk, as if the presence of Gus kept them away. Muñoz's girl is there with her friend, and I see them give each other the elbow when I climb into the ring. Boxing Valdes, I notice he's being a little more careful with me, backing away when I close with him, like he's fighting the killer from the newspaper and not the guy he had boxed for six long weeks.

Through all of this, Kirk is laying back, cool in his role as the trainer of a champion. But Gus is tough with me, catching every mistake. When I finish three rounds with Valdes, he brings in Muñoz. It's the first time I've boxed him since I came to the gym, and he fights like he's waiting for the chance. He really pours it on. He's bigger and rangier than me, a full heavyweight now, and a faster and more careful fighter than he used to be. I can't reach him with the hook, and when I throw the combinations he dodges and moves and gets away. I can't hurt him. After three rounds, it feels like huge rubber bags of water are tied to my legs. I want to get out of here and take a nap, but Gus signals that I'm not finished. He waves to a guy named Shotgun Taylor.

"Three more rounds?" I say.

"What's the matter, *champ?*" Gus says in a sarcastic way. "Too much for you?"

Shotgun Taylor is what the fight racket calls an opponent. About sixty fights as a professional and lost about half of them. Black, thick-muscled, with a shaved head and a flat padded face. He doesn't talk much and he only works out about three times a week, so I'm aware of him but don't really know him, as a fighter or as a man. He has no manager and Gus lets him work out for nothing. Every once in a while somebody calls from Boston or Pennsylvania or Ohio, and Shotgun is gone a few days, and we read in the papers that he's been knocked out in a couple of rounds, and a week later comes in quietly and unpacks his bag and goes out to loosen up. They say he's a tank artist, a tomato can, a guy who goes in the water for a few bucks, and that he was a good fighter once, a long time ago. But nobody knows for sure.

On this day, he steps into the ring and nods to me, then looks at Gus as if for instructions. Gus just blinks. The bell rings. And Shotgun comes out smoking.

He throws punches I've never seen before, coming from strange angles, bouncing off my gloves or going right through my defenses. Not hard punches, not punches that take your head off, but a lot of them, and they sting. Worse than that, they make me feel foolish. I try to close with him but get hit when I shouldn't get hit, and my body aches and my water-logged legs are dragging. At the end of the round, I feel terrible. Kirk rubs my back muscles, while Shotgun just walks around. I lean on the upper strand of the rope, and I can imagine the whole gym looking at me: Freddie, Muñoz, the two cigars, the two girls, Valdes, Smitty, Barker, all of them.

"You want to call it a day?" Gus says coldly.

"Up yours."

So he lets it go another round. I've never boxed more than six consecutive rounds in the gym. This would be round eight. The bell ring's and I go out to kill Shotgun. I hit him one right hand to the heart that seems to stop him, and then I pile in, the scream starting, bouncing right hands off his head and jolting him with uppercuts, and when he holds on I shove him back with both hands and bang him some more. A voice yells "Time!" somewhere, way off, far away, down some long corridor, but I don't really hear it, I don't want to hear it. I'm trying to kill this bastard. Chop him down. Hurt him. And I drill him with one right hand that jars my shoulder when it lands, and he starts down and I stay on him. And then there are hands and arms grabbing at me, and pulling me back, and shouts and the word "Time," over and over, "Time," and then its finished.

"Goddam you!" Gus says, slapping my face to stop me.

"Fuck you, Gus, fuck you. Fuck you," I say, my voice sounding strangled.

"Easy, boy," Kirk says. He plucks out the mouth-piece.

I look around and the whole gym is moving in slow motion, and I feel the anger leaking out of me. Shotgun is up and walking around. His lip is split and Freddie is holding a towel to it. I feel vaguely ashamed of myself.

"You pressed me, Gus," I said, taking it out on him. "Goddam you! Tryin' to teach me some kind of goddam lesson!"

"That's right," Gus says. And then his face begins to change, the toughness gradually lifting, like he's slowly taking off a mask.

Freddie says: "You get tired, you lose your temper easier."

"I know," Gus says. And he looks me in the eye. "Freddie's right. It's my fault. I shouldn't of let you box that long. You're too green." He smiles for a fraction of a second and then pulls the mask back on. "And too goddam thick."

We all get out of the ring and I go over to Shotgun and try to put my arm around him. He shakes it off.

"I'm sorry, man," I say. "I just lost my temper, is all."

"Fuck you, white boy," he says, and walks away.

Fuck you, too. Fuck all of you.

22

THREE DAYS LATER, I knocked out a flashy Puerto Rican in two rounds. The following week, I won a clear decision over a black dancer at Sunnyside Gardens. I had the dancer down in the first round and again in the third but I couldn't keep him down, although the *Daily News* said I'd won every minute of each round. The paper was now calling me "Irish Bobby."

The Irish started showing up at the fight with the flashy Puerto Rican. They had seen the picture in the *News*, with Carmine eating the canvas, and they started coming in a dozen at a time to see if I could do it again. They were heavy, tough-looking men, in rough clothes, with pink faces and beer bellies, and when I came into the arena they would yell at me in hoarse saloon voices: "Go get 'im, Bobby boy. Punch holes troo dis guy!" And I would wave and smile at them and go up to fight.

The Quarter-Finals were also at Sunnyside, and the promoters had to turn away more than a thousand customers. They said they'd never seen anything like it. The Irish had returned to boxing with a vengeance. When I came in for my fight, they were crowded around ringside, waving Irish flags, wearing shamrocks on their jackets and car coats, carrying cases of beer and smoking huge cigars. It was like they had all arrived at some great party, where they could let everything happen. Even mean things. The second-string sportswriters, assigned to cover amateur boxing, were dumbfounded. This was the amateurs. We were fighting for nothing: glory or experience, maybe, but not for money. And we were drawing more customers to Sunnyside Gardens than the professionals would draw. Kirk told me that some of the reporters had called their offices to explain what was going on and that they were told to make notes and file them, because the Golden Gloves belonged to the *Daily News*.

When I came in for my fight, it was clear why they were there. They stood up and roared, and started singing and shouting at me, beaming, laughing, full of argument and a kind of joy and a lot of beer. I looked around at them and smiled. But Gus hated what was going on. He said to me in the corner: "You're an amateur. You don't need fans." Freddie nodded. But Kirk smiled and waved back at the Irishmen, and they cheered him, too.

I loved it.

But that night, in the first round of the Quarter-Finals, a part of me started not to love it so much.

I was boxing a tough cool black kid named Jimmy Lyons, from the Salem Crescent Club in Harlem. For years, Salem Crescent was the best boxing club in New York, Gus told me, and when one of their fighters got to the Golden Gloves, he was ready. Jimmy Lyons was ready. He didn't try to be Muhammad Ali or Joe Frazier. He was just Jimmy Lyons and he was trying to kill me. He came in a straight line, shoulder-feinting and snorting, mean and hard and mechanical, working out of a bob-and-weave that made it hard for me to get a clear shot at him. He hit me and I hit him back, but because he was always moving I couldn't set myself to punch with power. I jabbed, trying to set him up for the combinations, but he walked right through the jab. Steady, snorting, fearless.

Halfway through the round, the Irish started chanting, "Fal-lon! Fal-lon! Fal-lon!" And I remembered Carmine, and the way his friends had chanted for him that night, and how it hadn't done Carmine any good at all. I turned to where the chanting was coming from.

And got hit.

There was a huge collective gasp, and I lurched away, my legs skittery under me. I hit the ropes, nodded out at the now silent Irishmen to let them know I was all right, and got hit again. I covered up, hands clamped to my face, while Lyons winged punches at me. I didn't go down. I didn't sag. But I didn't really fight back.

The bell rang and I went to my corner. Gus was staring at me.

"Now, listen to me very carefully," he said, in a soft, controlled voice. "Starting now, you forget everyone in this building except that guy across the ring. Everyone. Got it? Calm down, don't worry, keep your hands high, and jab. Use that jab like it was a spear. He can't keep going at this pace. And save the right hand. Don't show it to him. Keep him lookin' at that left hand. Jab, and jab. And hook off the jab if it's safe. But don't show him the right hand until near the end of the round. I'll yell, 'Forty seconds.' When you hear that, bust him good."

And I went out to follow instructions. In the first round, I had been flicking the jab, slapping with it, being cute with it. Now I began to punch with it. Stepping in, shortening the distance, and punching through, not at. The first few jabs smacked Lyons in the brow, so I lowered it, gauging the distance, adjusting for the bob, settling down and fighting more coolly. Lyons charged, and I jabbed and got out of the way. And kept backing up, backing up, my eyes always on Lyons. There was no chanting. Instead, people started clapping rhythmically, bored with what was happening, asking for a war. Gus yelled, "Forty seconds," but I was in the wrong position to do anything. I couldn't unload the right hand and so I saved it. The bell ended the round. Now there were scattered boos.

"That was better," Gus said.

"I didn't throw the right hand," I said. "There was no opening."

"That was okay. That was fine. When you see the shot, take the shot."

Kirk was quiet, his eyes worried.

In the third and last round, Lyons came out fighting. He had won the first round and lost the second, so everything was riding on this one, and he fought almost desperately, trying to overwhelm me with sheer energy. He leaped with one hook that I avoided, but then came back with a right hand that grazed my head. I didn't react. I just shifted position and jabbed. The crowd had begun to cheer again, seeing now that I could do more than just punch. I could move. I could think. I jabbed, almost taunting Lyons, waiting for him to make a mistake.

Lyons leaped with the hook again, and now I was ready.

I stopped, bent, and punched with the right hand. A perfect right hand. A picture punch. Short, hard, right to the point of the chin.

Lyons went over backwards and rolled.

In the neutral corner, I watched the referee begin to count while the Irishmen went berserk, whacking each other, hoisting the cans of beer, singing, the place full of terrific noise, and then, suddenly, Lyons was up.

It was impossible, but he had taken the punch, the perfect punch, the picture punch, taken it on the chin, gone back and over and then rolled, and he was up. And the referee was waving him in. The arena was dead silent.

He came right at me, and ripped a hook to my body and brought it up to my head, and sent me backwards. I felt my eyes tearing, a high white singing going off in my ears, something splitting the front of my skull.

And then I was in the shower and Kirk was staring in at me, with Gus and Freddie moving like shadows in the dressing room.

"You okay?" Kirk said.

"Yeah. Yeah, I'm okay."

I remembered the roaring crowd, Lyons getting up, the silence. Being hurt.

I said: "Oh, shit, Kirk. I'm sorry . . ."

"What the hell for?"

"I never thought he'd get up. I got fuckin' careless. Oh, shit . . ."

Kirk's mouth spread in a grin. "Hey, boy, you got nuthin' to be sorry *for*. You knocked that sucker *dead*."

"I *what?*"

"Hey, Gus! Come on over here, Gus. This poor boy thinks he *lost!*"

I turned off the shower and stepped out, and Gus came over with a towel.

"You won it, all right, Bobby."

"Jesus, I . . ."

"And you were good." He put his arm around my neck. "You were goddam good."

"I won it?"

"You won it."

I couldn't believe what I was hearing. "Jesus, he was tough."

"Yeah, he was tough."

"He was so fuckin' tough."

"He's a good fighter," Freddie said.

"Tough," I said. "So fuckin' tough. I knocked him out?"

"You knocked him out, all right."

"With what?"

"The right hand. He was coming in."

"Bango, on the chinola," Freddie said.

"Oh, my."

"A real good punch," Freddie said.

"I never thought he'd get up," I said.

"Neither did I," Gus said. "He's gonna be a hell of a fighter someday."

"He's a hell of a fighter now," I said.

"But you knocked him out," Kirk said. It was the first time he'd spoken since I got out of the shower. "That makes you a hell of a fighter, too."

"Is he still around?"

"They took him home," Gus said.

"That's where we oughtta go," Freddie said.

"Yeah," Gus said. "Let's go home."

23

You came out of the dressing room to the whirl
of lobby and corridor: to hands reaching out for you,
fat hands, rough hands, the hands of Irishmen and
Italians and some others you couldn't tell about, and
one of them reached over and pinned a fake shamrock
on you and another pushed a program into your face,
holding out a felt-tip pin, and you took it and signed
your name, and then someone tore a poster off the
wall and had you sign that, and you saw Gus bumping
people out of the way and his eyes all wide in alarm
and Kirk saying easy folks easy folks you'll all get a
chance and Freddie's head vanishing, and you heard a
harmonica and then singing and the voices coagulating
like blood, thickening, and beyond the glass doors you
saw that it was snowing, and then the singing was louder and the words were proud and noisy and defiant,
hurled against the walls, defying the cops, defying Gus,
defying the snow, even in some terrible way defying

you, singing that some have come from a land across
the sea, a fighting song, a soldier's song, and you were
caught in it, in the Irishness of it, you, who had never
felt very Irish, who had never been in an army but had
graduated from prison.

You, Bobby Fallon, who was good with his
hands.

Who had shown them all on this brutal evening
that you had heart.

They were lifting you, heading for the doors. The
ceiling seemed very close and Gus was yelling and
you were afraid they would smash your head against
the top of the door. But they were a river now, bobbing
and ducking and fading around and under all obstacles,
through one set of doors, into a great vestibule, down
four steps, the hands holding you, sitting on shoulders,
carried, elevated, made a part of motion and movement,
and the singing went on: Soldiers are we, who fought
and died for Ireland! Some! Have come! From a land!
Across the sea!

And out into the storm. You felt no cold. The
snow scattered across Queens Boulevard, the wind
too strong for it to stick, and you felt no wind. They
carried you to the right, heading for the bar. And you
looked back and saw that there were hundreds of them
now, and a dozen squad cars, and a cop with a lot of
braid and stripes standing out in the snow, and Gus
talking quickly to him and gesturing wildly with his
hands, and the cop not doing anything, just standing
there, looking at the wild Irish scene, and then, as they
carried you, and the car horns honked for passage, and
trucks and cars backed up down the boulevard, you
saw the cop's face open into a grin, his lips moving, as
if he had not heard that song for a long long time and
by God he was going to listen to it now and fuck the
traffic and fuck the rules and fuck Gus.

And then you saw her.

Leaning against a car. Dressed in a dark suede

coat with some fur on the collar, the snow driving at her red hair.

You yelled: Ma!

And she waved and tried to get through the crowd, and you yelled again, your words drowned by the chorus, and you kept your eyes on her and she was blowing kisses at you, and shaking both fists at you, her face full of happiness and triumph, and you knew that she had come here and gone into the arena and watched as you fought that tough bastard who would not quit: she had seen you get hurt: and get hurt again: until finally she had seen you knock him out,

You gestured to her, pointing at the bar, telling her to follow.

The bar was called O'Leary's, and as the first wave roared in the bartender turned, and three old men swiveled on their stools, and one of them stood up and reached for a bottle as if to resist some sudden ferocious invasion, and then the Irish tide slammed against the bar, and you were looking for her, hoping you could get to her, and you ducked under old ceiling dust and grease-covered fans as they carried you all the way down to the end of the bar, and someone shouted, Four hundred beers!

And then she was there. Beaming and happy, her hair wet, the coat stained, and she put her arms around you and hugged you and kissed you and you hugged her back, and she said she was so proud of you and you hugged her, and she said you were so good and so tough and so brave and it was the most exciting night of her life and you hugged her. A guy standing on a stool at the other end started singing Danny Boy and you waved to the bartender and she ordered a Scotch. You said if the Irish drink Scotch why don't the Scotch drink Irish? and she laughed, and the guy on the stool was now up to the part about Come you back, in sunshine or in shadow, oh Danny Boy, oh Danny Boy, I love you so. She took your hand and squeezed it, and you could feel her dampness and warmth.

The cop you'd seen with Gus came in and someone handed him a beer, and then he saw you at the end of the bar and shoved his way through.

Whaddya say, Fallon? My name's Corrigan.

You shook hands. He was looking her over with cop eyes.

I hear you fought one hell of a fight, he said.

You shrugged, smiled.

Let me ask you something, he said.

The cop eyes searched your face.

You said: No, you never arrested me.

And you laughed.

He said: Nothing like that. I wanted to ask you something else.

She said: Well, go ahead. Ask.

He sipped the beer. Are you related to a guy named Jack Fallon?

You felt her hand let go of yours. You were certain you felt her grow suddenly cold.

Yes. He was my father.

The cop bent his head to the side, cocking it as if he didn't know whether to believe me or not.

He said: Well, I'll be goddamned. When I read where you came from, I thought you might be related.

Did you know him?

He said: Did I know Jack Fallon? I grew up with Jack Fallon. I went to school with Jack Fallon. We were altar boys together in St. Stanislaus's church in Brooklyn. Did I know Jack Fallon? Jesus Christ. I loved Jack Fallon.

Her left leg was drumming nervously, the knee touching your thigh.

The cop said: When he left town, I really missed him. He was the toughest son of a bitch I ever met. Uh, no offense, ma'am.

She said: That's all right. He was a tough son of a bitch.

The cop said: You knew him, too?

She said: I married him.

You wanted to get out of there, to take her hand and hurry through the crowd and get out of there. But there was a part of you that wanted to stay. That wanted to know more.

You said: When was the last time you saw him?

He jingled some coins in his pockets and said: I hate to admit it, but it must be twenty-five years ago. Jesus, it's hard to believe. I mean, *nothing* happened twenty-five years ago. It was my goin' away party before I went in the Navy, and Jack was there. Jesus, he was a handsome son of a bitch. He had three girls at once. No offense, ma'am. But he was a good-lookin' guy.

She said: All the girls thought so. All three at once.

He said: I mean, he was a *dude*. He loved clothes, and he was always a sharp dresser. He didn't go for zoot suits and crap like that, or the pistol pockets and rises and pegged pants. That wasn't his style. But he loved clothes. And that night there was a guy named Jakie Morris from the Raiders. That was another bunch from down the hill. And this Jakie was supposed to be pretty good with his hands. He started cutting into Jack's action with one of the girls, and then he was doing a lindy with this girl and knocked a drink all over Jack's suit. I don't think Jack cared too much about the girl, but you just couldn't spill drinks on his suit.

She was listening carefully but not really looking at him, and you realized she wanted to know more, too.

The cop said: So Jack went to work. Jesus, he was a scary guy when the temper went.

You said: I know.

He said: And he went after this guy. He hit him with his hands, and knocked him backwards, and hit him some more and knocked him through the door of the place into the street, and then the guy hit back, and it became a war. The guy was good, but Jack had this other thing to him. Some kind of crazy thing. It would come from inside him, like . . . like some kind of . . .

Animal?

I didn't want to say that, but yeah.

And he would scream?

Yeah, it was like that. And Jack destroyed this guy. I mean, he beat him until I thought the guy was dead. Two squad cars arrived because the neighbors were screamin' from the windows. And when they got there Morris was out on the sidewalk and Jack Fallon was gone.

You stared at him, searching his face for the lie, the con, the deceit. But you couldn't find it. He knew. He knew Jack Fallon but he also knew you, your own reckless angers, the way, when the anger rolled through you, you were possessed and driven by the scream. Jack Fallon: you. Jack Fallon breaking his way up from your insides, from some dark and terrible prison, smashing his way out, demanding to be seen, respected, feared, loved. You sat on that stool, beside Jack Fallon's wife, talking to Jack Fallon's friend, and the crack opened a little wider than it had before.

The cop said: What do you hear from Jack?

You said: He's dead.

The cop blinked. He's dead?

That's right.

Jeez, I'm sorry to hear that. Well, uh, I better get outside and see what the guys are doing. Nice to meet you. Jeez, I'm sorry to hear that about Jack. He was a friend of mine. Good night, Mrs. Fallon.

He pushed his way back down through the crowd.

She said: I hope he didn't upset you, that cop.

No.

Talking about all those things.

It doesn't matter. He must be dead by now, anyway.

He's not dead. I told you that, Bobby.

To me he is.

That isn't nice.

I know.

I drive slowly and steadily in the car she rented, down to the Expressway, out to Brooklyn, with the skyline lost in the blizzard, and the docks empty and neat, and the road whipped by the wind.

She's sitting with her arms folded across her breasts, a cigarette in one hand, the window open a crack to let the smoke out. I can feel her looking at me, but she doesn't say anything and neither do I. I'm watching the road, driving very carefully, afraid that somehow it will end in some terrible crash, right now, when it's all starting. I get off the Expressway and keep going through the streets, slowly and carefully. I don't want to go straight home. I want to take her dancing. I make a wide turn around Park Circle and see a neon sign glowing through the snow. I pull over.

She smiles. "The Caton Inn? I haven't been here in years."

I lead her to a booth in the empty backroom and go up to the bar for our drinks. A TV announcer is saying there are storm warnings from Block Island to Cape May and that the city is bracing for a major blizzard. There's no picture. Just a voice and a sign saying CHANNEL 5 NEWS BULLETINS.

I sit down across from her in the booth. Her coat is off now, and she's wearing a silky turtleneck, and a black shirt, and in the shaded light of the table lamp she looks very young. Tony Bennett is singing "Because of You" on the jukebox, the song filling the room, and I take her hand and we go to the small deserted dance floor. She dances stiffly at first, holding herself away from me, and then Tony Bennett is singing "I Won't Cry Anymore" and she comes in close, and it's a snowy night in Brooklyn, and she puts her face in the crook of my shoulder and sings the words in a hoarse whisper:

> *I won't cry anymore,*
> *Now that you've gone . . .*
> *I've shed a million tears since we're apart,*
> *But tears can never mend a broken heart.*
> *I won't cry anymore . . .*

Her hand is on the small of my back. *I'll just forget you . . .* Her hair smells of soap and perfume, and the silk of her blouse eases against my jacket. *And I'm closing the door of memories . . .* You kiss her cheek. She who was twenty. She who danced with you on the darkened floor.

> *This is goodbye.*
> *I won't cry.*
> *Anymore.*

She finishes singing when he does and pulls back to look at me. She's crying.

"Hey, come on, none of that," I say.

"I can't help it," she says. "This place, this music . . ."

"Do you want to leave?"

"No. Not yet."

We sit down in the booth, me beside her, holding her hand the way she held mine earlier.

"Did you come here with him?" I say.

"I met him here," she says.

There's nothing I can do about it. The night has moved me around. It put me in the arena and into the street and into that bar in Queens. And it moved me to this place with her, where she and Jack were together once. There's nothing I can do.

"He was thirty and I was sixteen," she says. "We were sitting in that booth over there, a gang of us, six girls, and I was the youngest. My parents were dead and I lived with my Aunt Bridget. She's dead, too. They're all dead, one way or another. And he came right over to that arch, right there near the jukebox, and I thought to myself: Oh my God, that's the most beautiful man I've ever seen."

Her voice is changing: softening, growing timid, becoming even younger.

"He was wearing a dark blue suit and a light blue shirt. His tie was striped. He had a handkerchief in his breast pocket, and when he lifted his drink and looked into the back to see who was here, I saw light shining on his cuff links. He had on black shoes that were polished like patent leather. And I thought to myself: I've got to have him."

I look over at the arch and imagine him standing there in his dark blue suit and his polished shoes and his glittering cuff links.

The little girl's voice continues: "This place was always crowded then, every booth, the dance floor packed, the bar a madhouse. They had four bartenders out there, and a couple of waiters in the back. I didn't know how to meet him. Girls just didn't ask guys to dance in those days. They were supposed to sit around and look pretty and not come on too strong, because they would call you a whore if you did. But I was sixteen and what the hell did I know? I just watched him, standing over there, and saw him nodding to different guys as they came in, never saying very much, just nodding and sipping his drink and looking from time to time into the back. And so I went up to the jukebox and put a quarter in and played a couple of songs and asked him if he wanted to play a few. He looked at me and laughed, and said. How old are you, kid? I said I was twenty, and he laughed again. So I said, Hey, what's so funny? And he said, Kid, sixteen gets you thirty. And he walked away to the bar to refill his drink. Well, I wasn't about to let the son of a bitch get away that easy. So I played three more songs, they were six for a quarter then, and just waited in his spot under the arch with my arms folded. When he came back, I said to him, You got one more chance, big boy."

She smiles, remembering, and I wonder what I would have said to her if she'd come on that strong with me.

"He looked at me, staring at me, and reached past me without taking his eyes off me and punched the buttons on the jukebox. B-1. That was the number. It was Tony Bennett singing 'Cold, Cold Heart.' It didn't play right away, a lot of records came on before that one, but he told me I better have a draft card on me or he would turn me in to the Youth Board. I laughed and I went back to the booth. There must have been six of us sitting there, and four of us had guys in Korea. The war was on, and every other weekend there would be guys coming home in uniform and other guys going away, and some of the girls getting word that the guys just weren't coming home at all. So the place was packed with people who were half in love with dying and half in love with being permanent virgins. I mean, we had one girl who had a crazy affair with a Marine, who was married to a girl he met at some base in the South, and when she got her heart busted she went off and became a nun. It was either one thing or the other, one extreme or the other, nothing in between. It's different now. The kids aren't like that anymore."

She swishes the cubes around in her glass. I can feel her leg begin to bob again.

"Finally, 'Cold, Cold Heart' came on, and I got up and went over to him and grabbed his hand, and took him out to the dance floor. He kept his glass in his hand, behind my back, and he danced like a regular

Valentino. Very cool and very relaxed at the same time. When I saw you tonight, coming out at the beginning of the fight, it reminded me of the way he danced. Anyway, one thing led to another, and he took me home and that was the beginning of it all."

She takes a cigarette from the pack on the table. I light it for her, wondering how I looked coming out at the beginning of the fight.

"Why are you telling me all of this?" I say.

She smiles. "I don't know. This place. I guess that's what started it. This place."

I pick up her empty glass and go up to the bar for more drinks. Then I walk over to the jukebox. B-1 is now a Ray Charles record. The older records are on the right-hand side, the titles yellowed under their plastic strips. "Because of You" and "I Won't Cry Anymore." And down at the bottom, on the right, "Cold, Cold Heart." I play "Because of You" again, and then I play "Cold, Cold Heart" and take the drinks to the back.

She asks me if I plan to keep on boxing, and I say yes, of course I do. As a matter of fact, I say, I'm in the Semi-Finals in another eight days, and after that the Finals at the Garden. She asks me if I like it, and I say yes, I like it a lot. And she asks me if I'll be turning pro, and I say yes, sooner or later, depending on Gus. I explain how Gus is my manager and makes those decisions, and she smiles and sips her drink.

And then "Cold, Cold Heart" begins to play and I guide her to the dance floor.

> *I tried so hard my dear to show*
> *That you're my only dream*
> *But you're afraid each thing I do*
> *Is just some evil scheme*

I stand off from a distance, looking at her dancing with me, and me dancing with her, and I'm Jack

Fallon, leaning on the bar, watching her play the numbers on the jukebox. Her breasts press against me from under the turtleneck and I hold her close, looking at the young dark face in the mirror behind the booths.

Another love before my time
Made your heart sad and blue

And then she's moving away from me and reaching for her coat and handing me mine, and she's out through the door, leading me into the storm. The wind has softened and the snow is falling straighter now, and I'm Jack and wondering whether she's too young for me. We get to the car and I wipe the snow off the windshield with my bare hand and unlock the door on her side and help her into the seat, and I wonder whether I'm too old for her. Then I go around to the driver's side and get in and turn the key. The car won't start. I wait, try again, and it just lays there, and she starts to laugh.

"Beautiful," she says, and opens her door, and I open mine, and she's packing a snowball and so am I, and I wonder whether she's too young for me. She throws the snowball, and misses me and begins to run. I run after her, grabbing for snow, chasing her, laughing, remembering a sleigh that someone took, one of the big guys, a beautiful sleigh, with a sliver of that old fear moving through me, and then she's running past the tall stone columns into the park.

She's running as if she lived her life in that park, dodging over small hills, racing up snow-covered paths, circling behind something made of stone that looms dark in the blinding whiteness. Running until I can't see her anymore. Until she seems to have been swallowed up. I feel a shiver of panic and start calling her. Kate. Calling Kate. Wondering if she's too young for me. Kate. Hoping she's not hurt. Afraid I've lost her.

And then she's behind me, laughing, and when I

whirl around she socks me with a monster snowball and I lunge for her and we fall together into a drift, rolling and tumbling down the slope of a hill, until we're on the flats of the snow-covered meadow and her face is beneath mine and steam drifts from her mouth and her face is wet, and I wonder whether she's too young for me and I kiss her.

I feel her body tense. Feel tongue. Feel locked to her. Of her and with her and in her. The snow falls steadily and gathers on us, and I feel warmer than I've ever felt before. Until she moves. Rises to an elbow. We separate. I stand up first and offer her my hand and she takes it. She brushes snow off her coat. And I know something has been broken, the moment, the connection. The girlish laughing movement is melting out of her. She starts to walk towards Prospect Avenue. I walk beside her. There are no words.

Until we reach the house and I follow her through the outside door into the vestibule.

She stops, blocking the second door.

"I'd like to come up," I say.

She stands there. I kiss her cheek. It's cool and still damp from the snow.

"No," she says. "It's not right."

I can feel the strength flow out of me. A dull ache spreads around my head like yellow gas.

"Okay," I say.

"Please try to understand. It's because I love you."

"Is there anybody up there?"

"No." She smiles. "There's nobody up there."

The smile stays on her face. Part invitation, part rebuff. Telling me that I can come upstairs and fold back the covers and slide across cool sheets with her beside me. And telling me that I'll never be allowed here again. That something happened one Christmas afternoon out of loneliness and memories, and it would never happen again. Because it wasn't me standing in that archway when she was sixteen and he was thirty and he wore the handkerchief in the pocket of his coat. I look at that smile and turn quickly away. I run down the avenue, seeing nothing, refusing to look back.

On the subway, I fall asleep in the warmth of the car and dream of myself in a gleaming white bed. I'm very small. There are high bars on the sides of the bed, reaching high up to a pale blue sky. I can't move. I try to roll, to stand, to sit, but I'm helpless. And then a giant bird darkens the sky. It has a vicious beak, and dead evil eyes, and its neck is long and slimy. It hovers over me. And then it turns and shows me its ass. I try to scream but no words come out. The ass is red and purple and slippery, quivering at me from under the tail feathers. And then the tail moves, like a fan, and enters my mouth.

I wake up as the train pulls into 42nd Street. I've gone two stops too far. I get up and walk out of the car. The taste of the vulture lays in my mouth.

24

IN THE GYM THAT WEEK, as the city dug out of the great blizzard, I punished everybody, including myself. I hit one heavy bag until it came loose from its moorings. Gus laid me off for one day. I came back and was even worse. If I could punish things, I wouldn't have to feel.

I was like that the night of the Semi-Finals up at Felt Forum. I ignored the crowds waiting around the Eighth Avenue entrance, and I didn't speak to Gus or Freddie or even Kirk. I went to the dressing room with them, taped my hands and lay back on a bench to sleep. But there was too much noise as the lightweights and welterweights moved through the dressing rooms to go out and fight, and so after a while I sat up and asked Gus whether he knew yet when I was fighting.

"They're saving you for last," he said. "I don't

know yet who you're fighting. It's one of three guys. I just don't know yet."

I said nothing and lay down again. After a while a man in a gray suit came in and said that I was fighting Raymond North. He shouted this news into the dressing room and left quickly, slamming the door behind him.

"Damn," Gus said.

"It doesn't matter, Gus," I said.

"I wanted that kid Green. He comes right at you."

"This North is one of Jackie Bernstein's fighters, isn't he?" Freddie said.

"Yeah," Gus said.

"So what?" I said. "Who the hell is Jackie Bernstein?"

"You've seen him up the gym," Gus said. "He comes in with that creep Rogers. Always smokin' cigars and stinkin' up the joint."

"He's a pig," Freddie said.

"He means he teaches kids gutter shit," Gus said. "Laces. Elbows. A great left hook to the balls. A real pig. He calls himself a manager."

"They won't let no fighter do that number in the Gloves, will they?" Kirk said.

"In the Gloves, anything can happen. This is the amateurs."

Just before we all went out to the arena, Gus opened the equipment bag and handed me a new robe.

"Here," he said. "It's for doing good work."

The robe had a big green shamrock on the back and the words IMPERIAL S.C. stitched over the shamrock. I smiled and pulled it on, trying to keep from feeling anything, and then someone called my name and we all went out.

When the Irish fans saw the shamrock, there was a great huge pounding roar. They stomped their feet on the floor and raised their fists over their heads, and there was singing in the far reaches of the balcony, and more women with them now, their faces bright, their eyes gleaming, straining for a look at me and then chattering away when I went by.

"Nice and steady," Gus said in the corner as they pulled the gloves on. "Cool and steady."

I looked past Gus at North. He was a tall square-shouldered black, with a razor mustache and a flat shiny processed hairdo. There were three white men clustered around him. One of them was talking quietly to North, who nodded his head in agreement and stole glances at me.

"That's Bernstein, right?" I said.

"Yeah," Gus said. "But you're not fighting him."

Finally we were announced, and my name brought another huge roar, while North's was drowned in a sea of booing. The referee waved us to the center of the ring. North walked past the referee and stared down at me. He was at least three inches taller and his arms were a few inches longer.

"Hello, muthafucka. Gonna kick your muthafuckin' white ass, boy. They gonna be cryin' in them balconies."

"Yeah?"

The referee said: "Gentlemen, gentlemen. None of that, please."

"Gonna slice you up, boy. Gonna make you bleed and suffa, muthafucka!"

"Up your shit chute, cocksucker."

"Gentlemen, *please.*"

"You gonna look like hamburger, muthafucka."

The referee spread his hands between us. "Listen to me. *Both* of you. Keep that up and I won't let this fight take place. I'll stop it right now."

North went quiet. The referee, a small, neat man with slicked-back hair, ran through the instructions. I held out both hands and North slapped them away.

The crowd booed. A cardboard beer container bounced into the ring, and the referee picked it up and tossed it out.

I came out steaming, and North stepped aside quickly and tapped me on the back of the head as I went by. Then he backed away behind a long-armed jab, sticking, sticking. The jab wasn't a hard punch, but it was irritating and it was scoring points. And all the time he was talking.

"Come on, devil. Come on, muthafucka. Come get speared. Come get sliced, pretty boy. Come on. Come on, muthafucka."

And for the rest of the round I came on, walking like a sucker smack into the jab, lunging with wide swinging punches that the Irish fans loved but that hit only air.

"Fight like you got a pussy, boy. Fight like a fuckin' woman."

And the jab kept landing.

"Come on, muthafucka."

At the bell, I felt tired, and slightly foolish, as I finished the round standing in North's corner. He laughed at me.

"See you in a minute, muthafucka."

I said, "How about *fighting* me?" and stepped around him to walk across the ring to my own corner. I sat down hard.

Gus was angry. "You're letting him get to you," he said.

"Gonna kill that cocksucker. Gonna kill him."

"Listen, dope. He's doin' just what the corner told him to do. They know you gotta temper and they told him to talk to you, not to fight you."

"I'll shut his fuckin' mouth for him."

"No. Just go out and box him. Cut off the ring."

"I'll bust his ass."

The bell rang and I moved out.

"Hello, muthafucka," North said, snapping my head back with a jab. "Come on, blue eyes. Come on, devil."

I rushed, made contact, tried to punch and was gripped tightly in a clinch. The crowd roared and North kept talking. "You wanna ball me, boy?" The referee was prying us apart. "Hell, I'd like to give you a boff, boy. Right in the ass. Bet you like it there, don't you, boy? You got that kind of face."

His mouth was still open, still moving, when we finally pulled apart out of the clinch. His hands were down. He sneered.

And I leaped with the hook.

Suddenly North's eyes were scary and his broken mouth was hanging loose and he moved a glove to his neck, as if he was choking on the mouthpiece, and the crowd exploded and I knew I had the fight.

But it wasn't that simple. I had hurt him, but something else was happening: sound was coming out of me, the wild crazy screaming anger, high-pitched against the deeper darker roar of the crowd. I drove a punch into North's kidneys and bent him over, then straightened him up with the right hand, then saw him standing for a second with blood pouring from his nose and the jaw hanging from the hinges, and it still wasn't enough: I was hurling myself at him, grabbing him behind the neck with the right hand and pulling him forward and bashing him with hook after hook, when the referee rushed in.

And then there was a blur of movement, and the referee was stretched out on his back, not moving, and I was after North again. He pulled away, terrified, leaning out through the top two strands of the ring, and I hit him until he landed out on the apron with his shoulders on a typewriter, and then I started kicking at him through the ropes.

I turned and saw Bernstein rushing across the ring at me, swinging a pail, and then Kirk stepped in the way and knocked him down.

It was bedlam: cops charging into the ring, fans rushing the ringside, newsmen getting out of the way, and fights in the balcony, and whiskey bottles flying through the air, and Kirk and Freddie making a wedge to protect me as they pushed out into the riot. In the seats over the arch that led to the dressing rooms, about fifty blacks, Puerto Ricans and Irishmen were battling each other, throwing chairs, breaking bottles, while the arena filled with the sound of running feet and the bing-bing-binging of the ringside bell, trying to get order. I looked around one final time and saw three doctors still working on North.

Gus slammed the door of the dressing room and jammed a chair against the handle. Freddie pulled a table away from the wall and dragged it over to back up the chair. Kirk flexed and unflexed his right hand. I stood there, feeling unreal, like I'd walked into some movie, as Freddie came over and cut off the gloves with surgical scissors. The room felt very cold and I shivered.

"Get dressed," Gus said. "Forget the shower." His voice was flat and distant.

"That bastard," I said.

"Shut up," he said. "Just get your clothes on and we'll see what we can do about getting out of here alive."

I took off the trunks, cup and jock and stuffed them loosely in the bag, on top of the new shamrock robe. There was a lot of noise out in the hall. I pulled on shorts and a pair of chinos, and then heard a cop voice outside: "Clear this area! I want everyone out of this area!" I laced up the bridgeman's shoes and Kirk handed me my shirt. Someone pounded on the door but nobody made a move to open it. Gus put up his hand, indicating that we should hold everything, but he didn't say a word.

I heard the cop voice again: "Clear this area! You have two minutes to clear this area and that means *everybody!*"

I buttoned my shirt as the noise began to fade, and sat on the floor, with my back against the wall. Someone else banged on the door, and this time Gus moved the table and chair and opened it a crack. Then he pushed everything aside and opened it wide.

An older man walked in, neatly dressed in a blue blazer, gray slacks, a striped tie and a pair of shiny black leather loafers. He was holding my AAU card in his hand. He looked at the card and then at me. He was having a hard time controlling his anger.

"Robert Fallon?"

"That's me," I said, getting up slowly.

"Fallon, I have the distinct pleasure of informing you that you have been banned from amateur boxing for life."

I took a step forward. "What the hell does that mean?"

"The charge, Fallon, is grossly unsportsmanlike conduct," he said. Tension moved under the smooth pink skin. "The decision in tonight's fight has been awarded to Mr. North. All amateur boxing associations in the free world will be notified of your permanent suspension in the morning."

Gus stepped closer. "You mean you can do this without even holding a hearing? There was real provocation out there. That guy North was saying a lot of disgusting things. My guy was provoked."

The man turned to the door and touched the knob. "Your fighter struck a referee. He tried to kill another fighter. No provocation could be that terrible."

"But there should at least be a hearing, goddammit."

"The hell with it," I said.

I took two steps forward and the official backed away. I jabbed a finger over the heart of his blue blazer. "Get lost, pal," I said. "While you can still walk."

The man gave me a wintry smile, as if his worst opinion had just been confirmed. He ducked out the door, passing two young men on their way in.

"What the hell do you want?" Gus said.

The first man, short, with long dark blond hair, said, "I'm Bob Rothman from the *News*. This is Nick Siegel from the *Post*."

"We got nothing to say," Gus said.

"You gotta say *something*," Siegel said, laughing. He was going bald and had a soft voice. "They had a beautiful riot out there. The best one in years."

"How bad?" Gus asked.

"Fifteen arrests. A couple of guys in the hospital, stabbed. It was beautiful."

"Jesus Christ."

"I guess you heard about North?" Rothman said.

"No," I said.

"His jaw's busted in three places, his collarbone's fractured from the fall, and they think he has a busted nose."

Gus glanced at me. "That's too bad."

"How do you feel about that, Bobby?" Siegel said. North being busted up like that, I mean?"

"I feel good," I said.

"He doesn't mean that," Gus said. "But I'd like to say—"

"The hell I don't mean it, Gus. That son of a bitch *asked* for it and I gave him it."

Both reporters started writing furiously in spiral notebooks.

"Where are you from, anyway?" Rothman said.

"Brooklyn."

"And you're really Irish?"

"My father was Irish. Born here, but Irish. My mother's American, part Indian."

Rothman's eyes were really wide now. "Irish and Indian?"

"Were you drinking tonight?" Siegel said, laughing again.

"I don't drink."

"Hey, we gotta go," Gus said abruptly. "Thanks, gentlemen."

Kirk threw a coat over my shoulders and Siegel said to him: "Are you a fighter?"

Kirk smiled. "No. Just a lover."

"That was some punch you hit Jackie Bernstein."

"Now *that* was the only good thing happened all night," Gus said.

"I thought it was a little high," Freddie said.

We all laughed.

"You people are *crazy*," Siegel said.

"No," Gus said, pointing to me. "Only him."

"He's not crazy," Freddie said. "He's Irish."

Gus peeked out at the hallway. It was quiet, with a few cops standing around, smoking and drinking from containers of coffee.

"I guess you heard you're banned from amateur boxing," Rothman said. "For life."

"Yeah," Gus said. "And I say it was goddam unfair. We never had even a *chance* at a hearing. We never were able to explain what the other guy was saying to Bobby to make him go so . . . to lose his temper like that."

"Well, what are you going to do?" Siegel said.

Gus looked at me, and then at Freddie and Kirk. He pulled the door open wide.

"What can I do?" he said. "I'm turning him pro."

25

IN THE DREAM, I was in a canvas square, without ropes. I was naked. Fans were standing around in great hills of faces, chanting my name, applauding, singing. But my feet were glued to the canvas and I was trying to cover my nakedness, to find my trunks or the robe, but there was nothing near me. And then they were coming into the ring. Hundreds of them. Thousands of them. Moving like waves. And a black man was there. A pimp from Times Square. With a straight razor in his hand.

I didn't see him move. But suddenly my neck was open, sliced right through the Adam's apple, which didn't feel at all like an apple when I grabbed for it but was more like a corncob, and I was trying to hold the two parts together but they wouldn't join and the blood was streaming down my arms. All the people in the ropeless ring backed away and the singing stopped and the noise ended and I was there naked and I tried to scream, tried to call out, tried to say something.

And nothing came out.

I woke up alone in my room in the Cortelyou. The newspapers were in a pile beside the bed, and I turned on the light and grabbed for them. The front-page headline said RIOT MARS GLOVES SEMIS. There was a picture of me halfway through the ropes, aiming a kick at North's head, while the reporters backed away from his falling body and a large Irishman in a nylon jacket rose behind them, a plastic cup in his hand and a smile on his face.

I stared at them, thinking: Well, I've made the front page. And remembered that I hadn't called her, that I had closed down the telephone and gone to bed. I picked up the receiver and asked for messages. She had called three times. And I wanted to call her and go over there and sleep with her long body beside me. And to enter her warmth and her wetness. But I just thanked the operator and lay there with the light on until I fell away again into sleep.

A week later, I was given a professional license by the Ohio Athletic Commission, who sent it to Gus by mail. Three days after that, Gus told me I was fighting my first professional fight in another week in Newark. I was pleased as hell, and I told Gus I'd always liked Jersey and it was nice and close. And Gus smiled and said it wasn't Newark, New Jersey, it was Newark, Ohio.

We headed out in the cold winter morning along the turnpike for Ohio. Kirk drove the old Chevy, Freddie studied the maps and Gus sat quietly in the back with me.

"We're gonna do it right," he said. "It's not gonna be easy, but it's gonna be right."

"What the hell does that mean?"

"I mean that we're gonna go on the road. I'm gonna fight you in every hall and arena in this country. You won't come near New York, not even to train. We'll use all the gyms and all the sparring partners we can find, but I'm keeping you out of New York. You'll fight all kinds of guys with all kinds of styles, and when you come back to New York, you'll be a fighter."

Freddie said: "They don't do it like that anymore."

"That's exactly why we're gonna do it this way."

"You mean I'll be out of New York for a year?"

"Maybe longer."

"Jesus, Gus."

"We're gonna do it right."

We arrived in Newark late in the afternoon and spent twenty minutes trying to find the old American Legion Hall, where they were having the fights. When we walked in, some puzzled carpenters were still nailing the ring platform together and trying to get the slack out of the ropes. A man named Harding walked away from a group of people and came over with his right hand out, as if he were running for office. He was wearing a blue business suit with an American flag pin in the lapel.

"You must be Mr. Caputo," he said.

"Arnold Harding?"

"That's me. Nice to meet you." He looked at me and said: "You can strip down in the office over there. The other fighters have weighed in already and we held Soldier Bartlett until you got here. For the pictures, you see."

Over in the corner, Soldier Bartlett was sitting on a chair in a faded blue robe. A fat photographer with a veined nose was standing beside him, holding an old-fashioned Speed Graphic.

"Jesus, Gus," I whispered. "This guy's *white!*"

"Yeah? So what?"

"He's only the second white guy I ever boxed. In the can or in the gym."

"Would you feel better if we dressed him as a cop?"

I went into the office and stripped. There were pictures of generals on the walls, and a lot of plaques and a couple of softball trophies and a picture of Richard Nixon. I laid my trousers across a desk that was cluttered with baby pictures and brass elephants and a cigarette lighter disguised as a .45-caliber automatic. When I went out again, there were a couple of other men in suits standing with Harding. Soldier Bartlett was still on his chair, like a man waiting for a bus.

"All right, Soldier, we're ready," Harding said. "You can get on first, Danny."

"It's Bobby," I said. "Bobby Fallon."

"Right," Harding said, flashing a chilly smile. "Bobby Fallon."

I got on the scale with a towel wrapped around me and watched one of the men in the suits adjust the weights. Soldier tried to look interested. The fat photographer almost blinded both of us with the Speed Graphic.

Harding said, "Fallon. One seventy-seven and a half."

I stepped off the scale and Soldier got on. He had pads of scar tissue over both eyes, a nose without bone, dead eyes. He looked scary and tough.

"Bartlett. One eighty . . . three . . . and a quarter!"

"Hey, Bobby!" the photographer yelled. "Shake hands with Soldier. You know . . ."

I reached up and shook the limp hand of a pro. Soldier looked at me through the dead eyes, lazily chewing some gum.

"Good luck, kid," he said in a Southern drawl.

They finished the photographs and Soldier walked lazily to the office to get dressed. Then Gus grabbed Harding, his eyes blazing.

"When did you switch the goddam opponent?" Gus said. "We were boxing Charlie Holmes."

"I'm sorry, Mr. Caputo," Harding said nervously. "Charlie Holmes got sick. They sent me Soldier Bartlett."

"He's a main event fighter!" Gus said. "This is a four-round preliminary."

"Oh, it's much more than that," Harding said, with a phony jolly laugh and a wary eye on me. "Joe, give me the paper."

The lead story in the local paper was about me. NEW YORK'S "RIOT KID" TURNS PRO IN AREA BOUT. The main event, between two Pittsburgh lightweights, made the fifth paragraph. Gus tapped the papers, said, "Shit," and then to me, "Get dressed." We went into the office as Soldier walked out, dressed in a Johnny Cash cowboy suit, all spangles and piping. He nodded and kept going.

"Dude looks like he could fight," Kirk said.

"If he could fight, he wouldn't look like that," Freddie said. He gazed around the room, his brow creased with thought, and left.

"How you feelin'?" Kirk said.

"I'm okay. I'd just like to get it over with, is all."

"This is where it starts, Bobby," Kirk said.

"Naw. The start was in the Shamrock. That was where it started."

When we went out again, the carpenters had finished the platform but were still puzzling out the stanchions and the limp ropes. Gus said we would go somewhere to eat and find a place to rest before the fight. We had four hours to kill. Freddie was over on the side, talking very fast to Harding and pointing around the room with his cold cigar. Then he came over to Gus.

"Forget the fight."

"What?" Gus said.

"These hooples don't even have dressing rooms. It's worse than the amachiz."

"No dressing rooms?"

"He says all the fighters can dress in the office, but he ain't sure of that. I tell you, it's worse than the amachiz."

"Hey, you!" Gus yelled at Harding. The thin man walked over. "What the hell is this, no dressing rooms?"

"I'm sorry, Mr. Caputo. We just don't have dressing rooms. You know, we don't have pro boxing on a regular basis here. Just a smoker now and then. There's a men's room down at the end . . . I guess you could use that."

Gus looked crazy. *"The men's room? THE MEN'S ROOM?"*

"Well, it's clean . . ."

"You want my fighter to wait around where any drunk in the joint can come and piss?"

Harding went pale. "I'm sorry, I . . ."

"Forget sorry," Gus said. "We're leaving."

He turned and started to lead me out, but I stopped him.

"To hell with the dressing rooms, Gus. I want to fight."

My tone of voice must have surprised him. "I can't let any fighter of mine dress in a *shithouse,*" he said. "I'm sorry."

"Then I'll dress in the car."

And that's what I did. I sat in the front and stripped off my clothes and pulled on my socks, cup and trunks. We were parked near the side door of the Legion Hall and I could see a large crudely painted sign saying SMOKER TONIGHT PROFESSIONAL BOXING FORTY ROUNDS. Gus put an overcoat around my shoulders while I laced on the boxing shoes.

"Well," Freddie sighed, "when you're out of town, you're out of town."

Soldier is smirking when the referee calls us to the center of the ring.

"Find a soft place to fall, boy," he says. "This is only gonna take a few minutes."

Gus tells me to play it cool and easy. At the bell, I move out behind a jab and Soldier comes out leaning forward, his left forearm wrapped around his jaw, and heaves two big right hands. I take them on my gloves. Cool and easy. Bing with the jab. Bing. Bing bing bing. And I'm punching with the jab, not flicking it. Soldier lunges again and I back up behind the jab, then stop: hook off the jab, smash the hook into the unprotected body, then double the hook as Soldier's hand comes away from his face. The second hook almost takes his head off.

He goes down and I walk to the corner.

"Give me my robe," I tell Kirk.

The referee is at four. The arena is roaring, but I don't show anything on my face. They're stomping on the wooden floors and pounding on the chairs, but I just stand there listening to them. The referee gestures to the corner, trying to get a doctor. Soldier is still on the canvas. The sound of the crowd is building and I let it roll over me. Cool and easy: what happened with North won't ever happen again.

"One minute and twenty-nine seconds of the first round . . . Winner by a KNOCKOUT . . . Irish . . . Bobby . . . Fallon!"

We leave the ring and people lunge forward, trying to touch me. I ignore them, moving around past Soldier's corner. He's on a stool now, bleary and hurt. I just keep walking to the outside hall. Kirk drapes the overcoat on top of the robe.

"I'll be there in five minutes," Gus says. "I'm gonna get paid." He squeezes my gloved hand. "Good work."

"Yeah, I was really terrific," I say. "Spectacular. Tremendous."

"It's just that you kept your chin up too high when you threw that second hook."

We both smile, and he goes off and I go out to the car with Kirk and Freddie. Kirk starts the engine and turns on the heater while I strip off the trunks and the cup and change to trousers.

"Cream always comes to the top," Kirk says.

Gus comes out, looking angry in the blue fluorescent light from the doorway. He gets in the back seat next to Freddie.

"Let's go home," he says.

Kirk heads out to the turnpike.

"How much did we make?" I say.

"We cleared thirty-six dollars and forty-four cents," Gus says. "After taxes."

I laugh. "I'm rich. I can retire."

"Don't worry," Freddie says. "They'll get bigger."

"Much bigger," Kirk says.

We're out on the turnpike now, the countryside whizzing by.

"Forget the money," Gus says. "The money will come."

He doesn't even turn his head. It's as if he isn't talking to anyone in the car.

"The money is important," he says. "But you don't do it for the money."

"What *do* you do it for?" I say.

"The beauty," he says softly. "The beauty."

BOOK
FOUR

26

So BEGAN THE TIME that I'll always think of as my life on the road. One Wednesday morning, we piled into a car to go to a fight in Ohio and I didn't see New York or Kate Fallon again for seventeen months. We moved from Newark to Steubenville to Lorain to Pottstown, and then out into the West, living in motels, boxing local fighters, or fighters who'd just been imported, in Rotary clubs and hockey rinks and high school gyms. Poles came out of the mines to see me fight; Dutchmen learned to shout my name. And everywhere there were the Irish.

I knocked people out with straight right hands and left hooks to the chin and combinations. Gus booked three southpaws, to give me experience, and I knocked out all of them. I fought rough dirty fighters and sneaky careful fighters, and bangers and cuties, and old pros and raw hard guys. And I fought a lot of talkers: fighters who bad-mouthed, cursed, teased, taunted. In July and August, I fought nine fighters in eight weeks and knocked out all of them.

After my first eight fights, I was chosen Prospect of the Month by *Ring* magazine; after twelve, *Boxing Illustrated* made me the subject of a feature article. Gus booked me into six-round fights and then eight-round fights, and by the end of the eleventh month I was boxing main events and my name was in the fight results at the bottom of the sports pages in all the newspapers.

The reporters wrote about how there was no expression on my face in the ring and how you could never tell whether I'd been hurt. One of them wrote that I boxed like "a man imprisoned in solitude, unaware of the crowd, unaware of anything except the presence of an enemy." And that was what brought the crowds to their feet. I would come out clean and plain, with no tricks, no mugging, no wasted motion, and I would move and pause, move and study, move and wait, then move and explode. Every punch was a punch, nothing just for show. I punched to hurt. And I hurt to kill.

After the tenth fight, Gus started bringing a movie camera to the arena and the next day we'd look at the films, analyzing every move, every lost opportunity, the points where my opponent managed to hit me or avoid my punches. Then I would work on the corrections. I fought two men twice. One was a clutcher named Luther Mott, who went the full six rounds the first time and got knocked out in two the second. The other was a scrambling Puerto Rican named Davey Vieques.

Vieques was a clown, and the first time we boxed he performed his entire act. He went down in the first round from a soft punch, then twisted around and stood straight up in the air on his head; he was still that way when the referee reached eight. In the third round, he started singing opera. In the fourth, he did an about-face and started jogging away, throwing kisses to the audience. He came out for the sixth round with his trunks down to his knees. The crowd loved him. And so did I. I was so busy watching him that I didn't do much fighting, and some people thought I was lucky to even win a decision. Gus was furious: "He made you into an audience. Next time, fight him. Don't watch him."

Next time, I knocked him out in one round. He came in the dressing room afterwards, his right eye bruised and his lower lip split, but with a big grin on his face.

"Hey, man, you was in some kind of fuckin' hurry tonight."

"Hi, Davey," I said, buttoning my shirt.

"You gotta piece of ass waiting someplace or what?"

"Naw, I was afraid I'd lose the fight on a hernia. Laughing at your bullshit."

"Hey, man, life's a laugh, man."

"For you it is."

He shifted nervously and handed me a program. "Hey, sign this, Bobby."

"You mean autograph it?"

"Yeah. When you get famous, you might not remember."

I signed the program. Later, we took him out to dinner in some roadside joint and he kept us laughing until the place closed.

And while all this was happening, while I was fighting and learning on the road, the calls kept coming in from the big promoters. Madison Square Garden wanted me. The Forum in Inglewood wanted me. Sam Silverman wanted me for the Boston Garden. But Gus resisted, taking fights in small towns for small money, teaching me what New York and Los Angeles and Boston could never have taught me.

It wasn't easy for him to hold me back; my reputation was building faster than he could control it. All but three of my first twenty-six opponents were either black or Spanish, not because it was planned that way but because most fighters were either black or Spanish. White kids didn't have to bleed for a living anymore, and a lot of them were going to college or working in offices or taking big money in construction jobs. But I was a fighter. And I was Irish. And I was knocking out all the colored fighters. I was becoming what Kirk said I could become, all those months ago in prison. I was becoming a white hope.

But somehow, as I added muscle to my body, I didn't add many pounds. At 182, I was too heavy for the light-heavyweights and too light for the heavyweights. There was no money in the 175-pound division anyway, so Gus matched me with as many heavyweights as he could find. And from the waist up I was a heavyweight: I know I punched like one. But I had the thin waist and skinny legs of a middleweight.

When we had the money, Gus would feed me milk shakes, bananas, sixteen-ounce steaks, but I worked so hard in the gym that the fat burned off and I stayed right at 182. I knew 182 was the weight Floyd Patterson carried when he beat Archie Moore for the heavyweight championship, but it was still light. Not to go against Ali, who boxed like a bantamweight for all of his 220 pounds, but small for some of the big heavyweights. The ones who were coming up. The ones who would be in contention after Ali was gone.

Fighters like Walker Lewis.

The month that *Ring* magazine picked me as a Prospect of the Month, Walker Lewis became the number ten heavyweight in the world by knocking out Tommy Pynchon, of Albany, Georgia, in two rounds. I didn't pay too much attention at the time. Walker Lewis was just another name. But Gus looked at the detailed story in the back of the magazine and read how all of Pynchon's front feet had been knocked out of his mouth by a straight right hand. And he knew

Pynchon was a good fighter, a former St. Louis Golden Gloves champion. Gus started calling around and found out that Lewis was twenty-seven, had been boxing six years, had only eighteen fights behind him and lost two of them on decisions. He knocked out everybody else. Nobody wanted to fight him and Ali had turned him down as a sparring partner. He was what the trade called an animal. A murderous black puncher. A man who could neither read nor write, who had spent some time breaking heads for the teamsters in St. Louis, had worked as a collector for certain people in Vegas and, according to rumor, had broken a police detective's leg in Detroit when the cop tried to question him about his muscling for the shylocks. He also had a scar across his belly from a stabbing in Houston when he was sixteen.

The *Ring Record Book* showed that he'd fought only once the year before but suddenly he was getting fights. He'd fought twice in one month before knocking out Pynchon and already he was into the ratings. Gus said that meant Lewis was now connected. He'd found a goombah. An uncle. A protector. Someone who could move him and get him fights by making certain other things available, such as easy union contracts in arenas, a cut to the opponent's manager, a piece of a bottling plant or a reduced rate on tablecloths in a certain night club whose owner sometimes ran boxing shows in a certain town.

By the time I had my eighteenth fight, Lewis had moved up to number six in the ratings. And the sportswriters were beginning to notice. *Ring* magazine put him on the cover, with a caption saying LEWIS THE NEXT CHAMP? And *Boxing Illustrated* ran a long story on him, with pictures of him training and one of Tommy Pynchon laid out on his back with his teeth gone and the doctors working over him. Then Dave Anderson did a column in the New York *Times* that mentioned Walker Lewis and me together. Eddie Jorgenson, the matchmaker at the Garden, said Lewis and me were

the best of the division and a match between us would
be a natural, especially if I put on some weight. He
complained that Gus was keeping me out of New
York and offered to match me with Lewis anytime Gus
wanted to take the fight. For the first time, I began to
care about what was written in newspapers.

The Anderson story appeared in the local paper
in Albuquerque, where I was training to fight someone
named Herbie Pritchett, and I asked Gus about it.

"It's too soon," he said. "You're not ready yet."

"I'm ready for anybody."

"I don't mean you're not ready for Lewis," he
said. "I mean you're not ready for New York. For the
fans and the publicity and the rest of it."

"For Chrissakes, Gus, when *will* I be ready? We
been on the road over a year now."

"Soon," he said. "Soon."

Three days later, I knocked out Pritchett in three
rounds. It got a single line under "Fight Results" in a
New York paper, but the big boxing story that day was
about Walker Lewis making his Madison Square Garden debut in an all-heavyweight card. He knocked out
Billy Armstrong in forty-seven seconds of the first
round. Everybody predicted he'd be the next heavyweight champion of the world. And I didn't like it.

The last stop on the road was Providence, where
I knocked out a fast Cuban from Miami in seven
rounds. That made seventeen months on the road.
Thirty-three knockouts, three decisions and no draws.
When the fight was over, and the Cuban's white boxing
shoes were splattered with blood, and the Rhode Island
Irish were chanting my name as we went back to the
dressing room, I turned to Gus.

"It's New York next or I'm packing it in," I said.
He just looked at me.

"I'm serious, Gus," I said.

"I guess maybe you are," he said finally.

That night, he called Eddie Jorgenson at his home

in New York and told him he wanted to bring me home. Then he came to my room and told me not to go to bed because we were all going to New York: in two weeks, in Madison Square Garden, I was fighting Pineapple Anderson. I didn't learn until a long time later that he had turned down a fight with Walker Lewis.

27

YOU CALLED FROM A GAS STATION, and from a place in
Connecticut, and from the Howard Johnson's on the
Major Deegan when the car stopped for breakfast. She
was never home. And when you came down the FDR
Drive and saw the lights of New York, and Gus told
you to stay in a hotel that night, you said no, you
weren't staying in a hotel, you were going to Brooklyn.

Kirk stopped in front of the gym to leave off Freddie and Gus, then offered to give you a lift. But you
got in a cab and went over to the neighborhood. You
got out on the corner of Prospect Avenue, paid the
driver, rushed up the stairs and thumped on the door.
You heard the sounds of someone getting up and moving through rooms then diddling a lock, and your heart
was pounding, and the door finally opened and you
saw Charlie. His hair was matted, his face pasty and
older. He was hocking up phelgm and swallowing it,

and smiling the way fans do when they see you in the flesh.

And then he told you: Katey Fallon was gone. Had been gone for months. Headed south, to Florida or someplace, off on a trip, gone.

And would you like some coffee, Bobby?

No, Charlie. Thank you, Charlie. Did she leave a number?

No, she didn't leave no number. You know how she is, just ups and leaves, and when she went she just called me at the bar and gave me the house.

And you went away from that place, those streets, those people, knowing that something had changed again, just now or last month, whenever she went away, and you would never stare out the back window over the rooftops or watch the ships in the harbor or go with her to the darkened rooms at the other end of the flat. You went back to the gym and the reservoir, and you answered questions from reporters and saw the posters going up all over the city. And then you were riding to the Garden, feeling murder building in you, and the little boy moving right out of you to stand in a corner and watch and maybe cry. You lay there on the table in the dressing room. You had your hands taped. The commissioners came in, smiling and safe. An old face came in and smiled at you with a screw's sad eyes: Thompson, in a badly fitting brown suit, came down from upstate to see you fight. I heard you were in the Garden, he said, so me and some of the boys decided to come down. And a few minutes later you went out to fight. You threw a tentative jab, then another, then the right hand, without willing it, straight and hard, and Pineapple was on his back, his eyes all rolled up, and a referee was counting over him. Then they were grabbing you, the flash bulbs popping, the crowd roaring, and it was over: the easiest fight you ever had, less than forty seconds of the first round. And then you heard booing, and you looked around and the Irish guys were up on their seats, shaking their fists, and you saw a large black man, wearing dark glasses and a gold pimp's hat, moving up the aisle, a mink coat over his shoulders, coming closer, the booing getting louder, and then he was climbing up the steps, and it was Walker Lewis.

I'm gonna get you, muthafucka, he said. I'm gonnta get yore white ass, boy.

Shaking his fist, while the newsmen scribbled notes and pointed tape recorders, and the flash bulbs popped some more, and Pineapple came over to congratulate you. Saying it over and over, his chin stubbly with little iron hairs, his shoulders as wide as a door, his eyes shrouded behind the shades: as big and powerful and final as death.

You yelled back at him, told him how you'd kick his ass if you ever got the chance, how you'd cut him up and send him back to the cotton fields, and then you made a move at him, your gloves off but your hands still taped, knowing that Kirk and Freddie and Gus would hold you back.

And all the while you were afraid, babe. You were afraid.

And then you were in the dressing rooms, answering questions, with Kirk giving his own interviews on the side. They asked whether you wanted to fight Walker Lewis and you said, Hell yes, I'd like to fight Walker Lewis, go out there and get him and we'll do it now, 'cause I barely got warmed up. And Nick Siegel of the *Post* pushed his way through and said that Front Row Productions, the closed-circuit people, had just offered to put you on a double-header with Lewis, you fighting someone and Lewis fighting someone, with the winners to claim the vacant heavyweight title. You asked when and where, and Siegel said three weeks from now in Vegas, and you said, When do we leave? Then Gus came in and said tonight's fight was the big-

gest sellout in the Garden's history, almost 21,000, and
the reporters asked him about Walker Lewis and you
sensed the hesitation. We'll fight Walker Lewis when
the price is right, he said. Siegel asked about the offer
from Front Row and Gus said he hadn't heard any offer. Then Jorgenson came in with some television
people and they made the offer right there: the Double
Bill of the Century, Walker Lewis against Joe Norman
and Bobby Fallon against Gene Barstow, the winners
to fight each other for the title. Gus said, I don't know
about that offer, I'd have to look into it more, so let's go
over tonight's fight and we'll talk about Vegas tomorrow after we sleep on it.

And in front of all of them you said: Take it, Gus.
And he had no choice.

You got up and went to the shower, and when you
came out Gus was staring. It seemed like he wanted
to say something, to set something straight, but he
just stared. And then Kirk came over and said there
was someone to see you. Out in the corridor. You
opened the door and looked to your left, and way at
the end was Kate Fallon in a white plastic coat, her
face tanned, her teeth bright against her skin, her hair
done.

"Bobby!" she shouts, and comes at a run, slams into
me, hugs me, kisses me on the cheeks. "You were terrific!" she says. "You made me so damned proud! I
thought I'd bust a gut . . ."

She grabs my hands, her own hands warm and
damp, and I want to bury myself in her.

"Come on," she says, "We're buying you dinner!"

"Who's we?"

"Me and Mack. Hey, Mack!"

A guy comes down the corridor, looking a little
embarrassed as the special cops turn their heads. He's
wearing a gray suit and has steel-gray hair, broad
shoulders and a heavy tan. All gray and tan. There

are wrinkles under the tan but not as many as there should be.

"Mack? My son, Bobby. Bobby, this is Mack Ridgeway."

"Hello, Bobby," he says, squeezing my hand. "You sure were fantastic out there tonight."

"Thanks," I say, checking out the too-perfect teeth and the way he smiles like a man turning down a loan. His hand is large and soft-skinned but strong underneath.

"You sure were," Kate says.

Gus, Freddie and Kirk come out, and I introduce them all to Ma and then to Mack. Mack smiles, but there isn't much happening in his eyes. Freddie and Kirk wave and keep going, but Kate stops Gus.

"So you're the famous Gus Caputo," she says. "I heard a lot about you."

"Nice to meet you, Mrs. Fallon."

"Kate. Call me Kate, Gus." She nods at me. "Is he behaving himself? You know, he gets a little out of hand now and then, and you have to give him a good whack."

"He's a good man," Gus says, smiling.

"Care to eat with us?" Mack says.

"No, we've got some things to do. Thanks." He faces me. "I'll see you at the gym tomorrow, Bobby."

We say good night and Gus hurries down the corridor toward the Eighth Avenue end, trying to catch up with Freddie and Kirk.

"It's not much of a fight out there," Mack says.

In the arena, they're booing the last of the emergency bouts. "A couple of bums."

"Did you ever fight, Mack?"

"Oh, in college. And in the service."

"But not as a pro, right?"

"Well, no . . ."

"Then you really shouldn't call two fighters bums, should you?"

Kate looks uneasy. "Let's go eat," she says, an edge in her voice.

Mack says: "They can't fight very well. That's all I meant."

"You don't really know that," I say. "You might have two good fighters, but because of styles they don't look good against each other. Anybody who gets in a ring has guts. They aren't bums."

Kate takes my arm. "How's Gallagher's? I used to go there years ago."

"Gallagher's is fine."

We walk down the corridor together, her hand holding my arm. I can hear Mack's heavy step a few feet behind us.

Gallagher's was crowded, and as we talked and ate, and Mack drank vodka, people came over to the table to shake hands or have me autograph their programs or tell me how great I looked at the Garden. And in between all this, in broken sentences, Kate explained where she'd been. It didn't take long: she'd been with Mack. She was working as an office temporary and she met him one morning when he was in town on business and one thing led to another. He was in real estate, somewhere in Florida, and they'd come up to see the fight after reading in the paper that I was on the card.

"You should fight in Florida," Mack said. "Miami's a great fight town. They'd love you down there."

"I'll mention it to Gus. Where is it you live?"

"I have a place in Sarasota," he said. "Over on the Gulf. And we, well . . . there's another place in Lauderdale where Kate here stays and . . . Have you ever been to Florida, Bobby?"

"No."

Kate said: "It's beautiful, Bobby. You'd love it."

"Are you married, Mack!"

"Bobby!"

"I'm just asking."

"I'm separated," Mack said.

"I see. But not divorced?"

One of the waiters came up and handed me a *Daily News*. I'd never seen him before, but he put a hand on my shoulder as if we'd gone to school together. "Hey, look at this, Bobby," he said. He showed me a picture that filled the whole back page, with Pineapple's leg bent under him and me moving in the background with my hair sticking up like spikes. The caption said: "Going, going . . ." And the headline said: FALLON IN ONE!

Mack excused himself and got up. Kate took a drag on the cigarette and watched him cross the restaurant to the men's room.

"You didn't have to ask about the married part," she said.

"Why not?"

"He's a nice guy. Things are hard enough for him without other people being snotty."

"Did he buy you the coat?"

She crushed the cigarette in the ashtray, and looked up, her eyes blazing. "What if he did?"

"I guess he bought you the tan, too."

"Yeah. So what? Listen, Bobby," her voice sounded bitter. "I have the right to live with whoever I want. I didn't go on the road. You did."

It was as if she'd punched me, and I started to say something, but Mack was coming across the room. She lit another cigarette, her face rigid.

"I'm sorry," I said. "It's none of my business."

"What are you gonna do?" she whispered.

Mack was there, standing above us, moving his chair in an awkward way.

"First, I'm going home—"

"I don't mean tonight," she said.

Mack said: "Am I interrupting something?"

"No. Sit down, Mack."

"And then I'm going out to Vegas. There's a big doubleheader in three weeks. Me and Walker Lewis against two other guys."

"Las Vegas?" she said.

"Yeah. You ever been there?"

Mack sat down. "We're leaving for Florida in the morning," he said. He waved for the check.

"I don't think so, Bobby," she said. "I don't think I can go to Las Vegas."

"The two winners will fight for the title," I said.

"You and that guy tonight, right?" she said. "The one with the hat."

"Walker Lewis."

"He looks like a good fighter," Mack said.

"He didn't fight tonight, Mack," I said.

"I mean the way he dresses up."

"That's his act. Everybody has to have one now. He's got a pimp act."

"He looks bigger than you, Bobby," Kate said.

"They usually are," I said.

"What's your act?" Mack said.

"I knock people out. That's my act."

The waiter came with the check and Mack paid with a credit card.

"Well, I gotta go," I said.

I stood up and shook Mack's hand and leaned over to kiss Kate on the cheek.

"Where you staying, Ma?"

"The Americana."

"I'll try to call you."

I walked quickly to the street. Two hookers were standing near the penny arcade on the corner of Broadway and they smiled at me as I went by. Then I stopped and turned around. Someone was calling my name. It was Kate, alone and running. Leaving Mack outside the restaurant, waiting for a taxi, looking clumsy and sad.

"Bobby! Bobby, wait!"

She ran to me, up the street and past the hookers, and caught me at the corner.

"Okay," she said, her voice young and bubbling and happy. "Let's go!"

"Let's go where, Ma?"

"Las Vegas."

"When? Now?"

"Now," she said. "Let's drive. Right clear across the country. Just you and me."

"Ma, I'd have to rent a car, and call Gus, and get some money and . . . How long would it take? Must be like three days, right?"

"I don't *care*," she said. "Just let's *do* it!"

The sounds of Broadway banged around us. I watched Mack get into his taxi and pass us at the corner, slouched deep in the back.

"All right," I said. "Let's go to Vegas."

28

AND SO YOU DROVE, the two of you together, sealed into the world of cars and roads and highways: across rivers, through tunnels, over mountains, out onto plains; into strange towns late at night and out again in the morning; songs on the radio and news of disasters and Kate switching the dial away from the pain; holding your hand; eating sandwiches on the way; free of the gym, telephones, reporters and Walker Lewis. You made up names late at night: Mr. and Mrs. Charles Mermelberger. Freddie and Janice Isherwood. Igor and Florabel Spark. Names for the people at desks.

And all of it blurred into twilights and rainstorms and hammering sun; forests, farmlands, hills scarred by tractors; miles of neat houses and men shining their cars; trains rushing along sidings, whistles blowing, signals blinking at crossings, then more road ahead. She took the gold studs out of her ears and you touched her hair. In the evenings, she came to you wet from the bath. In the mornings, she was beside you, the long body huddled against you. You made love and drove on: the ashtray overflowing as she smoked packs of Marlboros, and one pack of Larks when the machine at a gas station was out of her brand; a roadside tavern; songs; a dance.

Until up ahead, under the empty night sky, you saw the low burning glow that said the trip was over. The glow at the end of the country. Las Vegas.

The promoters had a suite ready at Caesars Palace. But it was only for me: the basket of fruit was for me, the phone messages were for me. They didn't expect her. So I stood at the window, looking down at the fountains and the garish row of signs that made up The Strip, while we waited for them to find an extra room in the sold-out hotel. Ma smoked and looked nervous.

"Don't worry, they'll get one," I said. "You can stay there, and come here at night."

"I'm not worried," she said.

"If you stayed here, Gus would go bananas."

"We mustn't have Gus go bananas."

"You know what I mean. The newspaper guys'll be all over the place. Do you want to go downstairs and gamble?"

"Will Gus let you go downstairs?"

"I don't have to ask Gus."

"Ask anyway. He might be afraid of how it looks."

I rang Gus in his room. Freddie answered.

"Gus ain't here, Bobby."

"Where is he?"

"He went down to get Kirk out of the casino."

"What's the matter?"

"What the hell is usually the problem in a casino? He's down twenty-two thousand."

"Jesus Christ."

"Gus wants to have them put a limit on him. Put a top on his credit. No more than ten grand or something, so he'll stop showing off. He's got some Spanish broad with him."

"Is her name Yolanda Chacon?"

Freddie sounded surprised. "Yeah, that's her. She's singing here downtown. Down in one of the bust-out joints. You know her?"

"No. But Kirk does."

"You bet your ass he does."

I told Freddie to have Gus call me, then turned to look at Ma. She seemed drained and tired. It had been some trip.

"The hell with the extra room," I said. "Stay here."

"No. It won't look right. Gus will—"

"The hell with Gus."

I picked up the phone again. "Front desk, please."

"No, Bobby," she said. "I know what—"

A man came on and I told him I wouldn't be needing another room for Mrs. Fallon that night. She would be staying in the suite, I said, and I would double up with one of the other guys. He thanked me and said that would save them a lot of trouble because they were really full. I told him to cut off all the phone calls until I let him know otherwise.

In the morning, when I got back from running, she was in the shower. She stayed there a long time and came out fully made up.

"It's really sad out there, at the old race track," I said. "All the paint is peeling."

"It must be hard to run a race track in a town with a million crap tables."

"I guess so. But it's a great place to run. You look beautiful."

"I thought I'd go downstairs until they get me a separate room." She smiled in a nervous way. "You know, in case Gus or the other guys come up here."

"Come on, I'll go with you."

"Don't bother, Bobby. Get your rest. You've been running all morning while I've been sleeping."

"Yeah, but I still have to eat breakfast." She was sitting on the edge of the couch and I touched her face. "We can order from room service."

"Room service is always terrible. I don't care how great the hotel is. It's always better in the restaurant."

"I want to eat up here."

"I don't," she said.

I laughed. "Okay, I'll put on a shirt."

She lit a cigarette, and I went to the bedroom and took a shirt from the drawer. Then I weighed myself on the bathroom scale.

"I'm still only one eighty-two," I said when we were ready to go. "Gus wants me to gain ten pounds, so let's get everything. French toast, five eggs, and ham and bacon and English muffins and milk and toast."

"Pancakes. You loved pancakes when you were a kid."

"A ton of pancakes."

The door locked softly behind us. We walked to the elevator, holding hands. One of the maids looked up and smiled.

"With syrup," I said. "Maple syrup and a lot of butter."

We stepped off the elevator and she took her hand out of mine. There was a large boat to the right, with a trio playing on the deck, and to the left over a little bridge was a Japanese restaurant. Dead ahead was Vegas: crap tables, slots, keno games, wheels and blackjack tables.

"Wait," she said, opening her purse.

She started throwing dimes into the first slot machine, and quarters into the next, and finally hit with the nickel machine, the coins falling dully into the slot at the bottom. She scooped them up and I grinned at her.

"You gotta have at least two bucks there," I said.
"And I only spent eleven to make it."

A small man with a gnarled face came over.
"Hey, you're that Fallon kid, right? Pleased ta meet
ya. I hear you're a helluva fighta."

"Pleased to meet you, too," I said.

"Welcome to Vegas."

"You live here?"

"Naw, I'm from New York, but welcome anyway."

Kate laughed out loud, and I took her elbow and
moved her around the crap tables, nodding at people
who recognized me, watching the action, loving the
softness of her, and then we turned into a long arcade
and went through the entryway of the coffee shop. She
took her hand from my arm, and looked into the
crowded room, and suddenly made a little hurt sound in
her throat, a sound like oh, but more than that, and
her eyes closed and her face went white and she
fell.

And then waitresses were rushing over, and someone handed me a glass of water, and I had one hand
under her neck, and someone else began to pat her
cheeks, and I tried to get the water into her mouth, and
then stared into the room, at the place where she'd been
looking, and saw a man with handsome gray hair,
dressed in a dark blue suit and an expensive white
shirt. He was alone in a booth, a phone beside him,
sipping a cup of coffee and staring back at me.

29

You saw him, and you knew him, babe, but then the doctor was there and he asked if you knew her, and you said, yes, she was your mother, and he said, Well, we better get her upstairs. You helped lift her, and when you looked back in the room, the booth was empty.

You sat with her, beside the bed, while they took her pulse and gave her smelling salts and wrote out prescriptions. Finally she came around. Blinking at the doctor, at the walls and ceiling and then at you. And you told the doctor you'd take care of her now and asked how much was the bill, and he said, Don't worry about it, it's taken care of.

And when the door had closed, you felt your arms loose and weak and small, the way you'd been that time long ago, standing in the cold in a doorway across the street from Toots Shor's, and you knew that everything that had happened in the past week, all the things that had made you happy, were about to go. She would get up and pack and go out, down to the elevator, to the lobby. And she would find him.

She reached over and touched you, and you pulled away. You waited a long time and then you asked if she knew he'd be here. She said she wasn't sure, she didn't know, she was never sure. About him, she said, I was never sure. And me? you said. About you I was sure, she said. You were my own flesh and blood.

You walked out of the suite, leaving her there, taking the elevator and crossing the lobby, hitting the street and the white weight of the sun. You began to run and then you were aware of a car alongside and someone saying your name. But you didn't look: you kept running, and threw a combination at the air, and bobbed and weaved and cut to the left. Still: the car was there and your name was said. And finally you turned and saw Kirk in the car, with Yolanda Chacon, and heard Jack Fallon call you from the dark interior.

Get in, Bobby.

Go fuck yourself.

The door opened, and he stepped out into the dusty light.

Don't be stupid, he said, get in.

And you looked at him, while Kirk eased the car down the road a ways, leaving the two of you alone. And you remembered the climb up the stairs at the Statue of Liberty, and his rough beard, and the way he carried you on his shoulders, and you looked at him again: the elegant suit, the ugly-handsome face, the body that was still lean and graceful, and you thought about hitting him.

You son of a bitch.

And he smiled, his eyebrows moving, his forehead wrinkling, and he looked the way he had always looked, only bigger and smoother.

If you're thinking of hitting me, he said, you better do it right the first time. Because I get the second shot.

If I hit you, you'll stay hit.

You can try it, if you want to, he said.

You put your hands in your pockets, and turned away from him, and looked out across the flat empty town. But you didn't move. You couldn't. And he came closer, and then he put his arm around you.

I'm sorry, he said, holding you tight.

Sorry isn't good enough, you said.

You tried to find the words that had been in you all those years, the angry things you had hoped to say, if ever you saw him. You wanted to hammer him with accusations. You wanted him to answer the questions, to tell you why he had left, and where he had gone. But the words would not come. All you could say was son of a bitch. Murmuring the words, You son of a bitch. Thinking: *Now* you come back. *Now,* when I thought I had moved you out of the way for good.

And he said: Call me a son of a bitch. Go ahead. Call me anything. I've called myself worse from time to time.

You son of a fucking bitch.

And then he held you tighter, and moved you toward the car. The door opened and you got in together, and you were leaning into him, and he held you tight with the long hard arm, and you cried: for Jack and Kate Fallon, for all those journeys, those strange towns, for his sadness and hers, and for yourself, for what you wanted and thought you had, and now could never have.

Kirk drove the limousine through the hot dusty afternoon, turning left and right, heading into open country. After a while, he pulled up to a house made of two adjoining A-frames connected by a passage. There were three other cars in the driveway. Jack Fallon led us through the side door and into the kitchen and out past the sunken living room, with its stone fireplace and giant couches, and on out to the pool. Muzak washed over us, and I started to feel sick but not from the sound. It was the con. Something was going on here and I didn't know what. Eddie Jorgenson was sitting at a table under an umbrella, drinking a Tom Collins, a cigar in his mouth, and there were two other men with him. They were all in swim trunks, and they had Noxzema all over their noses.

"Hey, here he is!" Jorgenson said, getting up to shake my hand. "Whaddya say, kid? Whendya get in?" He made room for me at the table.

"Last night."

"Lass night? No kiddin'. I hear ya drove all the way, huh?"

"That's right."

"Hell, always wannid to do that myself. See America. I been to England, and to Paris France and Rome Italy, but I never really seen the U.S. of A. It's like a place you fly over all the time, goin' to the Coast." He turned to one of the other men. "Arthur, didden you always wanna drive cross-country?"

"Not really," the man said. "Hi, Bobby, I'm Arthur Youngstein."

"Arthur is with the fight," Jorgenson said. "And this is Lou Stevens, from the closed-circuit. I guess you heard the news?"

Jack Fallon interrupted, sliding dark glasses over his eyes. "I have some extra suits if you want to take a dip."

I said: "What news?"

"About Joe Norman."

"What news?"

"He broke a hand," Youngstein said. "The fight's off with Lewis."

Jorgenson eased in, rubbing a knuckle against his chin. "Unless, of course, something even better happens."

Jack Fallon sat down and waved to a Mexican in a white waiter's jacket. The Mexican nodded and went to the bar, just inside the pool doors.

"You mean you want me to fight Lewis?" I said.

"It could be the money fight of the century," Stevens said. "Look, we have about fifteen million tied up in the double-header already, but we already know that nobody's gonna fill the theaters to watch Norman or the other guy . . . whatsizname, the guy you're fighting."

"His name's Gene Barstow," I said. "He's a good fighter. The number four contender."

"Yeah, yeah, *Bar*stow. Well, anyway, we can move Barstow out of the way widdout too much grief, still keep the dates, print extra tickets and make you with Lewis."

"It'd do thirty million worldwide," Jorgenson said.

"And that's why we're here."

Kirk stepped out through the doors, in a paisley bathing suit, holding Yolanda's hand. They walked towards us. Her skin was dark from the sun and she had heavy thighs, but there was a breathy, dirty look to her that excited me. Kirk smiled.

"Where's Gus?" I said.

Jorgenson cleared his throat and said: "Well, that's one of the problems, Bobby. In fact, it's the *only* problem."

"He means Gus don't want the Lewis fight," Kirk said.

"Then what are *you* doing here, Kirk?" I said. "And where the fuck did you find *her?*"

Youngstein said to Kirk: "Take the bimbo someplace."

"She came with me, she stays with me. We're ole friends."

Yolanda's eyes smoldered and she twisted her mouth in an ugly way. Youngstein took Kirk by the elbow.

"Listen, Kirk, we're talkin' about thirty million bucks here. You undastan that number? Thirty million *large*. We don't want that fucked up over a piece of gash."

Yolanda smacked him. "Son of a bitch," she said. "Who the hell you think you talkin' to, Jewboy?"

"Easy there, sweetheart," Kirk said. "She ain't no piece of *gash,* Mr. Youngstein. She's one of the finest Latin singers in the *world* and she's an ole friend of Bobby. From *way* back. I mean from way, *way* back."

"Boy, is that bullshit," I said.

Youngstein sensed Kirk's weakness. "She's a lounge act, Kirk. Why don't you two go over there and jump off the board for a while."

Kirk and Yolanda drifted away. I didn't like what I was seeing in him but it must have been a long time coming.

"Goddam schwartze," Youngstein said.

"When did Norman get hurt?" I said.

"Who knows?" Jorgenson said. "Yestiddy, day before. We get a call from L.A. says the guy can't fight, he pulled a muscle, he broke a hand. I says to Plunkett, the manager, I says, Hey, you better get a doctor to write that in a letter or you'll never get a big-money fight again, pallie. He says he already had a letter. I think he just didn't want to fight Lewis. Lots of guys don't."

Youngstein came around the table and put his arm on my shoulder. I slid out from under him, starting toward the house and for the first time since he sat down, Jack Fallon spoke.

"You're not leaving, are you?"

I looked at him, wishing I could see his eyes behind the shades, and moved away from him into the house. He followed me. The rooms were chilly from air conditioning.

"The bathing suits are in the back bedroom," he said.

I looked around at the paintings of parrots and swans, the hotel-style furniture. It felt as if too many people had lived here, or too few.

"You live here?" I said.

"Sometimes," he said. "When I'm in Vegas. It's quieter than the hotels."

"You own it?"

"No, it belongs to a friend of mine. Sometimes he rents it out to the stars when they work here."

I stopped at the door to the back bedroom. "You were seeing her all those years, weren't you?"

"No."

"But you stayed in touch."

"I sent her some dough now and then," he said softly. "She knew how to find me. There were always calls she could make if she needed me."

"Why did you leave?"

"I wanted to."

"I should knock you on your ass, you know."

"That wouldn't be too smart."

"Yeah, why not?"

"Because you can make yourself a million bucks if you take the fight with Lewis. But if you hit me I'm gonna hit you back. And you could get hurt. What then? No fight. No million bucks. No future. Just a dumb fight in a house."

I went into the bedroom. The bathing suits were neatly laid out with towels under them.

"How do you get that million-dollar number?" I said.

"Listen to those assholes out there," he said. "They need you. They see the fuckin' dollars. And they already paid for the transmission lines. They already printed the advertising, made their deals with the foreign promoters. No matter what happens, there's gonna be a fight here. You might as well be in it."

"And what's *your* angle? How come all these people are sitting out there?"

" 'Cause I'm your father. They figure I can get you to make the fight."

"That shows how smart *they* are."

The phone rang while I was changing clothes and he picked it up. "Yeah? Well, what does he say? Tell him Bobby's here now. Yeah. Tell him that, and tell him to get his ass over here. We gotta get this thing straightened out *now*."

He slammed down the phone and I remembered the night he wrecked the apartment.

"Your guy Gus is a ball-breaker," he said.

"He's a great manager," I said. "If he doesn't want the fight, he must have reasons."

"He has reasons, all right. He doesn't think you can lick this jig."

"There ain't anyone in the division I can't lick."

"You ever see Lewis fight?"

"I don't have to. I seen him dress. Ain't any pimp in the world I can't beat."

I started out through the hall and again he was following me.

"Gus is coming out here," he said. "But I'm sure he won't take the fight."

"We'll see."

"What if he won't?"

I shrugged. "He's the manager. Not you. You're just my father."

Kirk and Yolanda were sitting on the diving board at the far end of the pool. I looked over at Jorgenson and the others, then walked along the edge of the pool and motioned to Kirk. He got off the board and met me halfway.

"What's this all about?" I said.

"Oh, just swimmin' an' drinkin' and fuckin'. The usual."

"I'm talking about this summit conference, Kirk.

I can see why Jorgenson and Youngstein are here. And that Lou Stevens. For them, it's business. But why are *you* here? And with *her?*"

His eyes made a funny move. "We gamble together."

"I hear you're down twenty-two grand at the tables."

"That's close."

"You mean it's more?"

He nodded.

"So they told you maybe you wouldn't have any trouble if you helped deliver me for the Lewis fight. Is that it?"

His eyes got suddenly bright and hot, and he hissed his words. "That's all it *ever* is, boy. Geetus, bread, the green. *Money!* Yeah, I'm down, but I been down almos' two years now, plus that fuckin' bit I did accounta you. Every place we went, I got the small stakes, babe. I'm the guy washes the tapes, cleans the robe, carries the water bottle, rubs your back, keeps you laughin', beats off the fuckin' fans, and what the fuck do I get outta this goddam thing? A piece of ass from a hooker every once in a while? A hundred bucks here, two hundred there? And why? 'Cause Gus wants to do it his way! He wants you fightin' in these fuckin' tank towns against these fuckin' stiffs for no fuckin' money and then when we get to the fuckin' Garden and you *really* score and it looks like we on our fuckin' way, then he starts gettin' chickenshit. He starts lookin' to duck. He don't want this fuckin' fight! He don't want this Walker Fuckin' Lewis. He wants you to come back on the road, in them little fuckin' gyms where you can beat up sheriffs and nuns and stiffs, and this Walker Lewis is gonna make all the fuckin' money left in America. *Yeah,* I wanna help make this fight. You bet your sweet *ass* I wanna make this fight, babe. I finally want all them things we talked about in jail. I want money and clothes and pussy. You make this fight and we got all that. We worked for it, Bobby. We busted our fuckin' balls for it . . ."

"Take it easy, man. Calm down."

"I don't even know *how* anymore."

I walked him away to the side and sat him down. The people at the far end of the pool were watching me, not talking, not even drinking. And Jack Fallon was more still and more silent than the others.

"Just go out and get in the car," I said. "Take Yolanda with you and go to the hotel and get laid. You don't have to hang around here."

"Yeah, I do. Your daddy tole me to hang here till you was finished."

"Did he tell you he'd take care of the problem at the casino?"

"He said he'd help."

"I see."

We heard a car pull into the driveway, and people getting out, and then a little guy in shades and a sport shirt was holding the door open for Gus and Freddie. The men at the table had all stood up and now they were going over to shake hands with Gus. I went up to Freddie, who was left out of the greetings.

"Hi, Freddie. Sorry I didn't see you at the hotel."

He nudged me. "What the hell."

"How'd they get you out here?"

"I'm not sure but I think they kidnapped us."

Then I shoved through the others and embraced Gus. He was stiff, uncomfortable, squinting at me like a cop looking for evidence of a crime.

"Hello, Bob."

"Gus."

"How was the trip?"

"Good."

Jorgenson pushed between us. "Wad about a drink, Gus? A TC or something?"

"I don't drink."

"A sandwich?" Lou Stevens said, his face gray and worried.

"No. I just want to know what the deal is, what the hurry was."

They told him. Jack Fallon was studying my face, but I didn't return his look.

"So that's *it*, Gus," Youngstein said. "Wuddya think?"

"I think we go home tomorrow."

There was a lot of talking at once, and hands waving, and drinks slamming against tables. Only Gus and Jack Fallon were quiet.

Finally, Jack Fallon said: "I think we should all calm down. I think we should make the offer clear to Mr. Caputo, *with all its implications,* and then we should let him sleep on it."

"Who the hell are you?" Gus said.

"I'm Bobby's father," he said. "I might as well cut through the chicken fat. I know you don't have a contract with my son. I also know that in many states even an unwritten contract, even an oral contract, isn't binding. In other words, I know that Bobby Fallon can talk for himself and make up his own mind. And since he's a minor . . ."

"You never mentioned your father was out here," Gus said to me.

"There was nothing to mention," I said. "I didn't know *where* he was. And besides, this bastard doesn't talk for me. You're the manager."

"That's what I thought I was when I got here."

"I just *said* you are."

"Just so these people know." He turned to Jack Fallon: "What do you mean, *with all its implications?* Explain me that."

Jack Fallon smiled. He lit a Lucky Strike and blew the smoke into the thin desert air.

"It's very simple," he said. "The Walker Lewis

people want you to know that if you don't make this fight right now, then Bobby Fallon will never get a shot at the title as long as Lewis holds it. And believe you me, if Bobby *doesn't* fight him, that title will belong to Walker Lewis."

"Oh, yeah? And just who are the Walker Lewis people?"

"We are," Jack Fallon said.

30

IT'S VERY DARK AND I'M ALL ALONE. She's been gone
all day, ever since I walked out on her. The bell captain had gotten her a cab, and now I'm in this round
bed, with the drapes pulled tight, my legs drawn up,
feeling small again. My skin is raw from the sun. I
wish I could lie here with just a sheet over me, but the
air conditioning is cold and I can't find the switch to
turn it off. We came across the country together, and
she saw him for a few seconds, and now her luggage is
gone, her smell is gone. She's gone away.

I doze off, and in the blackness I see the square of
canvas, the red ropes, and Walker Lewis across from
me. His body looks like a silky bag of rocks. And I
jerk awake, fumble for the light, turn it on. The room
is huge and very empty. I prowl around, touching
chairs and tables and the bar. I try to remember what
whiskey tastes like. Then I call room service and order
ham and eggs and a double English muffin. I settle

264

down on the couch in the living room. Ten minutes go by.

The food arrives. I eat too fast. I turn on the television. A movie, full of cowboys chasing each other past the same tree twice. I go into the shower and let it boil me for a while, the water hurting the raw skin. I dry myself and go back to bed and try to sleep. Her face drifts into my head.

The buzzer rings. I'm not expecting anyone. Maybe it's her. I open the door.

Yolanda Chacon is standing there. Her face is heavy with make-up, her hair curved around in front of one eye. She's wearing a tight white gown the way she did that first time I saw her.

"Can I come in?"

I step to the side and she walks across the deep-pile rug. I'm in my bathrobe. She kicks off her shoes and digs her feet into the pile, her bare toes splaying, like a cat testing new turf. Then she turns, smiles, runs her tongue over her lips and comes to me. She puts her hand inside my robe.

"I liked looking at you today, Bobby. At the pool."

"You looked good yourself."

"I don't remember you at the dance hall."

"I remember you."

"I'm sorry I don' remember you. Hmm. What's this?"

I laugh.

"I want to fuck you," she says.

The next day's newspapers were full of the story of what one writer called "The $15 Million Broken Hand." There were pictures of Joey Norman with his hand in a cast, and of his trainer looking sad-eyed, and there were quotes from Walker Lewis saying he would tie one hand behind his back and fight Norman anyway and still knock him out. Lewis was shown standing in front of Caesars Palace, holding up one big fist, and beside him were pictures of me, running alone that morning at the empty race track, dressed in a dark blue sweat suit and heavy bridgeman's shoes, my face all bunched up in concentration. There were no pictures of Jack Fallon sitting up in the stands, watching me run, and no reporters wrote about our talk, later, when the running was over.

"I want you to do this for me, Bobby. But if you think I'm gonna beg, forget it."

"Talk to Gus. I don't want to discuss it."

"Gus says there's nothing to talk about. He told me he's got a contract for a fight with Gene Barstow, not Walker Lewis. He says you'll fight Gene Barstow. Period."

"So I guess I'll fight Gene Barstow."

"No, you won't." He paused. "You see, Gene Barstow is going to get a bad back." His face went blank. He wasn't kidding.

"You miserable prick."

"That's no way to talk to your daddy."

"Not if my daddy's a prick."

I ran off, heading for the car where Kirk was waiting with the water jug. When I looked back, Jack Fallon was driving off. I told Kirk to follow him. We went for a couple of miles, hanging back a fair distance. And we watched him pull into a shopping center, park the car, walk across the lot and go into a pay phone. Kirk looked at me but I didn't say anything. We went back to Caesars Palace.

That afternoon, word came from Los Angeles that Gene Barstow had pulled a muscle in his lower back during training and that his fight with me was off. The late edition of the Las Vegas *Sun* carried the story. Near the end, Barstow said: "I'm sorry this happened, because I wanted to be the first fighter to teach this Fallon kid a lesson. He's been fighting stiffs and set-ups long enough. With me, he would've found out what a real fighter was."

And in a UPI story in another paper Eddie Jorgenson said that he was sorry, too, but he had dreamed up a perfect solution: "I think Walker Lewis and Bobby Fallon is the fight of the century. The hardest-punching white fighter against the hardest-punching black fighter. Sure, Fallon's a little light, but he punches like a guy 220 or more, and Lewis has never fought a guy with Fallon's speed. It'll be the bull against the matador." The story noted that I only weighed 182 and Lewis weighed 218 for his last fight, but the writer didn't expand on it.

On page one of the *Sun*, in an exclusive interview that was sure to be picked up nationally by the wire services, Walker Lewis said: "I want this Fallon boy so bad I can taste it. I'm going to chew him up and spit him out. I'm going to hit him so hard his feet are going to hurt. That is, if this boy gets in the ring with me. I don't think he'll do it. I don't think this boy has the heart."

Gus wouldn't discuss it. Not with the AP or the UPI. Not with the Front Row Productions people or Youngstein. And certainly not with me. When I went down the hall to his room, he just sat there and watched television.

Later that day, when I was taking my nap, Kirk came to see me. He didn't mention Yolanda and neither did I.

"What do *you* wanna do, Bobby?"

"Fight."

"Then *fight*."

I had no more to say. I just put the pillows up beside my head and went back to sleep. I didn't even hear Kirk slip out.

It was dark when the ringing phone woke me up.

"Bobby? *Cómo está?* It's Yolanda. You sound like I woke you up."

"You did."

"Can I come up?"

"No."

"I want to talk to you, Bobby. It's important."

"I don't want to talk to anybody."

"But this is *important*."

"How important can it be?"

"They're talkin' about hurting you, man. I mean it. Ask Kirk. He's in the casino."

"I thought they cut him off down there."

"Your father got him another five thousand worth of credit."

"Shit."

"And now there's a heavy rumor, man. Heavy. That maybe they gonna break your legs or something 'less you take this fight."

I laughed out loud. "Jesus Christ, this is a weird town."

"Yeah," she said, "but this ain't just weird, Bobby. This is true." Her breathy voice sounded childish over the phone. "We were out at your father's house again."

"Yeah?"

"And your mother was there."

"What the hell are you talking about?"

"I just wanted you to know," she said.

It was you, babe. Driving through the Vegas night, in a Plymouth the bell captain found for you; past the hotels and down side streets and through subdivisions; along broad avenues and past all-night supermarkets; into dead end streets, around and out again, like you were trapped in a pinball machine. Looking for the house with the double A-frames. The house out there somewhere in this strange city in the desert.

And all the time you thought about her. You had come across country, joined together, flesh and blood, and she would be there with you. Always. And then she saw him. You wondered if she saw him the same way he looked that night in the Caton Inn. And now that they were together, how many times had he made her laugh? Was she giggling right now at something he said, naked in a giant bed as he reached for a drink and lit her cigarette? They knew things you didn't know. That was the worst part. They had those years that you didn't share. Years when you just weren't there. And she came to him now full of those years that were maybe better than all the arrivals and departures, all the Charlies and Macks, the bad places where she'd done time. And maybe he was better than you.

You dozed in the car, in some empty parking lot, and when sunrise came you saw the line of the mountains, like a distant wall. And you remembered where the road was, with the mountains at the end, and the shape of the road, and you put the car in gear and moved out. And finally ahead you saw a sign saying RANCHO ESTATES, with a wooden corral style fence, and you drove in and found the house.

There were two cars in the driveway: one of them the silver Cadillac that Kirk had been driving: the other, a small red sports car. You sat, the engine idling, waiting, searching for words to say, plans of action. Imagining scenes: breaking doors, driving through plate windows, smashing him and hurting her.

And then you looked up and she was standing there in the kitchen doorway. Smiling. Looking bouncy and touseled and girlish. Wearing a flowered robe.

Hello, she said, coming over to the car. Come on in.

Is he here?

Of course he's here. It's his house.

I don't want to see him.

Don't be ridiculous. He's your father. Come on inside.

I don't want to.

Will you for God's sake grow up, Bobby?

You got out and she led you inside. To the kitchen, where she filled a kettle, and opened a coffee can, and spooned out coffee into the Chemex. Saying nothing, in the large clean wood-paneled kitchen. And you watched her, her bare legs, and the curve of her back under the flowered robe.

Where is he, you said.

He's in there, in the back. Asleep.

You knew he was here, didn't you?

No. I told you that. I told you I wasn't sure.

What happens now?

I don't know, she said. Will you be fighting Lewis?

Gus says no.

But the papers say you have to.

I don't have to fight anybody.

She brought over a glass of orange juice but she wouldn't look at you.

What do you think I should do? you said.

I guess you should fight him.

Why?

For money. There isn't any other reason, is there?

Sure there is.

What other reason?

And you remembered Gus after your first pro fight.

Beauty, you said.

She looked surprised, like I'd used a foreign word and I was a stranger from somewhere. And then she laughed: in a hard brittle blowsy early-morning way. She shook her head and said the word again. Beauty.

You watched her reach for a cigarette, and poke bacon around at the stove, not turning to face you.

And you hated her then.

You said: It's more than money.

I see, she said. She was looking at you now. Well,

I'm sorry, Bobby. I'm sorry I laughed. I didn't mean to hurt you.

You're always hurting me.

I don't mean to, I swear.

But you go away, Ma. You went away yesterday. You saw him and you went away, just like that.

He's my husband, she said.

No, he isn't. *I* am.

You can't ever be that, Bobby.

Yes, I can. I *can*.

No, but I love you, Bobby. You must know that.

Yeah.

Do you love me?

Yeah.

What do you want to do, Bobby?

I want to go home.

I woke up hours later on a red air cushion at the side of the pool. The water made a lapping sound in the light afternoon breeze. I could hear the steady hum of water sprinklers. When I looked up, I saw Jack Fallon sitting in a lawn chair in a blue bathing suit. He was staring at me.

"Good afternoon," he said.

I pulled myself up. I was wearing sweat pants, and someone had thrown a towel over my back and shoulders.

"You get a good sleep?" he said.

"I guess I did."

"Drink?"

My mouth felt furry. "Yeah. A tomato juice or something."

He called over the Mexican waiter, who was standing at the far side of the pool. He placed the order while I reached into the pool and splashed water on my head and shoulders. I couldn't face him. I wondered where Kate was and whether he had seen us together.

"Did you talk to Gus?" he said.

"He's not talking to anyone. I think we're going back to New York."

"Is that what you want?"

"No."

The waiter came back with cold tomato juice. I sipped it and stood up, peering into the chilly darkness of the house.

"She's gone," he said.

"Where?"

"Shopping, I guess. She didn't say. She just went."

"Like you."

"Don't talk like a punk."

"You ran, I didn't. Punks run."

He stood up. He was over 200 pounds and looked bigger with his clothes off.

"I'd like to make a deal with you," he said.

"What deal?"

"Take the fight. If you take it, I'll get out of your life for good. I'll just disappear."

He was staring hard at me now, and there was something in his eyes that said: I know about you, boy. And her.

"You're pretty good at disappearing, aren't you?" I said.

"It's my main act," he said, and smiled in a cold way.

I put my empty glass on the table. "Okay," I said. "I'll tell Gus I'm taking the fight. When it's over, I don't want to see you ever again."

He reached for the Luckies on the table beside his chair. "I'll tell your mother to stay at the hotel. You'll need her over there. Keep you from getting nervous."

He lit one of the Luckies and tossed the match into the brown grass.

"There's one other thing," I said.

"Yeah?"

"This," I said, and swung a hook. I hit him perfectly and he went over flat on his back. The cigarette rolled out of his hand, still smoking.

"So long, Dad," I said, and walked out to the car.

31

THAT AFTERNOON I WENT TO SEE GUS and told him I was going to fight Lewis. He sat very still on the edge of the bed in his small corner room.

"You're kiddin'," he said. "I don't believe what I'm hearin'."

"I'm gonna take the fight, Gus."

He squinted at me and I looked away.

"You can't," he said. "I'm the manager and you're the fighter and I say you can't. That was the deal."

"I'm sorry, Gus. I thought it all out and I'm taking the fight."

"Then I'm leaving."

I turned back to him. He seemed suddenly old.

"You can't *leave*," I said. "*Jesus*, Gus."

"I don't want you to take this fight. I want you to pack, go out to the airport, get on a plane and meet me in the gym tomorrow in New York. This fight isn't for you. Not now. Not in this town, with these people."

"Gus, it's for the title. All the commissions say it's for the title."

"A year from now it'll still be for the title. I want you to fight a few more guys, I want you to add some muscle. Then we'll fight this bum for a lot of money and the title, too. And you'll kick the shit out of him. But not now."

He got up and walked to the window, jingling the change in his baggy trousers. He waited for me to say something.

"I want to fight him now, Gus."

"Why?"

"I got reasons."

"You got *reasons?* Where the hell does it say that *you* can have *reasons?*"

"It doesn't say it anywhere, Gus. But I *got* them. And I'm gonna fight this fuckin' pimp!"

He looked at me hard, chewing something on the inside of his mouth. I thought he might want to cry. But then, his body sagging a little, he walked over to the closet, avoiding contact with me, and pulled down his suitcase. The battered blue cloth bag that had traveled with us to all the places on the road. He unzipped it and laid it out flat on the bed. And he opened the bureau drawers and started taking out clothes and putting them in the suitcase.

"Gus," I said. "Come on."

"I'm sorry, Bobby," he said. "I really am."

And so Gus went away, and you trained alone, and ran in the mornings while Kirk waited in the car. They brought in sparring partners from Los Angeles, and in the gym at the Convention Center you did all the things to them that Gus had taught you. You knocked down one long-necked white heavyweight and told Freddie to send him back to L.A. You hurt a lanky sad-eyed

Mexican with body punches and he didn't come back the next day. You broke bones in the face of some tall black dude. But you knew you weren't the same. And when the sportswriters asked you about Gus you said he'd gone back to New York, he had other fighters.

He's my friend, you said, and he's doing what he thinks is best.

But you missed him. He wasn't there watching you, off in a corner, and coming over later to tell you what you were doing wrong. Kirk still handled the water bottles, and Freddie stayed on. But the two of them together weren't Gus.

One of the reporters told you the fight was a big success in the money department, with long lines at the box offices all over the country. Youngstein's face glowed when he came to the workouts.

We got more press ticket requests for this fight than anything in history, he said. It's bigger than Ali and Foreman. It's bigger than Marciano and Moore. This is the fight of the century.

Fans stopped you for autographs when you walked through the lobby of Caesars Palace, and someone started selling green T-shirts with your face in the middle of a shamrock, and there was a souvenir book with pictures of all your fights.

Then Lewis came to town and set up across the street at the Aladdin, where he boxed on the stage of a big empty theater. He gave vicious interviews about you, telling the reporters what he'd do to you if you didn't run out on him. You looked at the stories and boxed hard in the gym, hitting the sparring partners, when you felt like it, getting ready to go fifteen rounds for the first time in your life. You boxed ten rounds two days running, then started adding eight-minute rounds at the end of a workout. You felt strong but the weight wouldn't stick. You started going across the street to Swenson's Ice Cream Shoppe and still the weight wouldn't come. Kirk looked worried but you didn't pay much attention. Kirk always looked worried.

From the day you had spoken to Gus and told him you were taking the fight, Kate was with you. She left the A-frame and came back to the hotel, where she stayed in the room next to yours. She watched over you. She ordered your meals from room service, she got you tickets for the dinner shows, she made sure you woke up in time for the morning's run. You stayed in the suite at night, but her room was connected and she always left the door open.

Sometimes you would lie alone, after she had said good night, wondering if she was there only because Jack Fallon told her to be there, and then you would imagine her waiting for you to sleep and slipping out the door to go down to the noise and lights of the casino, where Jack Fallon sat with his phone and his black coffee. And you would get up and cross the suite to the connecting door and go into her room. But she was there. She was always there. And some nights, you would be there beside her in the safe darkness.

Then, eight days before the fight, Freddie called you aside after a workout. Kirk stood nearby, silent but listening.

I want Gus to come back, Freddie said.

How come?

There's something wrong and I don't know what it is. Something's off.

You mean that kid I was boxing today? I was taking it easy, Freddie. That kid can't fight at all.

Not just today. I'd like Gus to come in. But I wanted to ask you first.

Gus wouldn't come out for this fight, Freddie. You know how he feels.

If I called him, he'd come.

Kirk walked over and stood next to Freddie.

I don't think you need Gus anymore, he said.

Who asked you? Freddie said. Get the hell outta

here.

I got somethin' to say, I'm gonna say it. And I say Bobby don't need Gus no more.

You don't get your ass outta here, I'll flatten you, Freddie said. I swear to Christ.

Kirk looked at you and then walked out of the dressing room to the gym.

That son of a bitch, Freddie said. I know he's a friend of yours, but he doesn't know nuthin' about boxin', except how to carry the goddam pails.

Easy, Freddie.

He took the cigar out of his mouth and said: Do you want me to call Gus?

No, I said.

Okay, he said. No harm in trying.

Nick Siegel came to see me run in the mornings, and I took him up to the suite and gave him little quotes that he made into big stories for the *Post*. He'd been there from the beginning, and I didn't know or like most of the other writers. He talked to me about what Lewis was doing at his workouts, mostly skipping rope to the sound of "Night Train" and getting his gut pounded by a medicine ball. Once he asked me about Gus and I told him I didn't want to talk about it. I respected him for never asking me again.

Then one morning Kirk didn't show up to take me to the race track, and Kate drove me out and waited in the car. When I came around the curve by the stands, I saw Nick sitting there, looking tired. I ran up beside him.

"I've gotta talk to you," he said.

"Sure, Nick," I said. "As soon as I'm through."

I finished up and went over to him. He handed me a container of orange juice that he'd picked up on the way and I sat down next to him.

"What is it?" I said.

"Something strange happened last night."

"Tell me."

"I watched Lewis work out and made a date to meet him at the Riv later on. He had an army of pimps hanging around, so there were six of us in a booth at the show, and afterwards we went back to Caesars. Lewis is wearing the usual: a hat with a big wide brim, and a black velvet suit, and a white shirt with enormous collars, and he looked, you know, gigantic."

"Doing his super nigger act, huh?"

"Yeah. And we walk into Caesars together, all six of us, and the room sort of chills. It doesn't stop cold, but it *chills*, as these five blacks walk in with one balding fat Jewish sportswriter. Anyway, over at one of the crap tables, he sees Kirk. He's shooting craps with this girl singer—"

"Yolanda Chacon."

"Right. Yolanda. And I said to Lewis, 'Hey, there's one of Fallon's people,' and right away I knew that was a mistake."

I laughed. "Right away."

"Lewis led the way over to Kirk's table and just stood there. This Yolanda was all made up from her show and she had on a silky kind of a gown, sort of rose-colored, with her boobs showing pretty good. And Lewis just stood there, big as shit, with the other spades behind him, and stared at Yolanda's jugs while Kirk shot craps. I went up and I said Hello to Kirk, and he introduced me to this girl, and she smiled, but then Lewis leaned over and put his hand under one of her boobs. And he sort of flipped it. Not hard. Just flipped it, right there in front of Kirk."

"Jesus."

"It was like he'd spit in Kirk's face. Kirk said, 'Hey!' but he didn't say it very loud, and the Yolanda chick didn't say anything. In fact, she looked pretty scared. The other black dudes started laughing, so Lewis leaned over and did it again. This time Kirk just sort of pushed his hand away."

"Should've taken a rap at him."

"Well, he didn't. Lewis just sneered at him and walked off. The girl looked like she was ready to cry, and Kirk took her hand and led her away. I stayed with them for a while. I said to Kirk, I said 'Kirk, how could you let that happen?' And he said, and this is a quote, ' 'Cause we all work for the same people.' "

"Say that again?"

" 'Cause we all work for the same people.' "

I stood up and looked over at the lot, hoping Kate wouldn't come around.

Nick said: "Well, what do you think he meant?"

"I don't know," I said.

"Is anyone doing business on this fight?"

"You mean do I think Lewis or me is gonna take a dive or something?"

"Yeah."

"Don't be stupid, Nick. That shit only happens in the fuckin' movies."

"But there's a lot of money riding on this fight."

"That's exactly why there's nothing going on."

I said goodbye and started to jog again. And I thought about what Kirk had said. I wouldn't know if there was something going on. I might not ever know. Money was pouring into the bookmakers all over the country. Whites betting against a black, and blacks betting against a white. They all knew that Lewis had thirty pounds on me. But they had made me an eight-to-five favorite, with the fight still five days off. Maybe something was going on. Or maybe it was all bullshit. I just didn't know.

Kate was still waiting when I got to the parking lot, and she left the car to come meet me. Her hair looked red in the sun, and she had on tight Western trousers and cowboy boots and a green Bobby Fallon

T-shirt. She was running when she reached me, and I picked her up and held her and kissed her on the mouth.

One more day. And out here, in the morning, on this empty track, I can run forever. They can't touch me here. They can't speak to me. Can't ask any more dumb questions. The whole crazy city is asleep, its people drained and exhausted, and all I have to do is run. One more day. Then I'll stop and wait. They'll pick me up at the hotel and drive me to the Convention Center. And then I'll be alone again.

Just me and Walker Lewis. Without Gus and without Kirk.

It was too bad Kirk turned out the way he did. I should have seen him for what he was. That day in the yard when he became an instant Muslim. Or the day he lost religion because he found a meal ticket. He doesn't even know what I know. What Kate told me. How Jack Fallon had found him the day he arrived in Vegas. How he took him downtown, through all the joints, and how he got him together with Yolanda Chacon. Jack Fallon could do that here. He had the friends who could do that. Jack Fallon just gave Yolanda to Kirk, the way he gave her to me not long after. Just told her to go with Kirk and be nice to him. And then he took the two of them back to Caesars and gave Kirk a line of credit and by dawn the next morning he had him.

He knew Gus would leave. That was part of it. He knew Gus would never take the fight.

He knew me, too. Make the fight, he said, and I'll go away for good. I'll never bother any of you again. And I believed him. The sun is up now. It's getting too hot to run. I'll go back to the hotel and close the door to the suite. And then I'll wait.

32

AT 7:02 I WAS IN THE RING, crunching resin with the boxing shoes, watching the clock, leaning back on the ropes to test their tension, looking down at the faces. When I'd come up the aisle in a Kelly green robe, with a white shamrock on the back and my name in big block letters, a pipe band started to play "Irish Eyes are Smiling" and the place went wild.

And then the band started a long rolling chorus of drums and congas and bongos, deep and primitive, and most of the crowd booed, and I could see a tall peaked black velvet hood bobbing ominously through the crowd and Walker Lewis was coming at me.

"He's gonna give you the glare," Freddie said, "but don't let it get to you."

I just moved, staying loose, and watched Walker Lewis come up the steps, coldly and deliberately, and bend through the ropes that were held open for him as if he were royalty. I saw the black polished forehead under the pointed hood, saw the whites of his eyes, the blank stare. And then I looked out at the press section. Nick Siegel was there, in the second row, and Dave Anderson from the *Times,* and I recognized a few other faces. I didn't look again at Walker Lewis.

"What's he doing?" I asked Kirk.

"He's just standing there."

"But how is he standing there?"

"Like he's waiting for the bus."

Kirk and Freddie tied the laces on my gloves and then Freddie put tape across the ends of the laces and I flexed my hands.

"Don't get fresh or stupid," Freddie said, while the announcer introduced a lot of old champions. "Just stick and move and stay out of his way."

"Okay."

"And when it's safe to hit him, hit him."

And then the building got quiet, and they sang the anthem, and the arena slowly darkened until the only light was in the ring. I remembered nights all over the country when I'd waited in the light like that and then went out and knocked people dead. With hooks to the body. With straight overhand rights. With combinations. That was what I did best. I hurt people. And now I was about to try to hurt a man named Walker Lewis, and if I hurt him badly enough I'd be the heavyweight champion of the world.

The announcer, a barrel-chested man in a tuxedo, waited for the microphone to drop from the ceiling pole. Then he started reading from an index card.

"In this corner . . . weighing two hundred eighteen pounds . . . in the black trunks . . . from East St. Louis, Illinois . . . the number one contender in the world . . . Walker Lewis. Lewis."

There was more booing and the drums rolled again, and Walker Lewis leaned back from the waist, letting his robe fall, and the crowd grew silent as the light picked up his rippling slablike muscles. He

moved his shoulders, stretched the strings and knots of
his back, feinted at the air, and leaned back again. He
looked like death.

"And in this corner . . . weighing one hundred
eighty-three and a quarter pounds . . . he's wearing
white trunks . . . with a green stripe . . . from Brooklyn,
New York . . . the number two contender in the world
. . . Irish . . . Bobby . . . Fallon!"

There was an explosion of applause, a skirl of
pipes, and the second "Fallon" was drowned in the
noise.

"Fifteen rounds . . . for the heavyweight . . .
championship . . . of the world!"

And then we were standing in the center of the
ring as the referee gave his instructions. Next to Lewis I
must have looked small and lean and light. I stared at
a point on his chest. The referee was talking about
counting after the bell, and the three-knockdown rule
being waived, and then:

"All right, boys, touch gloves and come out fighting."

We touched gloves and I went back to my corner. I looked at Kirk's anxious face, heard the bell ring
to start the first round, and turned to meet Walker
Lewis.

You were jammed, rushed and then lifted: you fell,
and you were lifted again: you threw punches. A roar,
and you were moving again: A shock, and one eye
was sticky, the lid gluey with blood, and you punched,
and a scream came from somewhere, and there was
another roar, and you saw Walker Lewis on his back:
and you thought you had won, leaped in the air, and
then were moved again: lifted: shocked: and then
emptied of air, vomit gagging you: and a film of red
covered your other eye: and then lights were in your
eyes: A roar: silence: A roar: silence: And you were
looking at Kirk, sponging at your face, and he was cry-

ing, and Freddie was reaching in and there were other faces: the referee, a doctor, cops. Walker Lewis, who said something and tapped you with a glove and turned away. And then you knew you had lost.

You were carried through crowds and down tunnels. The lids of your eyes sticky again. People shouted at you, and someone called you a bum, and someone else shouted, Next time, next time. And they had you in the dressing room, and you felt pain over the eyes again and looked up during a clear moment and saw that the doctor was stitching you. There were a lot of colors: reds, orange, a magenta. Then a cool sponge on your face. Soft voices. Murmurs.

And then it was quiet and you could smell her beside you. She touched your face and you asked, Are we alone? Yes, she said, they've all gone out. And you asked her how bad it had been and she said the sportswriters were calling it the greatest heavyweight fight since Dempsey and Firpo, whatever that meant. How the hell could that be? You had him down, she said, don't you remember that? Yeah. And was I down? Three times, she said. Well, did they count me out? No, she said, they stopped it because of the cuts.

Kate, I'm sorry.

There's nothing to be sorry for, silly.

You asked her to hold you, hug you, and she did. Fists started pounding on the door, but she didn't move, she stayed there a long time, pressing against you, soft, her hands touching your skin.

They're saying you got heart. You got more heart than anyone they know.

The fists pounded on the door, and her hands touched your lips, and then she kissed you and moved away. The door opened and there were shouts and voices and the room filled, and you were reaching for her, and she was going, and the doctor was there again, swabbing at your eyes, and suddenly you could see. The doctor was telling Nick Siegel that the cuts had required thirty-two stitches but they should heal, and yes, he would be able to fight again. Was the first cut from the butt? The doctor said he wasn't qualified to give an opinion on that. Then they were all shouting at you, asking about different punches, and what you felt when you knocked down Lewis and what you felt when you saw Lewis get up, and you said you didn't remember him getting up and didn't remember going down. Did you give away too much weight? Maybe. Do you think you should have waited another year. No.

You listened more and talked more, and tried to see them clearly, while Freddie told them, Come on, fellas, enough is enough, and you realized that Kirk wasn't there. And neither was Jack Fallon. Just Freddie, little, quiet, flat-nosed Freddie. The door opened and in came Jorgenson, and Youngstein, and Stevens, and the rest of the television people, and Howard Cosell was moving in behind them with a crew. The greatest fight I ever saw, Jorgenson said, and he sounded as if he meant it. Less than a round, but the greatest round in boxing history. You broke Lewis's jaw, you know that, don't you? We want a rematch, Youngstein said. We'll do a hundred million, worldwide. Maybe. Then Cosell beside you. Bobby Fallon, you have just fought the greatest single round in the history of pugilism but you have to face one overwhelming fact: Walker Lewis resoundingly defeated you. So tell us: What happened? You smiled at Cosell. He had never covered one of your fights before, and here he was, looking down at you, while a cameraman leaned over his shoulder to look at your bandaged face. You sat up. Well, you said, I guess I just got the shit knocked out of me. And they all laughed. Freddie started pushing them out the door so he could help you get dressed. He didn't know where Kirk had gone. You didn't ask him anything else. Maybe I would've done better if Gus had been here, you said, when the room was empty. He shrugged: Maybe. I guess I better call him, you said. And then he was packing the gear into the bag, the way he had done in so many other places, and you realized that this was just another fight for him, that it was just another fight for a lot of people.

Freddie?

Yeah.

Thanks for sticking with me.

Don't thank me for that, goddammit. Stickin' wit' you is my job.

He picked up the bag and helped you out of the dressing room.

33

WE WENT DOWN CORRIDORS and into a tunnel that came up into a parking lot. The lights were still on in the convention center, and a wedge of special cops took us through the crowd to a limousine. Four motorcycle cops were out front, and we rolled along the streets of Vegas, the sirens blaring, till we reached Caesars Palace. Kirk was standing in front.

"Where the hell did you go to?" Freddie said to him as we got out of the car.

"Takin' care of business," Kirk said. Then to me: "How you feelin'?"

"Okay."

"I got some food comin' up to the suite."

"I'm not hungry."

"Well, you should prob'ly eat somethin'."

"Kirk?"

"Yeah?"

"Get the fuck out of my life." I walked past him

and into the casino, and people stopped to stare at the heavy bandages over my eyes. As I came around the side of the pit, the gamblers stopped, put down the dice and cards, waited for the wheels to slow, and along the side, at the small tables in the Galleria, the drinkers stood up, and then the whole casino was clapping and applauding. I looked at them and touched the bandages, as if to explain.

"I don't get it," I whispered to Freddie. "I lost. I didn't win. I lost."

"Hey, they're all losers, too," Freddie said. "Remember?"

We kept walking and the applause faded and the gamblers all went back to their tables. Freddie and I turned past the keno game and went through the banks of slots, heading for Cleopatra's Barge and the Ah So Japanese restaurant. I heard someone call my name, and I turned and saw Kirk moving through the slots.

"Hey, Bobby, wait up, baby. Hold it."

I waited. "Yeah?"

"There's one more thing. You didden let me finish."

"What is it, Kirk?"

"It's your mother. She's checkin' out. She tole me if I saw you to say she was goin' to a place call the Caton Inn."

I put a hand on one of the slots and steadied myself and looked across the casino to the main desk. "Where is she?"

"Headin' for the back parkin' lot."

"I'll see you later, Freddie."

I went past the swaying barge and the Japanese restaurant, through the revolving door and into the parking lot. There were more than a thousand cars out there, and I started to trot. The lights were high and dim. I could barely see from under the heavy bandage. My head ached and my body hurt. I saw a man in a gray suit helping a blonde into one car, and a couple of people in cowboy suits getting into another.

And then I saw his car, long and gleaming. The door to the trunk was up, and he was putting suitcases in. She was standing with her back to me, watching him.

"Ma! *Ma!*"

She turned, and I could see her face in the light. She looked very young. He put down a final suitcase and stepped past her, coming right at me. I stopped and waited for him.

He gripped my arm. "That was a hell of a fight," he said, his voice choking. And then he hugged me.

"You made a deal," I whispered.

"I know. But she didn't."

And then it drained out of me: all the hoping, all the plans, all the need. I didn't want to hit him. I didn't want to hit anybody. I was empty.

"Are you okay?" he said.

"I'll be okay."

"Where are you going?"

"I don't know. Maybe California. Just rent a car and go."

"With that eye, you'll need a driver."

"So I'll get a driver."

I pulled away from him, and then Ma came over. The two of them were facing me, and I leaned back on the car.

"Hello, Bobby," she said.

"I wish you'd stayed around to say goodbye," I said.

Her face trembled. Jack Fallon reached over and gently touched her arm.

"Kate . . ." he said.

I stood up straight. "It's okay," I said to them. "I understand." I looked at them for a minute. "Well, I'll see you. Have a good trip."

And I turned to go out through the parked cars.

She called my name, but I kept walking. And then she was there, with tears streaming down her face.

"Bobby, I . . ."

"Go, Ma. He loves you. What else matters?"

"I love you, Bobby."

"I love you, too," I said, and kissed her on the cheek, and moved around her, heading for the casino.

Almost time to get up. How long have I been here now? A week? A month? My eye is itching under the bandage. The sea has moved up the beach, and I can see boats moving out on the horizon. The breeze is cool. A bird walks in the surf on long spindly legs, looking foolish. But not as foolish as standing in some arena in your underwear, in front of 18,000 people, getting ready to beat up a stranger.

A car door slams somewhere. The sky is still the color of lead, but it hasn't rained. Another car pulls away on the road above me.

And then a voice.

"Hello, Bobby."

It's Gus, standing there in the sand, pale as the New York sun.

"I've been lookin' for you. I've been in California two days."

"Jesus, Gus."

"Let's go," he says.

He gives me a hand, and I pull myself up. His grip is strong, the palm rough and hard.

"How'd you find me?"

"Freddie told me you were going to this Malibu. There's only three motels."

"You should've been a cop."

"Yeah," he says. Then, squinting: "How's the eye?"

"Itchy."

"It's healing. They always itch when they heal. Lemme see."

He peels away the bandage. The breeze feels very cold.

"Not bad," he says. "A really tight butterfly. I'd say you could get those stitches out whenever you feel like it."

"Let's do it today, Gus."

"Suits me."

We reach the top of the dune. "I'm sorry about the fight," I say.

"So am I," he says. He points at a maroon Ford. "Come on. I got a car."

He puts an arm around me, and we walk to the car. He stops and opens the door on the passenger side.

"Well," he says, "where are we going?"

I look back at the sea, the waves rolling endlessly across the Pacific. A girl in a flowered bathing suit is jogging in the surf, her blond hair bouncing.

"Let's go eat," I tell him. "We can talk about it later."

ABOUT THE AUTHOR

Born in Brooklyn in 1935, PETER HAMILL left high school after two years to become a sheet-metal worker in the Brooklyn Navy Yard. In 1952 he joined the Navy. Later he studied painting on the G.I. Bill at Pratt Institute and Mexico City College, worked as a designer and started writing for newspapers in 1960. Formerly a columnist for the New York *Post,* he now contributes to the New York *Daily News* and other papers, and has also appeared in many major magazines. He is the author of two previous novels, *A Killing for Christ* (1968) and *The Gift* (1973); and a collection of his journalism, *Irrational Ravings,* was published in 1971. He has lived in Mexico, Spain, Italy and Ireland, and now lives again in Brooklyn. He has two daughters, Adriene and Deidre.

WE DELIVER!
And So Do These Bestsellers.

REACH ACROSS THE GENERATIONS

With books that explore disenchantment and discovery, failure and conquest, and seek to bridge the gap between adolescence and adulthood.

Bantam Book Catalog

Here's your up-to-the-minute listing of every book currently available from Bantam.

This easy-to-use catalog is divided into categories and contains over 1400 titles by your favorite authors.

So don't delay—take advantage of this special opportunity to increase your reading pleasure.

Just send us your name and address and 25¢ (to help defray postage and handling costs).